Education

Edukation

EDUKAZHUN

An entertainment

James Rainsford.

James Rainsford was born in Kent and attended school in Essex. He spent two years as a seaman in the British Mercantile Marine, prior to attending the University of Sussex, where he read Philosophy, English and History. He also gained an Advanced Diploma in Special Education from The University of Wales. His subsequent career has mainly been in education. He has been a teacher in both primary and secondary schools and has held senior positions within educational publishing. His most recent teaching position was as Head of Year in a large comprehensive school.

He is married with two daughters and currently lives in Devon, where he is working on his next novel.

Education

Edukation

eDukaᴢHun

An entertainment

James Rainsford

Education

Edukation

eDukazHun

An entertainment

Olympia Publishers
London

www.olympiapublishers.com
OLYMPIA PAPERBACK EDITION

A CIP catalogue record for this title is
available from the British Library.

ISBN: 978-1-905513-90-1

This novel is a work of fiction. Names of places, characters and the events
portrayed in the narrative are a product of the author's imagination and any
resemblance to actual places, actual persons, living or dead, or to particular events,
is entirely coincidental.

Front cover design by Debbie Jones

First Published in 2009

Olympia Publishers part of Ashwell Publishing Ltd
60 Cannon Street
London
EC4N 6NP

Printed in Great Britain

To Wendy, with thanks for all her support, understanding, encouragement and love.

"It is a terrible thought, to contemplate that an immense number of mediocre thinkers are occupied with really influential matters."

Friedrich Nietzshce 1844 – 1900

Foreword

Hi! I'm Dave Falconer, a fifty-six year old English teacher and Head of Year at Gruffudd ap Cynan Comprehensive, a school, so neglected and mismanaged, it shimmered like an oasis of incompetence and squalor in a desert of educational mediocrity.

Accompany me now, as I take you on a short journey through the final four years of my teaching career, before my eagerly anticipated retirement. I hope you will find it an account both edifying and entertaining. In the following chapters you'll be taken on a tour down some of the mysterious and most inaccessible corridors of current educational practice. You will meet characters, situations and events which would never be acknowledged in the platitude filled atmosphere of a typical school parents' evening, yet, you will learn more of the true nature of British secondary education, than you could hope to discover by reading the educational press, listening to politicians, or studying learned journals.

So, whether you're standing, sitting, or lying, just relax and enjoy the trip, as I introduce you to Gruffudd ap Cynan Comprehensive School and its terrible team of senior managers.

Chapter 1

The School

Gruffudd ap Cynan Comprehensive School was named in honour of an XI century Welsh King. It was located on the level floor of a wide break in an otherwise narrow South Wales valley, just on the edge of the declining town of Abercwmtwerp. Once blighted by the dust and mountainous slag heaps of two active pits, it now stood as a fitting memorial to Margaret (Milk Snatcher) Thatcher, who robbed the kids of their free school milk and the valley of its mines. Fortunately, it had also lost its dirty and dangerous slag heaps, which had blighted the valley with the ever present prospect of sudden death, but this failed to compensate for the loss of its close and co-operative sense of community. Many of the values, forged in the harshness of a life characterised by danger and self reliance had disappeared with the death, or departure of the old established mining families. Their lives and their family cohesion had, like in so many similar communities, been replaced by a high level of unemployment, despair, mistrust of neighbours and suspicion of those in authority.

One consequence of these changes was a loss of respect for teachers, and in many cases, an unwillingness to believe that teachers were to be valued, or trusted. This made working with many of the local parents in a collaborative way very difficult, and there was a partially justified perception among a number of the teaching staff that parents were at best an unwelcome annoyance, and at worst, meddlesome, ill-informed trouble makers.

Any government vision of parents and teachers working together, in some utopian partnership for the benefit of the nation's children, was simply that: a vision! Not that I'd ever imagined politicians actually believed this vision themselves; most teachers knew it to be

17

just another empty sound-bite, designed as a smoke-screen to conceal the true agenda.

The major part of the school had been constructed during the 1960's and apart from the main teaching block, was a collection of uninspired, poorly constructed, square concrete buildings of three or four storeys. In addition to these hideous eyesores, there were also a number of neglected so-called temporary demountable classrooms, which had been erected at various times to accommodate some now long abandoned educational initiative or hastily deployed in response to some other unexpected crises, like "The Great School Flood of 1984".

The main teaching block had been built in 1994 to house an influx of additional pupils caused by the closure of another secondary school in a neighbouring valley. Its construction was reported on at the time as an opportunity to build a functional and modern addition to the school, which would inspire all those who worked within it to value their environment and be proud of the exciting new facilities which it provided. It was praised by councillors, the press, leading figures in the L.E.A. and local dignitaries as a shining example of what could be achieved by using the best architects and the finest materials.

This was of course over ten years ago, and in the intervening period this shining beacon of civic pride had been allowed to deteriorate to the point where it now resembled a conflict ravaged warehouse in some Eastern Block war zone!

Since its construction there had been absolutely no maintenance beyond the occasional replacement of a blown light bulb, or a broken window and even these small repairs usually took months to be effected.

It very quickly became apparent after the building enjoyed its first taste of teenagers that, the architects, so lauded for their imaginative innovations, had absolutely no conception of how to design a building which could withstand the kind of care and attention it was going to receive from a bunch of destructive yobs, whose idea of looking after their environment had been fostered in the dirty, graffiti and litter strewn streets of a community suffering from terminal neglect. The finest materials, which had been so eloquently praised at the time of construction by incompetent 'design gurus', had proven totally inadequate in the face of the onslaught they suffered at the hands, and often the feet, of twelve hundred unconcerned and un co-ordinated kids, who valued nothing; in many cases not even themselves!

The list of the building's features which were not fit for purpose was a very long list indeed, and included such necessary items as: door and window hinges and fastenings, doors and door frames, windows, desks, chairs, carpets, stairways, window blinds, floor and ceiling tiles, notice boards, light fittings and, most serious of all the deficiencies, the pupils' toilets!

To be fair, it was not totally the fault of the pupils that the buildings and its contents were so quickly damaged or destroyed. It was also the result of awarding the contracts to construct such an important community asset to architects and builders who were forced to tender the lowest possible price, and who were obliged to work to specifications, produced by well-meaning local authority personnel, who would have been challenged by the task of designing a durable shed for an allotment.

As if this were not bad enough, the appalling situation was compounded by passing responsibility for the building's maintenance upon its completion to a local authority which was as short of funds, as it was minds, and to a headteacher and senior management team too weak and self-serving to insist upon civilised standards.

Thus the whole sorry story of the buildings' transformation from potential palace to actual pig-sty, aptly illustrated, yet again, the fact that we frequently entrust projects of consequence to mediocre thinkers.

This whole collection of shabby and uncared for buildings was the work place of over twelve hundred students aged eleven to eighteen, and also, some seventy-plus staff, including, caretakers, mid-day assistants and administrative personnel. Responsibility for the entire site, plus all the staff and students, fell upon the weedy and inadequate shoulders of Dr. Michael A. Douglas, a relatively recently appointed ex-deputy head from a failing inner city school, which had been closed following one of the worst reports in the entire history of school inspections.

He had been appointed, after several failed attempts by the over-ambitious and unqualified Board of Governors to select a successor to Mr Trevor Littlejohn BSc, O.U., (Open University) an unprepossessing career educationalist who was head for only four years. Upon appointment, Mr. Littlejohn was publicised as the new broom, who was going to sweep away the tradition of old-fashioned values, principles and achievements of the immensely well liked, charismatic and respected previous Head; Mr Harry Morgan. Mr Morgan, who enjoyed the support of the parents and affection of the students, had been in charge of the school since 1962. He had, through conviction and strength of character, defied the wishes of the newly appointed Chairman of the Governors, Mr Rodney J. Field, a self-opinionated and supercilious accountant who believed passionately in the educational clap-trap expounded by the one-time Secretary of State for Education, The Right Honourable Kenneth Baker, M.P. Mr Field viewed Harry Morgan as an educational dinosaur intent upon thwarting his authority and blocking his desired reforms for school improvement. Harry, who was close to retirement and far too intelligent to work under a governor of such obvious deficiencies, told Rodney Field to stick his desired reforms up his arse!

And, so it was, that the school passed into the obsequious hands of Mr Trevor Littlejohn. Mr Littlejohn was like many who achieve headship, a third rate science graduate who, being unsuccessful in his attempts to gain a position with a large international chemical company, had entered teaching as an alternative to unemployment. He very quickly realised however, that he lacked the talent and personality to motivate the unfortunate children in his chemistry classes and therefore, he turned in desperation to educational administration as an escape route from the difficult and demanding challenges presented by trying to teach large groups of totally disinterested pupils.

In his desire to be free of the classroom, he was not different from many other inadequate teachers, who pursuing promotion like heat seeking missiles, voraciously absorbed the theories and jargon of the educational elite, and then presented themselves for selection before panels of gullible governors and educational prima donnas who, flattered by the deference and apparent gravitas of such knowledgeable candidates, offered them the opportunity to climb the next rung on the ladder to educational incompetence.

As evidence for this, it can be stated that the only attempted change for the better introduced by the now departed Mr Littlejohn was the purchase and strategic placement of thirty supposedly vandal-proof waste bins in his doomed efforts to tackle the mounting litter problem. The only other noticeable change he made was to delete from the School Prospectus the designation 'hons' (honours) printed immediately after the university degree achieved by most of the teaching staff. It was rumoured that he ordered the deletion of these marks of distinction because his own BSc, being only an undistinguished 'pass', was awarded without honours.

His departure, to take up the position of Deputy Director of Education in a large metropolitan authority, was only regretted by Sandra Love, the always absent, immensely unattractive and hypochondriac Head of VI Form whom he had appointed to this important post soon after his arrival and with whom he had been having a supposedly secret affair, ever since he had first encountered her when he was temporary acting Deputy Head in a private school for the educationally delicate in Dorking.

His promotion to take up his administrative responsibilities in a far distant L.E.A. was, apart from the distraught and abandoned Miss Love, universally approved of by the remainder of the staff who were, understandably, delighted to see the back of him. They would not, however, have been so thrilled had they known that his replacement was to be Dr. Michael A. Douglas, an even more inept and inefficient escapee from the responsibilities of the classroom.

All staff knew of him initially was that he had originally hailed from somewhere near Doncaster and that he had been the only candidate whose academic qualifications would appear impressive on the school's stationery and the cover of the prospectus.

Upon his first arrival at the school most teachers had been encouraged by his seemingly friendly and open personality. Unlike the devious and untrustworthy Littlejohn, he at least made eye contact when spoken to. What no-one appreciated at the time was that this

21

apparent focus upon the opinions of his staff was not an expression of interest, but a struggle to remember who was addressing him and to recall the position within the school which they occupied. It was said that, the only reason he had his own name printed on his office door in such large block capitals, was not due to a wish to see his academic achievements writ large, but because he required a clear, unambiguous and visible reminder of who he was!

He was certainly no improvement on Littlejohn in the sartorial elegance stakes. His working wardrobe consisted of three crumpled, worn and ill-fitting lounge suits in slightly varying shades of brown. These he invariably partnered with a soiled checked shirt with the top button missing and a stained knotted woollen tie, in a bilious shade of green. The trousers on all three suits were at least two inches too short, which was very unfortunate as they simply allowed his odd socks and scuffed and dirty suede Hush Puppies to become the fashion feature of the ensemble. As if this vision were not enough to bear, it was made considerably less appealing by the fact that his head was far too small for his body and was perched precariously on a scrawny tortoise like neck, which tapered off into a pair of almost non-existent shoulders reminiscent of a Guinness bottle. He was indeed, so atrociously dressed that it was extremely difficult to treat with respect the educational utterances of such a man, who had obviously failed to learn how to use a mirror and who had married a woman who thought so little of him the she allowed him to leave the house less well attired than the Guy, annually created and burned, by the Third Abercwmtwerp Scouts.

He possessed many other negative attributes, but probably his most serious deficiency as a leader was his total inability to make a decision and stick to it! He was a vacillator of monumental indecisiveness and was, therefore, subject to the conflicting demands of a factious and divided staff, who challenged his every decision, knowing that by the application of a little pressure he could be persuaded to change what passed for his mind. This had the consequence of creating an ever changing interpretation of the school's aims and objectives and promoted a complete lack of confidence that anything decided upon today, would still hold true tomorrow.

In this atmosphere of mistrust and uncertainty the school quickly descended into a spiral of decline, where staff morale was non-existent and where the behaviour of the pupils' steadily deteriorated until it matched the appallingly managed and uncared for environment in which they were taught.

To compound matters, the ineffectual Dr. Douglas was assisted and supported in his important leadership role by a Senior Management Team of breathtaking incompetence.

This team consisted of two Deputy Heads and Head of Key Stage Three. The first of the two deputies was, Vic Davies, a recently appointed, idealistic, ex-head of Chemistry from West Wales, who believed in peoples' innate goodness and who viewed all children as virtuous innocents trapped in an unfair system. He was a woolly thinker of the first division and he possessed about as much zip as a pair of button-fly Levi's. Much to their contempt he tried to befriend the pupils with inane stories of his own childhood and reminiscences of his disastrous career in previous schools.

The other and more senior of the two deputies was Frank Baldwin, a profoundly deaf, bombastic 'call-a-spade-a-spade' northerner who'd left his native Durham years ago and who'd been passed-up for promotion to Head every time he'd applied. He had, consequently, been at the School since 1968 and was now so close to the end of his tenure that he had effectively retired from any active or visible role and spent most of his time cloistered in his office reading educational journals. At least, he always claimed they were educational journals whenever he was unexpectedly caught reading one by some member of staff who had entered without knocking. His other prime occupation was his efforts to eliminate a persistent and unsettling whistling noise which plagued his notoriously unreliable hearing aid.

The final member of this ineffectual quartet was Bert Bowen, a balding, myopic physical wreck, who'd been at the school so long that many of the new pupils in year 7 viewed him with awe and amazement because he'd taught their grandparents. Bert was, at base,

23

a well intentioned buffoon, who would have been out of his depth in a car park puddle. He had long ago been promoted so far beyond his abilities that he existed in a constant state of panic and nervous exhaustion. He was affectionately known as 'Dogsbody Bowen', due to the way he was constantly abused and exploited by the other members of the Senior Management Team. If there were any controversial or thankless task to be undertaken, they would invariably delegate it to Bert who would always try his best to carry out their wishes, but inevitably fail, due to the lack of time, stamina and most critically, talent.

It might be thought unusual and somewhat remiss in these times of feminine ascendancy and political correctness, not to have a female serving on the Senior Management Team, particularly in view of the fact that over fifty-five percent of the pupils were girls. The reason for this was difficult to assess, but I suspect that, in part, it was down to the powerful and uncompromising personality of Kay Wallace, the charismatic one time Head of VI Form who had served on the Senior Management Team in the days when Harry Morgan had been Head. Kay was an intelligent and extremely capable Scot who did not suffer fools gladly and who voiced her opinions with withering perception and authority.

Upon Harry's retirement she had continued as a member of the S.M.T. during the first few terms of the Trevor Littlejohn era. It quickly became apparent to everyone that now Harry's skill and experience had departed, she was the only member of the team with any degree of competence. In fact, her ability was so awesome that it threw into sharp relief the hopeless inadequacies of the others and resulted in most staff by-passing them and taking all issues and concerns directly to her.

While this was unquestionably the only certain way that staff could ensure their problems were dealt with and concerns addressed, it was also a threat to the male members of the team who were all too aware of her popularity and were helpless in the face of her obvious talent and scornful contempt of their shortcomings.

At the time she was approaching sixty and when she announced her retirement, they must have breathed a collective sigh of relief. At her retirement, they all made appropriate expressions of regret at her departure but it was obvious to all that they were more than a little relieved to be losing this formidable fire-brand, who shone like a beacon of sanity and illuminated their many failings with the accuracy of a surgical laser.

Subsequent to her retirement there was never any mention from the S.M.T. of the need for a female replacement. It was assumed, probably correctly, that their experience of working with a competent and confident woman had so disheartened them that they had no desire to appoint another possibly perceptive and capable female who may expose their disastrous deficiencies.

These then, were the four members of our Senior Management Team, Douglas, Davies, Baldwin and Bowen who were collectively charged with responsibility for managing a budget of millions, the welfare, aspirations and career prospects of some seventy plus staff, and most worryingly of all, the education and social development of over twelve hundred children.

It was in this depressing, yet often farcical and humorous environment I was to spend the last four years of my working life, the details of which, I now take very great pleasure in sharing, hopefully to illuminate the darkest corners of life in Gruffudd ap Cynan Comp.

Chapter 2

Two Lunch Luke

It was almost at the end of lunchtime registration when the phone rang. A small group of my Year 8 pupils had just left my classroom after having collected the bags they invariably dumped on the desks during lunch, to remove the burden of having to carry them into the feeding frenzy of the school canteen.

The phone ringing anytime during registration nearly always signalled trouble. It was usually one of my form tutors reporting a non-attender, or an incident requiring my intervention, so when I put the receiver to my ear and barked an impatient 'Dave Falconer' I was not surprised to hear the voice of Mandy Jones, Form Tutor to the notorious 8/MJ and my Assistant Head of Year 8.

'It's Luke Lowe,' she said without introduction.

'Luke Lowe?' I repeated, 'what's the matter with Luke Lowe?'

'He says he can't move.'

'What do you mean he can't move? Why can't he move?'

'He says he's full.'

'What do you mean he's full?'

'Full up! He says he's full up.'

'Full up? Full up with what?'

'Well food, I suppose,' said Mandy, who by now, was obviously becoming fraught by trying to maintain order and talk to me as her form class were leaving to begin the first lesson of the afternoon.

I waited, the receiver still pressed to my ear, as I listened to Mandy shouting. 'Don't push Darren! Amy, stop throwing sweets! David! Give Emma her bag back and don't rub that in her hair!'

Eventually the chaotic noise of the form's departure subsided and Mandy returned her attention to the phone.

'Has he left?' I enquired.

'Left?' she questioned, struggling to recall our interrupted conversation.

'Luke Lowe,' I clarified. 'Has Luke Lowe left?'

'No!' she exclaimed in exasperation. 'That's what I've been trying to explain to you he says he can't move because he's too full!'

'Well,' I replied, 'he managed to get to your room, so when he decides he can move I suggest you send him to me.'

'Right,' Mandy acknowledged, now obviously keen to end this slightly surreal conversation, as the chaotic noise returned, signalling the arrival of her Maths class for period 6. I just caught the admonition 'Nicole don't…' before the phone went dead.

I replaced the receiver and pushed my chair back slightly from my desk, grateful that, for me, this was a free period. This was, of course, a total misnomer. As Head of Year, with the pastoral care of two hundred and forty pupils in Year 8 to attend to, the possibility of a free period was zero. However, I had been looking forward to a brief period of uninterrupted time to finish writing some report comments due to be completed by 4.00pm, so I was not happy having to deal with Luke Lowe, even if he was full and couldn't move. I considered how much slower a slowed down Luke Lowe could possibly be, since even without the handicap of being full he only had two speeds, slow and stop. If indeed he was now so full, that he had slowed from his usual pace, then perhaps I would be spared an interruption and would be able to complete the waiting pile of reports.

Luke was, without doubt, the most disorganised and bemused boy in Year 8. He was the only pupil I'd ever known to have been medically diagnosed with half a disorder. His mother, concerned at his lack of academic progress and whose neighbour's son, had recently been diagnosed with A.D.H.D. (Attention Deficit Hyperactivity Disorder) had decided that this must be Luke's problem also and had badgered the family G.P. into arranging an assessment for Luke with Dr. Darius Dimpole, a renowned local child psychiatrist, who favoured a diagnosis of A.D.H.D. in almost all cases of under achievement in school. Consequently, our school, being close to his consulting rooms, enjoyed the reputation as the A.D.H.D. (All

27

Discipline Has Disappeared) Comp. A place where it was rumoured, that 'Ritalin,' the childhood chemical cosh of choice, was added to the burgers served in the school canteen. This wasn't true of course, though it might have proved an interesting experiment in pupil behaviour management.

What was true was that a considerable number of pupils had been diagnosed with A.D.H.D. and had been prescribed the drug 'Ritalin' in an attempt to improve their behaviour. From my experience, 'Ritalin' didn't seem to improve behaviour so much as slow it down. Pupils on 'Ritalin' still misbehaved, but they just misbehaved more slowly. An effect which might have been amusing, had it not resulted in the common confrontations with pupils taking twice as long.

Anyway, when Darius Dimpole assessed Luke he informed Mrs Lowe that Luke was so inactive that he couldn't possibly have the hyperactivity element of the disorder and therefore, he didn't have A.D.H.D. Dimpole was however, shrewd enough to realise that Mrs Lowe would be disappointed by this, so by way of compensation he suggested that Luke may have A.D.D. (Attention Deficit Disorder). Mrs Lowe still felt slightly aggrieved, but thought that on balance it was more satisfying to learn that Luke had half a disorder, rather than no disorder at all, which would have left him with the lowly status of normality.

Almost all of period 6 had passed and I'd managed to complete over half of the reports before there was a timid knock on my door. I had to shout 'Come in!' three times before the door slowly opened to reveal the dirty and tear stained face of Luke Lowe.

'Ah, Luke. At Last!' I exclaimed. 'Come and sit, Miss Jones has told me of your troubles. She said you couldn't move because you were full.'

'Y-Yes Sir.' He mumbled, using his familiar I've been hard done by voice.

Luke was, unfortunately, what all teachers would recognise as a natural victim. He seemed to attract bullies like flies to excrement. He was only ever really animated when attacked and was once described as only truly fluent in five bandages.

Of course, all the staff and a number of senior pupils involved in the school's bully watch scheme did their best to try and mitigate the worst effects of this, but no sooner had one group of bullies been identified and dealt with, than Luke set about securing another tribe of tormentors. He seemed to relish making the task of helping him a perpetual and increasingly difficult challenge.

As he sat now, in the chair opposite my desk, it was obvious that he'd suffered another trauma, which would probably prove intractable, problematic and necessitate correspondence and meetings with his unfortunate mother.

I tried to summon what I hoped was my most caring and concerned expression, as I asked him how he came to be so full that he couldn't move.

'W-well,' he stammered, 'w-when I w-went home, my m-mum gave me a very big dinner an' I was very hungry, so I eat it all up, an' then my mum was going round my Gran's, so I come back to school early, an' J-J-Jamie F-Fisher saw me and said "Where's my 50p?" '

'Did you owe him 50p?' I enquired gently.

'N-no, I have to give him 50p when he finds me.'

'Are you telling me,' I asked, 'that Jamie Fisher has been extorting money from you?'

'N-no, he just says I have to give it to him or he'll beat me up.'

How early it begins, I thought. Jamie Fisher, a Year 9 thug with all the charm and attractiveness of a flatulent baboon and a reputation for classroom disruption had now graduated to demanding money with menaces.

'How long has Jamie Fisher been asking you for money?' I asked.

'I don't know, a long time,' Luke responded as if trying to remember.

'Well, how long? Since the start of term, or longer?'

'Longer.'

'And how much do you have to give him?'

'50p.'

'Always 50p?'

'Sometimes, if I haven't got it, he says I'll have to pay a pound next time.'

'Does he!' I exclaimed, my voice rising with incredulity. 'I'll deal with Master Fisher,' I said, trying to reassure Luke that the situation would be resolved.'

'So what happened today?' I continued.

'I didn't have 50p today 'coz my mum said she'd had to pay the milkman and she didn't have any change.'

'So what did you tell Jamie Fisher?'

'I said I hadn't got 50p.'

'What did he say?'

'He said, I could go to the office and tell Mrs Williams that 'coz I hadn't got any money, I hadn't had any dinner and he said Mrs Williams would give me some money for dinner and then I could give the money to him.'

'And did she?'

'What?'

'Did Mrs Williams give you money for your dinner?'

'N-no, she said she wouldn't give me any money.'

'What did she do then?' I asked, the reason for his fullness now beginning to dawn.

'She marched me over to the canteen and told the dinner ladies to give me a really big dinner.'

'And you ate it?' I enquired incredulously. 'Why didn't you tell Mrs Williams you'd already had a big dinner?'

''Coz I'd already told her I didn't have any dinner, so she'd give me some money to give to Jamie.'

'But why didn't you just leave the dinner?'

''Coz Mrs Williams stayed there. She said she wanted to make sure I had a really good feed 'coz I was so hungry and then she sat down and asked me if I often missed my dinner 'coz I didn't have any money, and she stayed to make sure I ate it all up, and then, when she went, I had to go to form 'coz the bell went and then Miss Jones called the register and then I couldn't move and then Miss Jones phoned you, and then she said I had to come and tell you all about it and that I had to tell the truth.'

I looked at Luke for several moments before I spoke. His eyes were downcast and he looked small and lost, even for a twelve-year-old boy.

His tale was, without doubt, highly amusing and I felt, just for a moment, my compassion struggling to subdue a fit of the giggles, but empathy can be a powerful suppressant and imagination an effective antidote to mirth. So, instead of collapsing in laughter, I asked Luke if he now felt sufficiently recovered to return to lessons, or would he rather go and see the school nurse.

He responded immediately that he wanted to go to his lessons because the nurse would only give him a bag of ice to hold on his stomach and he didn't think that would do any good.

I felt reluctant to argue with his assumption, since it did seem to be the case that every pupil sent to the nurse ended up wandering the school holding a leaking bag of rapidly melting ice to whichever part of their anatomy seemed to be causing a problem. It had occurred to me that the school nurse could have been offered a job share with an automatic ice dispenser. An opinion, I once inadvisably expressed in a staff meeting, when the topic under discussion was something like, 'School First Aid Developments for the New Millennium.'

'Right then Luke,' I said, 'I want you to promise me that you won't give Jamie Fisher any more money and if he asks you for money, or threatens you in any way, then you must come and tell me immediately. Do you understand?'

'Yes Sir,' he replied.

'What lesson are you supposed to be in now?' I asked.

'I think I'm in History.'

'With Mr Pritchard?'

'No, with Miss Jenkins.'

'OK, you go to Miss Jenkins. I'll phone her and let her know you've been with me.'

'Alright Sir,' he responded, as he slowly moved towards the door. He cut quite a pathetic figure and for the first time in a long while, I actually felt quite sorry for him.

I checked my internal phone list for Miss Jenkins' number and keyed in her three digit code.

Miss Megan Jenkins was a recently qualified, vivacious History teacher, who was still possessed by an enthusiasm for her subject and an optimism that her pupils would benefit from her instruction. Her attitude was pleasantly refreshing, particularly when contrasted with the more cynical realism of many of her older and more experienced colleagues. Her Head of Department for example, Mr Geoff Pritchard, (MA Cantab) was a short, dark, disillusioned and demented Welsh demigod, who detested children and was counting off the days to his retirement on a large calendar located on the wall behind his desk. His classroom was on the opposite side of the corridor from my room and just as Miss Jenkins answered her phone, I heard his door open, as yet another unfortunate pupil, who had probably failed to appreciate historical significance of Hitler's Third Reich, was roughly ejected into the corridor under a torrent of uncontrolled and vindictive verbal abuse. His outbursts were becoming louder and more frequent as term progressed and I had to shield the receiver so that Miss Jenkins could hear me.

'Hi!' I said, 'It's Dave Falconer, sorry to disturb your lesson, but Luke Lowe has been with me over a pastoral matter and I didn't want him to get into trouble for being late.'

'Late for what?'

'Late for your History lesson.'

'He's not in my History lesson.'

'Oh Christ!' I exclaimed. 'Sorry Megan, he said he was supposed to be with you now. When he arrives, send him back to me would you?'

'Yes OK.' Megan responded, obviously keen to quell the mounting chaos of Year 8 History.

As I replaced the receiver I could still hear Geoff Pritchard ranting in the corridor and just for a moment, I debated with myself over the wisdom of interrupting him in full flow, but I decided that, on balance, it was preferable to risk incurring his displeasure than to have to endure his continuing tirade.

As I pulled open my door I could see Geoff's back, draped in the same tired and baggy tweed jacket he had worn every day during the five years since I had arrived at the school. He was still shouting, his shoulders shaking in apoplectic rage as he berated the cowering form of Huw Hopkins, Year 8's most notorious numbskull, a diminutive weasel-like creature, whose classroom behaviour was so disruptive that he was spending most of his school life languishing in corridors.

I coughed loudly to attract Geoff's attention and he spun round to check who had the temerity to interrupt him.

'Oh!' he exclaimed, 'it's you!' glowering at me from beneath the bushiest eyebrows in the school and obviously annoyed and perhaps a little embarrassed at being observed bullying Huw with such unrestrained vehemence.

'Yes.' I replied. 'Sorry to interrupt you when you're having fun, but I wondered if Luke Lowe is supposed to be in your lesson?'

'I bloody hope not!' he said, still red faced and panting with the exertion of trying to remind Huw of his school and civic responsibilities.

'If you imagine I want to try and teach that disorganised clot on top of having to deal with twerps like this you must be joking! Discipline is wasted on him,' he barked, waving his hand at the obviously relieved Huw Hopkins, who now, had risen slightly from his previous cowed position. 'Wasted on him, totally bloody wasted!' he continued. 'He is a right royal pain in the class and other places that rhyme with it!'

'Right!' I responded, 'I'll leave you to it then,' anxious now to return to my room and discover where Luke was really supposed to be. As I closed my door I heard a muffled comment from a still defiant Huw Hopkins followed by Geoff's rising response of 'Don't you argue with me boy! Don't you argue with me! I've told you, and told you, and told you, not to argue with me! Haven't I told you not to argue with me? Well, haven't I! What gives you the right to argue with me? Who told you, you could argue with me, hey? Did I tell you, you could argue with me? Well did I? Did I? Did I!' All this, shouted at an ever rising volume and increase in rage, made me think that, Geoff would be very lucky indeed to reach his so desired retirement.

I was pleased to re-enter the relative calm of my room, where I phoned Sue Williams in the school office to ask her to look up Luke's timetable to determine his correct lesson.

At the mention of his name, Sue began to relate the story of the missed lunch. I quickly said that I was fully aware of what had occurred and that I would tell her the whole story later. Like many school secretaries, being at the hub, gave Sue a unique and valuable perspective. She had access to a pretty complete picture of school life and not being a teacher, often gave her an uncluttered view of events. However, I was keen to conclude the saga of 'Two Lunch Luke,' so I pressed her for the timetable information and concluded the call with a repeat of my promise to update her later.

It turned out that Luke had Geography with Miss Davies. Just as I discovered this, he returned, with his usual timid knock and a crestfallen expression, as he reported that Miss Jenkins had sent him back.

'Of course she sent you back. Of course she sent you back,' I repeated in exasperation. 'You didn't have History did you?'

'I thought I did.'

'Well we all know what thought did, don't we?' I replied, instantly regretting my response, as I realised that sarcasm was as wasted on Luke as discipline was on Huw.

Who, from the now silent corridor, I inferred had been abandoned by Mr Pritchard to reflect upon his argumentative behaviour.

By now, lesson 7 was drawing to a close and being almost afternoon break, it hardly seemed worth sending Luke to Miss Davies in Geography, particularly as her room was on the 4th floor of S Block. So I told him to sit quietly at the back of the room until the end of the lesson.

I still had to resolve the problem of what to do about Jamie Fisher. As I was teaching English next period to 7/RS, (a form, only half jokingly known as Psycho Ward 7) dealing with Jamie would have to wait until tomorrow.

Chapter 3

Rock Hard Regan

In 'Nice Work' by David Lodge there is a consummate description of the therapeutic and quietly enjoyable nature of the early morning drive to work. His character, Vic Wilcox, enjoys his experience in the opulent and leather lined luxury of a large and powerful Jaguar saloon. Vic valued this time of quiet isolation where, cocooned and insulated from the clamour of the world, he could relax to soothing music and gather his thoughts in preparation for the day's trials and challenges.

When I first read the description of Vic's journey, I instantly empathised with his response to this valued period of calm in his hectic and often trauma filled day. My enjoyment of the morning drive to work was, unfortunately, taken in the less sumptuous interior of an M.O.T. failing, frequently vandalised, five-year-old Vauxhall Cavalier, with ill-fitting windows and a spaghetti like wire filled hole in the centre console, which had once housed the recently stolen radio. Despite this contrast, I still managed to take comfort from the morning journey to work. Like Vic, I valued the isolation of the locked and inviolable space which my car provided. It is obviously the major reason why all attempts by governments to persuade us to use public transport are doomed to failure. Anyone who is able to travel to work alone, uninterrupted by the company and clamour of others, is going to require a far more powerful incentive to abandon the practice, than simply making motoring increasingly expensive.

I would have given serious consideration to stopping work entirely, if I was forced to endure the dirt, noise, discomfort and unreliability of the bus and even though the drive to work was occasionally marred by heavy traffic, or the lack of intelligence of other road users, it was infinitely preferable to any possible alternative.

This morning, the early October day had dawned clear and crisp, with a bright sun and a chill intimation of the forthcoming winter. As I left home for school I recalled yesterday's saga of 'Two Lunch Luke' and my promise to deal with Jamie Fisher and his extortion racket. Chances were, that if he'd been extracting money from Luke, there'd be other unfortunate victims. Problem was, that in dealing with Jamie, I would, almost certainly, also have to deal his mother, the formidable and gargantuan Mrs Bunty Fisher; a woman so universally feared that even our recently appointed Headteacher, had ensured that, when making an appointment with her he had instructed 'Free-Fall Evans,' our ex Paratroops' Regiment caretaker, to be present in case of trouble.

Mrs Fisher had four children at the school and four more being incubated in the 'child centred' thug factory of one of our feeder primary schools. Unfortunately, one of her offspring, the inappropriately named 'Grace' was in Year 8 and was therefore, one of my charges. Not only was Mrs Fisher prodigiously and dangerously fertile, she was also of the belief that her children were the misunderstood victims of a vindictive and partial teaching profession. Not that Mrs Fisher, like many other parents, was remotely impressed by our frequent and doomed pleas to be considered 'a profession'. She had, unfortunately, been far more influenced in her opinions by the decades long, persistent and relentless campaign by both government and media to denigrate and vilify teachers as lazy, incompetent, left-wing loonies, who were massively over rewarded with indefensibly short hours and undeserved long holidays. It had always amazed me that politicians and media commentators blamed ill-discipline in schools upon the decline in respect shown to teachers by pupils. They often made such statements without any apparent irony, or any acknowledgement of their own culpability in the public's very low opinion of the nation's teachers. However, no analysis of the reasons for Mrs Fisher's contempt for teachers was going to help in dealing with her, and I mulled over this potential problem as I left the city to drive the eighteen miles to work.

My journey took me from the city suburbs to the Welsh valley town of Abercwmtwerp. This had the advantage of being in the opposite direction to the majority of traffic, which was heading into the city centre. Equally, my journey home in the evening was also blessed by being against the flow of those returning home.

This particular morning however, I was too preoccupied with how I was going to tackle the Jamie Fisher issue to fully appreciate the welcome solitude of the journey.

My first task upon arrival at school was to take my Year 8 assembly. This was always conducted in the canteen, which was euphemistically referred to as 'The Small Hall'. This stark, uninviting space consisted of a square wooden floored hall in a nineteen sixties built block, which also housed the Art and Technology Department and the inappropriately named Music Department; from which issued an unimaginable cacophony of sounds; none of which, could even be loosely described as music!

Year assemblies were held once a week and were designed to foster a sense of belonging to the Year Group and identification with the school's aims and objectives. They were invariably taken by the appropriate Head of Year, usually, with the desultory and unenthusiastic support of the year's Form Tutors, who were always a very mixed bunch, with varying levels of commitment and skill.

In my own year there were eight Form Tutors and by far the most reluctant to attend year assemblies, or to fulfil any of the other key duties expected of a Form Tutor, was Mark Collins, a forty-year-old balding and talentless lecher, who fancied himself as both a comedian and singer. In addition to his lack of commitment as a Form Tutor, he also displayed a monumental lack of awareness of his own shortcomings and a misplaced belief in his own worth.

Unfortunately, for the pastoral well-being of his form class, he was also the Head of the Technology Department and this gave him a ready bank of excuses not to attend assemblies. His favourite, and by far the most commonly employed, was that he couldn't attend as he was expecting an imminent delivery of timber.

I once pointed out to him that, if the timber deliveries were as frequent as he claimed, then not only would the World's forests be very soon depleted, but that he would need a timber yard the size of Texas, instead of the few old tea chests in his stock cupboard, containing the misshapen off-cuts left over from Year 7's failed attempts to construct plywood nest-boxes.

Enough, however, of Mark Collins and his excuses: of which we shall learn more later.

Unusually, on this particular morning my Year assembly passed without major incident and with all my eight Form Tutors in attendance.

The moment assembly was over I headed off across the yard towards the gym, to see Steve Regan, the huge, slightly malformed monster, who was second in the Boys' P.E. Department. Steve, who was now approaching fifty, was universally known by the kids as 'Rock Hard Regan' due to his ability to withstand repeated punches to his stomach and his reputation for flattening school bullies on the rugby pitch. In addition to his role within the P.E. Department, he was also Head of Year 9, and consequently, the person who had the unenviable responsibility for Jamie Fisher's pastoral welfare.

He had been awarded his nick name years previously, when he had been a young, fit and newly qualified teacher. It's true, that he still retained most of his physical strength, due to his huge frame and large bulk, but he'd long since lost the stamina, agility and toughness of spirit which had made the boys fear and respect his sporting prowess. In fact, he was increasingly absent from school with various ailments brought on by the rigours of his chosen role and by being forced out into the elements, even in atrocious weather. Most staff thought he was only a pale shadow of his former self and that he'd lost the motivation required to run successful sports teams.

He had for example, only recently returned to school after a period of sick leave, occasioned by an unfortunate confrontation with the notorious and demented dwarf, Huw Hopkins, who, a few weeks previously, after a disagreement with one of Steve's refereeing decisions during a Year 8 rugby match had sunk his teeth deep into Steve's left buttock and despite Steve's frantic efforts to dislodge him, had hung on like a rabid terrier. Reports by others in Year 8 had confirmed that the harder Steve tried to extricate himself from his unfortunate predicament, the more securely Hopkins attached himself. Steve had, apparently, first spun round and round like a whirling dervish and then, ran the length of the pitch, with Hopkins still firmly clamped to his arse and streaming out behind him like a swallow-tailed pennant in a high wind.

Boys scattered as Steve careered wildly around the pitch frantically trying to remove Hopkins by striking out behind him and smacking Hopkins on the head with his chrome plated 'Thunderer' patented whistle which hung at the end of his scoutmaster's lanyard. Hopkins however, was determined not to be dislodged and tightened his grip with every blow to his misshapen cranium. Just when it seemed as if this macabre spectacle might continue forever, a large black labrador, which until then had been watching the match with only a desultory interest, suddenly became extremely animated when Steve hurtled past with Hopkins' spindly legs flapping wildly in his slip-stream. The temptation of such an exciting chase proved too much for the dog to resist, and it set off in pursuit of its quarry with an excited yelp.

There was of course, no contest. Despite Steve's size and strength, his top speed was severely reduced, due to his age and the handicap of having a five stone maniac firmly fastened to his arse. According to later reports, there were a few moments, after the dog had caught up, when all three were attached in a surreal high speed procession, with Steve still running, Hopkins' teeth tenaciously embedded, and the dog clinging to Hopkins' right foot, as though it were a fleeing hare. This was just too much of a burden, even for Steve's renowned endurance, and so, all three collapsed into an untidy and chaotic heap, from which Steve finally emerged, free at last from Hopkins' vice like grip and relieved at his release from a most painful and distressing situation.

I hadn't spoken with Steve since the incident and his subsequent return to work. The drama was first reported in the staff room by Geoff Pritchard at afternoon break on the same day it happened. He had, apparently, witnessed the whole event from the window of his classroom, which was located on the first floor of the main teaching block, and from where he had an excellent view over the school field. He had arrived in the staff room as usual; nonchalantly swinging his disgustingly stained coffee mug, and loudly announced that there was going to be an urgent need for more bloody cover in the P.E. Department.

'Why's that Geoff?' I asked, knowing that he was bursting to tell all the assembled staff some piece of newly acquired information.

'Because Regan's gone home sick, boy! That's why,' he exclaimed in a loud voice. 'I've just seen 'Horrible Hopkins' sink his teeth into Regan's gluteus maximus! Regan was running round the rugby pitch like someone had rubbed horse oil on his bollocks; with Hopkins' clinging to his arse like a demented ferret: couldn't dislodge him though. He was finally saved by the timely intervention of that bloody black labrador that's always hanging around in the yard at break times. Quite a sight it was, yes indeed, quite a sight! Hopkins is one of your Neanderthal louts, I believe,' he continued, looking pointedly at me, as though I was somehow personally responsible for all Hopkins' misdeeds.

'He's in Year 8, if that's what you mean,' I replied, thinking about all the additional work this most recent incident was going to generate.

I recalled all this, as I turned into the litter strewn corridor outside the gym and approached the door marked, 'Boys' P.'. It had of course, once read, 'Head of Boys' P.E., but like most signs in the school it had been thoughtfully altered to be less informative, but more emotionally satisfying.

I knocked the door and then entered, to find Steve Regan gingerly perched on a large rubber-ring of the kind used in hospital after an operation for haemorrhoids.

'Still sore then?' I enquired.

'Bloody sore! He replied. 'I heard that you'd insisted on a period of exclusion for Hopkins.

'Yes,' I said. 'He's still not back. I tried to get Douglas to exclude him permanently but you know how jelly livered he is when it comes to the issue of exclusion.'

The jelly livered Douglas in question, was the aptly initialled, Dr. Michael Anthony Douglas, BSc, Med., our relatively new Head teacher; who, like many head teachers, was terrified of upsetting parents, governors, or the L.E.A., and who had jumped on the latest educational bandwagon of 'Pupil Inclusion' with an enthusiasm bordering on the criminally irresponsible. It was now so difficult to have a pupil excluded that even good teachers were leaving teaching altogether, or took periods of extended sick leave due to stress.

I had heard it remarked, by Free-Fall Evans, our bolshie and cynical caretaker, that to get yourself excluded from our school you'd have to kill a member of the Senior Management Team, and then, because this might not prove a sufficient misdemeanour, you'd have to bury the corpse in full view of the Governing Body, preferably during a parents' evening, to ensure the maximum number of witnesses. Even then, he thought some bleeding heart do-gooder would argue a case for tolerance and understanding.

Evans was of the opinion (shared by some on the teaching staff) that, we were all too bloody soft on kids and that we should bring back the bloody cane! After all, he said by way of illustration, it had never done him any bloody harm. Although, those of us with even a modicum of perception, questioned the validity of *that* claim!

Anyway, I had argued a powerful case with Douglas for Hopkins' permanent exclusion, which I'm sure, is why he was sent home for four weeks: a punishment of almost unheard of severity and harshness.

Steve, of course, was less than happy with the decision, but had been advised by his union that, in the current climate of educational cowardice, it was the best he could hope for; so he had reluctantly, returned to work, despite feeling that Hopkins' punishment was lamentably inadequate.

As he sat now, with one cheek carefully positioned in the empty centre of his rubber-ring he looked up at me with a kind of weary resignation and said:

'I heard from one of the kids that you wanted to see me.'

'Yes,' I replied. 'It's about Jamie Fisher.'

'What's that little sod been up to now?' he enquired.

So, I related the saga of 'Two Lunch Luke,' without too many humorous embellishments, and said I'd be grateful if he could have appropriate words with Fisher to ensure that the extortion stopped.

This, he promised to do, and anxious to have the matter resolved without a major confrontation with Mrs Fisher, he said he'd deal with it quietly the next time Fisher had P.E. Not wishing to know too much about Steve's dubious methods of control; I thanked him, and headed off to the staff room to pick up any messages left in my pigeon-hole.

As I waded back though the litter, it struck me that Steve was looking very tired and was probably well on the way to a nervous breakdown and eventual redeployment as a teacher in the Special Education Department. Secondary schools throughout the land are invariably possessed of an old, demountable, temporary classroom, that had been speedily and shoddily erected during the baby boom of the fifties, and which now stood in a woefully dilapidated state, in a neglected and remote corner of the school; well separated from the main school buildings and used as a base for babysitting those pupils identified as having 'special educational needs.' It was equally likely that, such a base would be staffed by an aging ex-P.E. teacher, who, like an old broken down cab horse, had been put out to end their days in unfamiliar pastures.

I could comprehend how finding meaningful employment for old P.E. teachers, who were too worn out to referee matches, but were still too young to retire, was a major headache for the Senior Management in most schools. However, it always struck me as singularly perverse and incompetent to give them the task of trying to educate the most challenging and difficult pupils in inadequate and poorly equipped premises which were as remote from the main life of the school as possible. Yet, this is undoubtedly what happens in many schools, and can only really be explained by the very low priority given to those pupils whose academic achievements were inevitably going to depress the school's ranking in L.E.A. League Tables.

If anything in education is true; but almost never achieved, it is that, the most deprived and vulnerable children require the best educated and most skilful teachers; teachers who are highly intelligent, sensitive and extraordinarily perceptive and resilient.

The fact that this state of affairs is not only rarely achieved, but not even consistently striven for, is an indictment of our entire system of so called education.

It was now almost at the end of period 1, and as I re-crossed the yard to reach the staff room I could just glimpse in the distance, tucked away behind the science block, the corner of our own example of this all too common Special Educational Needs classroom. In our case, this sad and scruffy building was currently the teaching domain of Lofty Lewis, the ex-Head of Boys' P.E.

Lofty was an extremely short, fat, irascible and disillusioned whinging Welshman, close to retirement; who had been moved into the S.E.N. Department after a slipped disk and early onset arthritis had forced the premature end to his days as a teacher of P.E. He had, unfortunately for him, been set to work under the non-existent direction of the Head of Special Education, Miss Pamela Potts. Miss Potts was an ex-R.E. teacher who, much earlier in her career, had experienced a crisis of faith upon the break-up of her only romantic attachment and had, as a consequence, felt unable to teach a subject in which she no longer believed. It being almost impossible to dismiss a teacher for something as trivial as no longer being able to do their job, the distraught Miss Potts was offered a short retraining course and then re-employed as a special needs teacher. Within a very short time, the Head of the Special Education Department had taken early retirement due to stress and, it's rumoured, the pressure of having to supervise the work of Miss Potts, and Miss Potts, who was perhaps, the most opinionated and idle teacher in the school, was duly promoted to Head of Department.

Lofty, who had a vitriolic hatred of her, undermined her at every opportunity. He ignored her pleas to attend departmental meetings and aggressively sabotaged her desire to be respected by ignoring all her schemes to get him to acknowledge her authority.

Like Pam, Lofty was ill-equipped for the task assigned him. He was supposed to teach basic literacy and numeracy skills to a carefully selected group of eleven to thirteen year olds who were unable to cope with the levels of reading and maths skills required in mainstream classes. In reality, the kids mostly played games on the few ageing computers which had been donated when the I.T. Department had recently upgraded its obsolete machines. His classroom was also used by small groups of dim and disruptive older boys, who found his lack of interest in teaching a refreshing change from some of their more demanding lessons.

Lofty only had a couple more years to go before retirement, so it was quite likely that his place would be taken by Steve Regan, especially if Steve's ability to cope with the rigours of P.E. continued to decline.

It was certainly true that Steve's recent encounter with 'Horrible Hopkins' had taken its toll and probably hastened the day when he would be consigned to the educational graveyard of 'Special Needs', to serve out his time child-minding the ever growing ranks of the educationally disaffected!

Chapter 4

Uniform Issues

Almost a week after my conversation with Steve Regan about Jamie Fisher's extortion racket, Fisher stopped attending school and despite his mother's forceful attempts to persuade him to attend, he was adamant in his refusal. Unusually for Fisher, he was not revealing any reason for his sudden school phobia, but I suspected that Steve's strategy for ending Fisher's extortion had involved the threat of some action which he was not brave enough to face.

In any event, his absence provided a blessed relief, for both staff and Fisher's victims. I noticed that Luke Lowe had perked up considerably since Fisher's absence and when Luke's mother had phoned to thank me for sorting out his problem, she had mentioned that Luke now seemed much happier about attending school.

Due to Fisher's unpopularity, no-one enquired too closely as to the reasons for his absence. Eventually, his refusal to attend was referred to Sylvia Coombs the E.W.O. (Educational Welfare Officer) with a strong recommendation that the remainder of his education would be better undertaken elsewhere.

I'd asked Steve why his handling of the Fisher case had been so effective, when I next saw him at one of the regular Thursday evening pastoral meetings, but he indicated that I didn't really wish to know. The pastoral meetings were interminable gatherings held once a month in a classroom located in the ever deteriorating Main Teaching Block. The meetings were usually attended by the five Heads of Year, plus the Head of VI Form and an assortment of others, depending upon the issues under discussion. These others normally included: Pam Potts, the Head of the Special Educational Needs Department,

Sylvia Coombs, the E.W.O., and Chris Reed, the teacher in charge of the Pupil Referral Unit.

The P.R.U. was housed in a large, old dilapidated ex-P.E. changing room known as 'E Block', due partly to its shape, but also as an indicator of its function as a place for the internal exclusion of disruptive pupils.

The pastoral meetings were invariably chaired by Bert Bowen and had been delegated to him, because the pastoral aspect of education held a very low priority among other members of the Senior Management Team who were always reluctant to attend, on account of the fact that, collectively, the five Heads of Year were always vocal and articulate in their criticisms, and not frightened to lay the blame for the school's failings fairly where they belonged.

As I entered the meeting on this particular evening, I noticed that we had the usual attendees. Bonny Butler, the new Head of VI Form was present for her first meeting after having been recently appointed from her previous position as Head of Girls' P.E. She was yet another example of Douglas' talent for placing square pegs in round holes. She was, according to Mark Collins, a desperate spinster who needed a good seeing to; although it's very doubtful that Collins was the man for the task. Bonny had a very attractive face and, in certain lights, also a rather seductive one. Unfortunately, it was set upon a body which had failed to respond to the rigours and disciplines of the P. E. Department and was no advert for the benefit of sport as the route to a desirable figure.

As one of my lithe and outspoken ex-Year 11 girls had once accurately, but inappropriately observed, she was 'a fat arsed old cow!'

Also present, as usual, was Pam Potts, another spinster of considerably less appeal than Bonny, and who was consumed by a need to be considered important. She possessed a precious and quite erroneous perception of her own worth and ability, and was almost universally despised as a deluded non-entity. Staff viewed her with only slightly less contempt than that harboured by Lofty Lewis who was almost paranoiac in his hatred of her.

Chris Reed, who was also supposed to report to her in her role as Head of Special Needs, totally ignored her, and refused to acknowledge her claims of authority. Chris had his own subversive agenda, and was a volatile maverick of high intelligence and unconventional morality: I liked him enormously!

He smiled at me as I entered, and announced in a loud voice 'Here's Falconer! Now the brains have arrived we can commence the usual fruitless discussion regarding matters of no consequence!'

I cast him my usual quizzical look of mild amusement and took my place next to Mandy, my young, enthusiastic and popular Assistant Head of Year. Bert, who was already sitting at the head of the table passing out copies of his miss-spelled agenda, tried to call the meeting to order.

'Can we make a start?' he said, casting a look of impatience in my direction.

By way of reply I pointed to my watch to indicate that, in fact, I was not late and nodded towards the door, which had just opened to admit Steve Regan, who was always the last to arrive, due he claimed, to the pressing responsibilities of his P.E. commitments.

Finally, we were all assembled apart from Bruce Lloyd, the idle Head of the current Year 10. Bruce had only managed to attend one pastoral meeting in the last three years. He had long since stopped sending his apologies, with some lame and fictitious excuse for his non-attendance. Bert still sent him a copy of the agenda, but of course, failed to take him to task for refusing to adhere to one of his duties.

I glanced down at the agenda for this evening's meeting, which Mandy had kindly placed in front of me. It was, as usual, brief, predictable and the product of a pressured mind.

ADGENDA
PASTORIAL meeting
4.00pm 10.11.05..
Room M18

1.　　Minites of prevbious meeting!
2.　　The Chrismas fare
3.　　Pupils' Matters
4.　　Year Assembys
5.　　Uniform Issues.
6.　　The Schools' Councel!
7.　　Uniforn Issues
8.　　A>O>B>

I would often try to alleviate the crushing boredom of these occasions by correcting the agenda in red ink and passing it back to Bert in the vain hope that it would help him to improve his grammar and punctuation. His problem was, that, being under constant and unrelenting pressure, he inevitably left the preparation of the agenda until the last possible minute and therefore, was forced to undertake the task himself. This he did, a few moments before the meeting was due to begin, using a word processing package, so antiquated that it made an IBM Golf-Ball typewriter seem the height of sophistication. I'd often advised him to write it up earlier and pass it to Sue Williams in the office for proof-reading, correction and printing, but he claimed he never had the time. So we were collectively subjected each month to an always interesting example of his last minute illiteracy.

Once Bert managed to start the meeting we rattled through the agenda at a cracking pace. This was quite normal, due to the fact that the agenda usually reflected the issues which the S.M.T. were keen for us to discuss, but which generally failed to generate any enthusiasm, as they were, inevitably, items which had been debated numerous times at previous meetings without any resolution. Most members of the Pastoral Committee simply wished to raise matters of genuine concern to themselves under A.O.B. and then head for home. For some reason however, we became stuck this evening on items 5 and 7.

This probably was because Laura Price, the young, vivacious and inexperienced Head of Year 7, had asked why item 5 had been listed twice. Laura was new, both to her role as Head of Year and as a member of the committee and she had not yet realised that to draw attention to an agenda item in this way gave Bert just the window of opportunity he was waiting for.

'Good question,' he responded to Laura's enquiry. 'It's listed twice, to remind me just how important it is! We must start to tackle the kids who are flouting the uniform rules.'

'What all twelve hundred of them?' asked Chris.

'Oh, it's not as bad as that,' Bert responded, sensing that Chris was about to make some condemnatory comment about his, and the S.M.T.'s failures. 'There are some who wear the correct uniform.'

'Yes,' agreed Steve Regan, 'there's one in my year.'

'Who's that?' I enquired, amazed that, with Steve's slack grip on uniform issues, there would actually be a Year 9 pupil who obeyed the rules.

'That new girl,' he replied, 'what's her name?'

'Trudy Wilson,' offered Sophie Millar the Head of Year 11 and the teacher responsible for those pupils who were in foster care.

'Christ!' I exclaimed, 'I'm not surprised she's in the correct uniform, she's just been placed in foster care and provided with a brand new uniform by Social Services after losing all her possessions in a house fire started by her drunken father. The only reason she's in the proper uniform is because the poor little sod, has nothing else to wear!'

There then, followed a general discussion of the uniform, or the lack of it, which culminated in a round-robin where, Bert asked us all to name which pupils in our respective year groups regularly wore the designated uniform. Needless to say, we all struggled to name one; thus, conferring absolute validity upon the inference in Chris's original question.

The uniform was supposed to consist of: black shoes, black socks, black plain tailored trousers, or plain black knee length skirt, (as optional wear for the girls only), royal blue polo shirt embroidered with the school badge and motto, chocolate brown sweater embroidered with the school badge and motto and, as an optional extra, a plain chocolate brown regulation school baseball cap embroidered with the school badge and motto. This last item had recently been introduced in a moment of insane innovation by the S.M.T. in an attempt to prevent pupils wearing the wide variety of headgear which they obviously favoured. It proved an innovation too far; for the only persons I ever saw wearing this sartorial abomination were Dr Douglas and Vic Davies, who wandered the school wearing the cap for the first few weeks subsequent to its introduction in an attempt to publicise its availability. Their endorsement gave the cap all the street-cred required to ensure its demise.

All in all, the uniform was a totally uninspiring outfit and therefore, most kids attempted to brighten it up a little with their own individual interpretations. These ranged from the commonest deviations, such as wearing trainers, or hooped earrings to the most extreme examples of gothic, or punk fashion, including make-up and body piercings, which would not have looked out of place on the set of a horror movie.

Every term there came a point where, even the normally unobservant members of the S.M.T. became aware of the fact that, the rules regarding the wearing of the appropriate uniform were being totally ignored. When this point was reached, instead of taking a lead and insisting upon the uniform rules being enforced, they simply noted their concerns and asked that the matter be discussed at the next pastoral meeting. This gave them the comfort of appearing to be doing something, without actually having to do anything.

I had repeatedly asked why, if the wearing of the correct uniform was important, the S.M.T. never took any effective action to enforce the rules. Like most issues, which may have placed them in a situation of potential conflict with the more truculent parents, the uniform issue was never confronted.

Personally, I ignored the rantings of the S.M.T. on the uniform issue and simply used my own unsanctioned strategies to deal with the problem.

I had consistently pointed out at both pastoral meetings and full staff meetings that, if it was desirable that pupils wear the designated uniform, then, all that was required was that the Head and other members of the S.M.T. ensure that all pupils obey the rules. After all, the solution to the problem was not one which required high intelligence or exceptional ability, so it ought really to have been within the limited talents of the S.M.T. to solve.

However, my confidence in their ability to tackle the uniform issue was severely undermined when Vic Davies introduced 'Trainer Permission Notes' as a strategy for solving one of the commonest transgressions. His idea was that, if a pupil arrived at registration in their form-room wearing trainers, they were to be sent to him immediately to explain why they were not wearing the regulation black shoes. Then, depending upon the validity of their explanation, they would either be issued with a signed trainer permission note or – and that's where the idea ended; for there was never any 'or', not at Gruffudd ap Cynan Comp!

And so, we all faced the new situation of confronting pupils in trainers, who now, had not only a reason for being inappropriately attired, but also a note to excuse it!

I had occasion to enter Vic's office a few days after the commencement of his new 'Trainer Permission Note' initiative and was less than encouraged to see, on his desk, a huge pile of just printed notes, all ready and waiting to be signed and issued. I remember that, I commented to him at the time.

'You're obviously intending to issue a lot of Trainer Permission Notes then Vic,' I observed. He cast me a blank look of incomprehension.

'The notes,' I said, pointing at the large pile. 'I'd have had more confidence in your intention to deal with the problem, if you'd only printed a few for distribution. Judged by the evidence however, I suspect that Trainer Permission Notes are about to become as common as seagulls on a waste tip!'

'No – well,' he responded, obviously incapable of appreciating the conflict between his stated determination to stamp out the wearing of trainers and the printing of several thousand permission notes authorising the very behaviour he wished to eliminate.

In the event, my prediction proved absolutely accurate. At ten to nine each morning there was a very long line of trainer wearing kids outside Vic's office, queuing for Trainer Permission Notes, which were being issued with the frequency of arrows at Agincourt.

This well publicised initiative resulted in pupils, not only wearing trainers, but now wearing them with the swaggering confidence of Chicago mobsters who had the Chief of Police and the D.A. on the pay-roll.

The number of pupils wearing trainers increased exponentially once they were sanctioned by an official note. Previously, when I'd stopped a pupil to ask why they were wearing trainers, they would offer me an explanation. Now, they simply said that they had a Permission Note, usually accompanying their statement by aggressively brandishing a dirty and dog-eared piece of paper bearing Vic Davies's illegible signature. I pointed out to them that the answer 'I have a Permission Note,' was not an explanation as to why they were wearing trainers.

As far as I was concerned, the great 'Trainer Permission Note Experiment' was not going to impact upon the pupils in Year 8. The school rules clearly stated that the wearing of trainers was not permissible and my job description clearly specified that, as Head of Year I was expected to uphold and enforce the school rules. So that's exactly what I did!

I queried every Trainer Permission Note issued to a Year 8 pupil. I requested a detailed written explanation from Vic, asking that he specify the exact reasons which had influenced his decision to issue the Permission Note in question. I further requested a list of Year 8 pupils who had been refused a Permission Note, again with an explanation of the reasons for the refusal. Of course, as there had been no refusals, this did not present Vic with any additional work, but it did serve to remind him of the need to have criteria for refusal built into any system which required permission.

I also told all of Year 8 in my next Year Assembly that, as Head of Year, Trainer Permission Notes, cut no ice with me, not even if they'd been issued by the Almighty, and that I required, as a minimum, an official letter from their doctor specifying the exact medical condition which necessitated the wearing of trainers.

I further instigated a break-time and lunch-time rest regime for all pupils whose doctors were gullible enough to issue a medical explanation justifying the wearing of trainers. I wrote to all Year 8 parents, informing them that pupils arriving to school with medical justification for the wearing of trainers would be kept in each break and lunch time with their feet resting upon a cushion placed on a chair of suitable height, so that they could benefit from the care and attention which their poor feet obviously deserved.

In addition, I confiscated all trainers worn without an appropriate doctor's letter, and I tore up all Trainer Permission Notes which had been issued by Vic without considered and acceptable medical reasons.

Within three weeks I had reduced the wearing of trainers in Year 8, from epidemic proportions to the rarity of 'hens' teeth.'

When, at the next pastoral meeting, I was asked for an explanation as to why the wearing of trainers in Year 8 was practically non-existent, I replied that it was simply a gift I had for communicating with the kids, in a way which made my intentions clear.

In truth, the pressure placed upon the system by my request for written explanations for the issue of each Trainer Permission Note had quickly lead to the schemes demise and only six weeks after the great Trainer Permission Note initiative began; it ended.

So many notes had been printed that we were, eighteen months later, still using the blank side of them to record telephone messages and inter-departmental memos.

The whole failure of the initiative stood as a shining example of the incisive and innovative skills of our Senior Management Team.

Anyway, the final conclusion of the Pastoral Committee, arrived at after much discussion, was that Bert was to report back to the S.M.T. that the Year Heads would enforce the rules on the wearing of the correct uniform, when they had confidence that their decisions would be totally supported, and that sanctions would be employed to punish transgressors. As this was extremely unlikely to happen, another long and fruitless debate had ended, with no conclusion for positive action.

The meeting finally ended after the usual groans and gripes under A.O.B. and we were all blessedly free to head for home and the relative sanity of our ordinary lives.

A couple of months after the failed Trainer Permission Note fiasco, a new and worrying adaptation of the uniform began to emerge among a small group of disaffected boys in Year 10. I noticed that a few of them had taken to wearing belts which were far longer than necessary, and where the excess length was allowed to hang down the front of their trousers, like a pet snake. At first, the length encouraged to dangle was only about eight to ten inches, but like all fashion trends it developed adherents, who took it to extremes; so that, within a very short time, there were boys with the end of their belts hanging down, well below their knee, and in the more easily influenced devotees, almost to their ankle!

Of course, it was not long before this new innovation began to be copied by boys in all the other years, and very soon there were boys reporting to the nurse with various injuries suffered by having their belts trapped in doors and desks, trodden on by jealous rivals and even pulled by over enthusiastic girls who began to employ 'the belt tug' as a new weapon in their attention seeking armoury.

By the time I'd decided that this was a dangerous and unacceptable departure from the correct uniform; it had already captured the limited imaginations of the boys in Year 8, and was, unfortunately, a well established trend. I decided to tackle the situation head on at my next year assembly in the canteen.

These occurred each Tuesday for Year 8 and on the morning in question the pupils arrived in their normal half awake and disinterested state. The canteen was only just large enough to accommodate all two hundred and forty plus pupils and it was a tight squeeze to fit everyone in. They of course, did not have the luxury of chairs as in the main hall and so had to sit on the dirty and litter strewn floor. There were however, chairs provided for my eight Form Tutors.

Once everyone was seated, I called for their attention as usual, and greeted them with my normal salutation of: 'Good Morning Year 8!' to which the expected, and only acceptable response was an audible and eager 'Good Morning Mr Falconer!'

Needless to say, I very rarely obtained the genuine and sincere greeting I desired, and so, I had to repeat the exercise several times, until I heard 'Good Morning Mr Falconer' uttered with a moderate degree of enthusiasm.

All my Form Tutors were present apart from Mark Collins who, for a rare change, was not having timber delivered, but who was waiting for the anticipated arrival of an engineer to repair a drilling machine, which had apparently been recently destroyed in an unequal contest with Horrible Hopkins.

Once my morning greeting had been answered with acceptable volume and clarity; I began.

'It's become apparent to me that we have a problem!'

A few audible groans issued from the front couple of rows. I waited for the return of silence, and then continued.

'The problem is one of evolution and extinction!'

More groans, this time louder, and from an identifiable group of intellectual pigmies in 8/MJ: 'Stand up Mark Plowman, John Griffiths and Matt Thomas,' I barked.

Once they were standing and order was re-established, I expanded and elaborated my theory.

'When I say the problem is one of evolution and extinction, I'm not talking about dinosaurs and dodos here. Oh, no, I'm talking about belts and trousers!'

Now, an audible snigger from Dr Simon Moore, Form Tutor to 8/SM, who was the brightest member of my team and had guessed where this was heading: I flashed him a look of wry disapproval and surveyed the blank and uncomprehending stares of the pupils and began to suspect that the theory I was about to expound was going to miss its target.

'Yes!' I repeated. 'Belts and trousers! You must all be aware by now of my concern regarding this ridiculous new trend of having several feet of belt end hanging down the front of your trousers. Well, I've been doing some research, and guess what I've discovered?'

'That you're brainy Sir!' shouted the unmistakable voice of Ben Jacobs, the observant class clown from 8/SM and whom I'm sure, was being encouraged in his increasingly flippant insubordination by Simon Moore, his bright, but unconventional Form Tutor.

'Yes Ben,' I agreed, 'I am brainy, well spotted boy! But I was not researching my incredibly high intelligence. I was researching the evolution of the trouser and I discovered (it was a mistake to pose a rhetorical question to pupils younger than sixteen) that it has taken some four thousand years of trouser evolution to produce: The Belt Loop!'

No gasps of amazement greeted this announcement of my discovery. My Form Tutors were, collectively, now incapable of paying attention, and most had lowered their gaze to avoid eye contact.

'My fear is that, by having the end of your belts dangling down the front of your trousers, you are depriving the belt loop of its valued and noble function. Now, there is a well known evolutionary maxim that says: 'if you don't use it you'll lose it!'

I tried to obtain confirmation of the validity of this statement from Joanne Monk, Form Tutor to 8/JM and a well respected Biology teacher, but she had covered her face with her hands and was rocking on her chair as though she were undergoing some sort of seizure.

'Miss Monk obviously knows all about losing it!' I observed. This remark had the effect of focusing all the kids bemused attention upon the unfortunate Miss Monk at the precise moment that she slowly slid from her chair to collapse in a giggling and undignified heap right next to the stunned Ben Jacobs who by way of helpful commentary, shouted, 'Miss Monk's on the floor Sir!'

'Yes, thank you Ben,' I acknowledged. 'Perhaps Dr Moore you'd be kind enough to help Miss Monk regain her seat.''

'Certainly Mr Falconer,' Simon answered, as he stepped forward to assist Joanne, who was struggling to regain her composure and was waving to me a signed apology as she fought to suppress her fit of the giggles.

This short distraction had certainly woken up the kids, who had gone from disinterested apathy to rapt attention. Unfortunately, their attention was upon the battle Miss Monk was having to prevent her shoulders from shaking.

When finally, I'd managed to restore order, I returned to my theme.

'I don't intend to allow your cavalier treatment of the belt loop to result in its extinction. From now on, all belt ends will be threaded through your belt loops, so that they are prevented from hanging down the front of your trousers. Any visible belt end will, from today, result in the confiscation of the belt. If this means that your trousers fall down: tough!'

This grabbed the attention of Stacy Fowler and her gang of precocious girls, who, from their whistles of approval, obviously gave their unqualified endorsement to the idea of boys' trousers falling down.

Although, I cannot judge the message of my assembly to have been an immediate success, it was the beginning of the end for the dangling belt end fashion trend. After only a week, and a large box full of confiscated belts, the trend withered, and finally died.

It only remained to maintain a constant vigilance to spot and suppress the next inspired uniform adaptation.

Chapter 5

The Christmas Fayre

All parents should be cautioned that, when choosing names for their offspring, there are certain names which may seem a mark of distinction when considered in the fevered anticipation of the 'happy event,' but, when recorded in the revealing light of a school register, leap off the page to sound alarm bells among teachers as signifiers of potential problems.

For girls, these would include all hyphenated names: Lindy-Lou, Sarah-Jane, Jamie-Lee etc. Also, all names paying homage to songs, or singers: Layla, Lucille, Lulu. Antipodian imports, such as: Kylie, Keeleigh, Sydney are best avoided. So too, should all place names: Chelsea, Paris, Dallas, even if the child *was* conceived there! Especially feared are those with names misspelled through ignorance, or a belief in the value of eccentric individualism: Natalee, Zoey, Cloey, etc.

For boys, the range and boundaries of the ridiculous are somewhat more limited, but generally, names indicating an enthusiasm for the iconic, or famous, spell real trouble: Elvis, Tyrone, Keefer etc. Boys can also present with names best reserved for popes, or polo players: John-Mark, John-Paul, Tarquin, Tudor, Warwick. Such names usually signify parents with an inflated and unrealistic view of their child's character, class and charisma.

I mention this because I was reminded of its importance when I took morning registration for Mandy Jones one morning in early November. I had agreed to take a morning registration period with each of my seven forms in Year 8, to try and generate some enthusiasm for becoming involved in the forthcoming School Christmas Fayre. The burdensome duty of organising this annual

58

money raising event, traditionally, fell upon the shoulders of the Head of Year 8. This was because Year 8 pupils were considered the best placed to organise the event, due to their being young enough to still have the necessary gullibility and enthusiasm; old enough to possess the required ability and talent; yet not quite old enough to view the whole enterprise with the cynical contempt which inevitably sets in by the time pupils reach Year 9.

An example of this transformation, from being an innocent and co-operative pupil to an implacable enemy of all teachers, can be succinctly illustrated by the fact that, if a teacher, upon hearing a familiar noise and detecting an odious smell in a room full of Year 7 pupils, asks the question 'Who broke wind?' all pupils will noisily name and point to the culprit with loyal enthusiasm. However, the same event, and the same question asked in a room full of Year 9 pupils, will produce a contemptuous silence so profound, that a whisper in a library would seem the loudest sound on Earth! For, by the time children reach thirteen-plus, their desire to please their teacher has been superseded by a wish to conform to the authority-hating attitude of their peers. This is of course all quite natural and not a cause for concern, but it does illustrate the wisdom of not trying to involve older pupils in events which require an unquestioning acceptance of the value of projects initiated by adults. Even by Year 8 there were some pupils who were already showing signs of identifying with the hormonally afflicted in Year 9, and so, were reluctant to participate in any event organised by the school. Fortunately, this only affected a few of the more mature pupils and the majority of Year 8 were still innocent and trusting enough to involve themselves in The Christmas Fayre.

Upon my arrival at Mandy's form room I was pleased to see that she'd already admitted her class, including Horrible Hopkins who'd now returned to school after his four week exclusion for biting Regan's bum.

'Hi!' I said, 'thanks for getting them seated. Have you called the register?'

'No, I thought I'd leave that pleasure to you, after all, there's no point in your doing only half the job.'

She winked, to endow her comment with the warmth of approval. 'Thanks for taking reg for me Dave; it will give me the chance to phone Mrs Lowe about Luke.'

'What's the matter with Luke now?' I enquired, casting a quick glance around the room to check if he was present.

Seeing my look, Mandy said. 'He's not here, at least not yet. He's been turning up late to reg, especially in the mornings. I just need to tell Mrs Lowe, because I'm sure she's not aware of his lateness.'

'Fine, you get off, I'll deal with this lot. Let me know what Mrs Lowe says and I'll see Luke if you feel it would help.'

'OK,' she said, with her usual engaging smile, as she left to make her call.

I closed the door and stood behind her desk surveying the mixed bunch of twelve and thirteen year olds that comprised 8/MJ.

Stacy Fowler and her group of girlie grotesques occupied a large table at the rear of the room and close enough to the windows to enable them to shout abuse at all those pupils arriving to school late. The most sinister of Stacy's mob was Tracey-Ann Smith, who, although only just thirteen was already beginning to show signs of her future destiny as a fearful and accomplished predator. Even boys several years her senior were wary of her and would cross the school yard to avoid her. Next to Tracey-Ann was Crystal Devine, an aptly named, heavily adorned bottle blonde siren, whose future definitely lay within the entertainment industry; which branch only time would tell. She was already a self-aware little vixen, whose cuteness was beginning to disappear under her died hair and purple eye-shadow. I made a mental note to tackle her about her make-up at the end of the period. Opposite Crystal were the identical and notorious Turner twins, Dixie and Trixie. These two should never have been allowed to attend the same school, let alone be in the same form. They were a pair of talented troublemakers, who could communicate in a private language of clicks, grunts and whistles, and who reminded me of the young, blond, vacant eyed aliens in the film, 'Village of the Damned'. They would often make strange and inexplicable noises, and greeted every enquiry regarding their well-being with a malevolent stare of terrifying intensity. They were a part of Stacy's gang only because she and Tracey-Ann, were the only girls who could control them, and who were not fazed by their weirdness. Stacy kept them in reserve as a backup which could be employed if her enemies (of which, she had quite a few) failed to respond to her usual tactics of bullying and intimidation. 'You'll get a visit from the Turner twins' was a threat most pupils understandably dreaded.

Opposite Stacy's table were 8/MJ's most troublesome boys, chief among whom was Horrible Huw Hopkins, who Steve Regan now always referred to as 'Horrible Hopkins the Hobgoblin from Hell', a piece of alliteration, of which, I would not have thought him capable. Also on this table was Jack Reynolds, a fat, unpleasant slug of a boy, who always smelled faintly of urine and stale cabbage water. Next to Jack was the truly dangerous Nathan Hyde. Nathan was the only boy in the form who was not frightened of the Turner twins. He was a violent misfit, whose temper was controlled by maximum strength 'Ritalin,' which was relatively effective in modifying his behaviour as long as he remembered to take it. Past incidents of his aggressive episodes were so memorable that, all his teachers made it their first task to ask him if he'd taken his drugs. Next to Nathan was Kyle Bowman, an intelligent manipulator who, although small in stature, featured large on my list of pupils to watch. He was a budding classroom lawyer who knew all his rights, but failed to acknowledge any of his responsibilities. He was sly, mean, underhand, and a pathological liar. In fact, he possessed all the qualities necessary for a successful career in politics. Most of the moronic thugs in Year 8 respected him because, although it was obvious that he knew considerably more than they, he nevertheless seemed to share their disparaging and negative attitude to learning; a fact which I, and other staff knew to be unfounded; for his work was exemplary, his school exercise books neat and well presented and his knowledge extensive. His father was chairman of the planning committee of the local council and his mother was an ex-tax accountant, now running a car clamping firm, following a short spell in prison for fraud. He possessed therefore, the perfect combination of nature and nurture to ensure success, possibly as a future chairman of The Conservative

Party. I considered him to be potentially one of the most dangerous pupils in the school.

On the closest table was Luke Lowe's empty chair and a mixed group of the dim and inept; while in the farthest corner, well away from the windows and potential trouble were the small group of bright pleasant and co-operative pupils who made teaching a joy. The most noticeable bloom in this oasis of talent was Hannah Austin, a polite, pretty, popular girl of immense charm and intelligence. Five minutes in her company was sufficient compensation for the hours of grief and despair occasioned by contact with the low-life losers who consumed most of my time.

The form was now beginning to chatter noisily, waiting for me to commence registration. Unlike Mandy, I was formal and less forgiving than her in style. Like my assemblies, I insisted upon starting a form period with a greeting, so I began registration with: 'Good Morning 8/MJ!' and received the expected desultory response. It took four further attempts before their 'Good Morning Mr Falconer!' reached the required level of volume and enthusiasm. Once the register was marked I revealed the reason for my presence.

'Right,' I began, 'we've, and by we've, I mean you lot in Year 8, have been selected to organise this year's School Christmas Fayre. I know most of you attended last year when you were the new kids in Year 7, but now it's our turn to run the event and decide exactly what stalls and attractions we're going to put on.'

'Let's have 'Duck the Teacher!' shouted Lance Morris.

This suggestion was greeted with universal approval; an approval, which I immediately quashed by informing them that there would not be any events which harmed, damaged or embarrassed any member of staff. After this announcement it was very difficult to generate much enthusiasm for any alternative attraction which did not, in some measure, involve the humiliation of their teachers. After wasting further time explaining to them why it was not acceptable to cover staff with water, grease or rotting fruit, I finally heard a sensible suggestion from Simon Carter, who volunteered 'Splat the Rat' as a possible idea.

'Good!' I agreed, ' "Splat the Rat" is a successful money-spinner and it has proved very popular at previous fayres.'

'We could use real rats Sir,' suggested Melanie Cole 'it would make it more interesting.'

I looked at Melanie in a new light at this remark, not having realised that this normally quiet and polite girl, would find the killing of rats with a large mallet, as they emerged from an inclined length of old drain pipe; interesting.

'Yes Melanie,' I agreed, 'it may make the event more interesting, but I'm not sure that most parents would appreciate the successful rat splatters arriving home covered in pulverised rat guts. Anyway,' I continued, 'it's doubtful that real rats would just willingly slide down the pipe, especially when they realised that there was an eleven-year-old homicidal maniac with a mallet waiting at the bottom to smash them into oblivion. Rats are quite intelligent you know.'

'Probably better at Maths than Luke,' observed Lance Morris, who obviously, had a very low opinion of Luke's academic ability.

'We could poke them through with a stick,' offered the mild mannered Melanie, trying to maintain the momentum of her idea.

'Possibly Melanie,' I replied, 'but the use of real rats is totally out of the question. Not only would it be illegal and attract the attention of the R.S.P.C.A., but from where, do you imagine, we'd get the rats?'

I sensed at once that, this question was a mistake, for it was answered immediately by Stacy Fowler with the information that the Turner twins kept rats, and that they had dozens of them. Upon hearing Stacy's revelation of their obviously little known pet rat collection, the twins began to make strange rat like gestures, which they embellished with little squeals and squeaks, disconcertingly like a couple of cornered rats caught in the torch beam of a man with a salivating terrier and a large club.

It was with some difficulty that I restored order and persuaded the twins that their rats were in no danger of making their final and bloody appearance at the Christmas Fayre.

Lance tried to revive the scheme by suggesting that, real rats could be persuaded to descend the pipe if it were filled with running water, like the water-chute he'd experienced during his holiday in

Florida last summer, but this proved to be the last attempted innovation in his desire to inject an element of realism into the event.

Finally we agreed that 8/MJ would organise and run, 'Splat the Rat,' with cloth rats as usual, they also selected to stage, 'Guess the name of the Teddy Bear' and 'Stick a flag in the Map to find the Buried Treasure'. I divided the class into three roughly equal groups and delegated responsibility for organising their individual events, telling them that all had to be ready before Saturday 14th December, when the great occasion would occur. By the time everything was decided the form period came to an end and I dismissed them to attend their first lesson of the day, only pausing myself to have my intended words with the prettily painted Miss Crystal Devine.

I just managed to prevent her slipping from the room, as she tried to escape my attention by trying to hide behind Stacy and Tracey-Ann.

'Look at me Crystal,' I commanded.

At this she lowered her eyes, providing a spectacular display of her purple eyelids. I hadn't realised that her eyes were also decorated with silver glitter and a heavy black layer of mascara. Finally, she looked up and impatiently asked, 'What's wrong now?'

'Well, for a start young lady,' I responded, 'you're wearing more make-up than a Las Vegas showgirl. You've got three pairs of hooped earrings in each ear, you've a ring through your right eyebrow and you're wearing foundation and purple lipstick, and you've a stud in your left nostril. You have a ring on each finger and one on your right thumb. Your shirt is three inches too short for your trousers, revealing another stud in your navel and you're wearing some kind of high heeled fashion boots. There are probably other things which are wrong, but that'll do for a start!'

Lance Morris, who'd been trapped behind Crystal when I barred her exit, said. 'And she's got a tattoo on her bum Sir, and you can see her thong when she sits down.'

Before I could respond appropriately to Lance's revelations Crystal had half turned towards him, to give him an aggressive one fingered salute. She also added to this crude insult, by sticking out her tongue, revealing a shiny, spittle covered gold stud.

64

'Ah!' I exclaimed, 'you seem Crystal, to have more piercings than the cling film cover of microwavable moussaka.'

'What?' she asked, in understandable incomprehension.

'Never mind,' I said. 'Let's just say you're wearing too many rings, studs and earrings.'

'You can't do nothing about the one in me tongue,' she argued, 'can't even see it most of the time.'

'I think Crystal,' I replied, 'it's time your parents and I had a little meeting to discuss your inability to follow the school rules on jewellery. In the meantime, you come to my room at twelve-thirty today for a lunchtime detention, and make sure before you arrive that all rings, studs and earrings are removed; otherwise, they will be confiscated, and only returned to your parents when they come to the meeting.

I gave her no time to argue, for Mandy had just returned to her room and I was anxious to get to my first lesson of the day, which was a P.S.H.E. (Personal Social & Health Education) lesson with 8/AS.

Before I departed Mandy told me that Mrs Lowe was unaware of Luke's habitual lateness, so she intended to escort him to school for the remainder of the term.

I informed her of the three events which her form had agreed to organise and I knew that, when she said that all would be ready by the fourteenth that I could leave all the arrangements in her very capable hands. I doubted that I would receive the same level of commitment from my other form tutors.

Over the next couple of weeks I repeated the exercise with my remaining six Year 8 forms, so that, by the week prior to the fourteenth, all the preparations for the Fayre were complete.

The School Choir, under the very able direction of Karen Owen, was booked to sing carols. Karen was our incredible Head of Music and Drama and was, like very few other members of staff, an undervalued, talented and innovative teacher of considerable skill, who encouraged her pupils to perform far beyond their usual levels of attainment. She was one of those individuals whom occur in many schools, but never in sufficient numbers; a dedicated, and inspirational professional, whose considerable achievements were only limited by

65

the myopic vision and life denying agenda of the Senior Management Team, whose motivation was rarely to inspire and motivate children to reach beyond the narrow limits imposed by Government dictate and career educationalists: those lauded experts who could debate every educational theory from Plato to Piaget, but who knew little about life, and even less about children.

Karen was like a light reflecting gem in a desert of tumbleweed and dust. I held her in very high regard, and knew that, now she had agreed to organise the musical entertainment for the Christmas Fayre that, like Mandy's, her contribution would be of the highest possible standard.

The money raised by the Fayre was destined for the coffers of the P.T.A., who used their funds to support a significant number of school projects and activities. Currently, they were organising a number of events to assist in the purchase of a new school minibus.

It amazed me that, a minibus was considered a non-essential item which schools had to fund themselves, yet, the Government, willingly spent millions upon millions funding a school inspection system, which was unhelpful, unwelcome and essentially, counter productive. The only standards raised by OFSTED (The Office for Standards in Education) were those it carried into its battles to undermine and demoralise the nation's teachers.

We had recently been informed that we were going to be inspected early in the New Year. It was an event which I relished with the demob-happy attitude of one close to retirement, and with no longer any promotional ambitions. For the very first time in my varied career I could tell the truth without any concern for the consequences. It was a powerful, refreshing and liberating feeling. How much better would the world be, if those of us who knew the Emperor had no clothes, possessed the courage to actually tell him?

In addition to raising the money to support various items for school use, the P.T.A. also gave valuable assistance at events like the Christmas Fayre. They always ran a refreshment stall and provided much needed adult supervision at all school functions which involved the pupils. At the Fayre they had agreed to provide their usual stall selling hot and cold drinks, mince pies, Christmas cake and mulled wine, plus this year, for the first time, they were also going to provide roast chestnuts.

As the time for the Fayre approached, I was reminded, as I was every year at Christmas, how teaching provided a powerful link with the emotions of childhood. The excitement of the kids was infectious and cut through my usual armour of cynicism, to reawaken memories of Christmases of long ago. There is an atmosphere of palpable anticipation in a school during the last few weeks of December, which recreates the mystery and magic of our own lost illusions. There is no place on Earth which better evokes the sense of wonder and the guileless intensity of feelings, still to be corrupted by age and fevers, than a school at Christmas time. It was yet another of those experiences, where daily contact with the young, engendered hope.

Finally, the day of the Fayre arrived. The Saturday morning dawned clear and very cold. The buildings, trees, fields and hedgerows were covered in a glistening layer of white frost, which sparkled in the intense light of the low winter sun. Driving to school I experienced an unfamiliar, and probably unwarranted premonition, that this was going to be a perfect day; a premonition, which was only marred by a very slight feeling of unease concerning Mrs Hopkins.

A few days previously I had reluctantly agreed, after much pleading from Horrible Hopkins and one of his deranged older sisters, to allow Mrs Hopkins to rent a stall at the Fayre to sell some unspecified paraphernalia for the garden. This was not a new departure, as a number of parents used the Fayre as an opportunity to sell various items. Mrs Jacobs always took a stall to sell her excellent homemade jam and chutney and Mr and Mrs Cole, Melanie's parents, were selling their charity Christmas cards and printed T-shirts in aid of the hedgehog hospital, which they ran from a converted garage in the garden of their bungalow. The legend on the T-shirts read: 'I HELPED A HEDGEHOG HAVE A HAPPY CHRISTMAS', this was printed below a picture of a hedgehog in a hospital bed with a thermometer in its mouth, peering from beneath the sheets with its front claws bandaged and a lone tear of sadness on its prickly cheek. It was all *most* distasteful!

67

Parents who ran a stall were charged a flat fee of £20.00 by the P.T.A. by way of rent, and I'd specified in a letter of agreement which I'd sent to Mrs Hopkins that she could sell her garden items under the same terms. I hadn't been unduly worried until Mandy had expressed her concern that, if Mrs Hopkins was flogging anything at the Fayre, then it was, almost certainly, knocked off. By the time I arrived at school I'd managed to put my nagging concern regarding Mrs Hopkins to the back of my mind.

The Fayre was held in the main school hall, which was a very large and high room with an impressive proscenium arched stage. I was pleased to note that Free-Fall Evans had, unusually, kept his promise to put all the tables out ready for all the stalls and attractions. I was also delighted to see that Karen was already on the stage, taking the school choir through a final rehearsal before the official opening.

The Fayre was due to open at 10.30am and scheduled to finish at 2.00pm. Previous experience had shown this to be the best timing to attract the maximum number of visitors. By 10.20 most stalls were ready for business. The VI Form students were staging their usual attraction of 'The Human Fruit Machine,' where three extremely attractive and provocatively dressed VI Form girls popped up from three very large dustbins, holding aloft a symbol of a lemon, a strawberry or an apple. They charged 20p a go and three of a kind won a prize. This consisted of a bottle of bath essence if the winner were female, and a hug and a Christmas kiss from the girl of choice if the winner were male. This attraction always proved immensely popular, particularly with young boys and granddads. Most men who attended with their wives were positively discouraged from wasting their money on this event, but quite a number of the Year 8 boys spent a fortune, rejoining the rear of the queue for their next go, time after time. Very few bottles of bath essence were ever won. However, some of the young boys won far more often than any statistical analysis would have predicted. I had more than a slight suspicion that the girls colluded to let the boys win, so as to encourage the gullible youngsters to spend the maximum amount of money. I'm sure this was instigated by Bonnie Butler, the new Head of VI Form, who had made it a condition of the girls participation that fifty percent of the proceeds from 'The Human Fruit Machine', were to go to the fund for the refurbishment of the VI Form Common Room.

I had also noticed Horrible Hopkins, two of his feral older sisters, three scruffy younger brothers, a wailing infant in a dilapidated pushchair and his awesomely well-endowed mother, setting up their stall just inside the main entrance to the Hall. They were assisted in their efforts by several of the school's most notorious villains and numbskulls. These included Nathan Hyde, Jack Reynolds, and hovering by the stall, with what looked like a cashbox, the suspicious figure of Kyle Bowman.

I was also surprised to see Jamie Fisher, who'd only recently been found a place on an alternative curriculum scheme, run by a charitable trust on a local farm, which had been specifically established to cater for school phobics and other rejects from mainstream education.

For the last half hour, this mixed bunch of juvenile reprobates had been delivering to the stall by wheelbarrow, dozens and dozens of ornaments, mainly consisting of a bewildering variety of garden gnomes.

There were gnomes of all shapes, colours and sizes. Some were sitting, some were standing, some were fishing, others were perched on toadstools, several were pushing wheelbarrows, and one, an obvious novelty gnome with a salacious grin, appeared to have his hand thrust up the skirt of a fibre-glass fairy. However, before I could go and have a word with Mrs Hopkins, Mandy opened the main doors to allow in the waiting throng of parents and kids. The choir began to sing 'We Wish You a Merry Christmas', the lights on the large Christmas tree began to flash, and the Christmas Fayre was underway.

The first few minutes were chaotic, as young children, freed from parental restraint, ran excitedly to their chosen attraction. There was a Coconut Shy and a Wheel of Fortune, both loaned for the occasion by the local Rotary Club; plus stalls running raffles and offering various prizes for games of skill and chance. Philip Wainwright, a talented boy in Year 11, had transformed himself into a magician and was appearing as 'The Great Grimaldi Master of Magic'. He had already attracted a large crowd of youngsters and was busy relieving them of their money with the three card trick, 'Find the Lady'. The VI Form girls in 'The Human Fruit Machine', who were dressed (or more aptly, undressed) as harem slave girls, had drawn a very large number of open-mouthed males, some of whom were being reluctantly dragged away by their wives and girlfriends.

I suddenly had to make an early intervention at 8/MJ's 'Splat the Rat' stall, when I discovered that Lance Morris was trying to persuade his younger sister's pet hamster to descend the four foot length of drainpipe to take its chances against Melanie Cole with an upraised mallet. She'd apparently paid extra for the privilege of being the first to try and flatten the poor creature. By the time I'd been alerted to the possible tragedy, Lance was trying out his water-chute idea by pushing the terrified little rodent into the pipe and then pouring in coke from a can which he'd just purchased from the P.T.A. refreshment stall. It was only his younger sister's screams of distress which had prevented the hamster's bloody demise. I finally managed to free the hamster from its ordeal by gently inserting a broom handle into one end of the drain pipe while Lance's tearful sister called 'Fluffy Fluffy' from the other end. Eventually, after much coaxing and pushing Fluffy emerged, coke stained and trembling, to be reunited with its distraught owner.

It transpired that Lance had taken the unfortunate Fluffy from its cosy cage in his sister's bedroom without her knowledge, or approval. It was only when she'd come running up to the school to enlist his help in finding it that she discovered the awful truth. It did of course teach her not to trust her sibling.

I immediately took Lance and Melanie off the stall and provided them with a large black bin-liner each, and ordered them to go around the hall picking up litter for the duration of the Fayre. They both grumbled at first, until I told them that, if they didn't get on with it without moaning, the rodent loving Turner twins would hear of Fluffy's terrifying adventure. This had the desired effect, for they made no further protest and set to litter picking with an unexpected energy and enthusiasm. It's amazing what an appropriate threat can sometimes achieve in situations where instruction, or pleading, fail.

By the time this incident was satisfactorily resolved the hall was packed full, and the Fayre was alive with excited noise and activity. I walked slowly back towards the stage taking in the sights and sounds of this obviously successful event. I felt immensely pleased and not a little relieved that everything was going so well. The Fayre seemed set to make a very handsome profit for the P.T.A., and the choir was creating exactly the right seasonal atmosphere with a superb rendition of 'Once in Royal David's City'. They'd just sung the line 'Mary was the mother mild' when there was an ear piercing shriek, so loud that, the choir faltered, and everyone in the hall turned to try and identify the source of the sound.

The shriek had obviously emanated from an agitated woman standing in front of Mrs Hopkins' stall of garden gnomes. My first thought was that she'd seen the obscene gnome groping the fairy, but she was clearly pointing to a large florid faced gnome with a blue hat and bright yellow trousers. By the time I arrived at her side to try and calm the situation, she had picked up the gnome in question and was cuddling it with an unrestrained passion. She began shouting excitedly to her male companion.

'It's Norman – it's Norman, I'd know him anywhere! Look Les, Norman! It's *our* Norman! Oh! I've missed him so!'

Les, who I assumed to be her husband, looked acutely embarrassed and was obviously reluctant to identify 'Norman' as a long lost member of his family, although there most definitely was a family resemblance.

Before I could enquire what exactly the problem was, it became patently obvious. A large and very irate woman pushed past me to loudly proclaim that the gnome sitting on the big red toadstool with the white spots, holding a fishing rod was called 'Nobby' and had been stolen from beside her garden pond over a month ago.

Quite quickly, the area in front of Mrs Hopkins' stall filled with a crowd of angry parents identifying and claiming ownership of gnomes, miniature wheelbarrows, toadstools, plastic frogs, ceramic ducks, a sundial and a large bird-bath made of Cotswold stone. Mrs Hopkins, who was usually a force to be reckoned with, found herself trapped and besieged behind her stall, by this vocal and threatening mob of extremely furious victims.

I battled my way back out through the angry mob to try and apprehend Horrible Hopkins and his gang of accomplices, but unsurprisingly, they had fled the scene the moment the first shriek had signified that their thieving had been exposed.

I spotted Mandy by the main doors, desperately trying to reassure parents, fleeing from the chaotic melee which had now erupted across the hall, that order would soon be restored, and pleading with them to return and enjoy the Fayre. A prospect which seemed increasingly unlikely, as Mrs Hopkins beleaguered stall collapsed under the weight of the attacking hordes.

Even the normally sedate and well disciplined members of the school choir, had broken ranks, and were excitedly attempting to leave the stage and join the riot raging below. Karen was vigorously attempting to re-establish control and return them to their designated places.

Just as I began to despair of the possibility of recreating any sort of order from the mob hysteria which seemed to have gripped the increasingly violent crowd, the situation was rescued by the timely arrival of the cavalry. The cavalry consisted of P.C. Phil Hobson, our local Community Police Officer and the person responsible for police/school liaison. Fortunately, he'd arrived with four other officers and two large and intimidating dogs. They very swiftly restored order and led the unusually subdued, and I suspect grateful, Mrs Hopkins from the hall.

I followed them out into the School Foyer and as I did so, I was relieved to hear behind me the choir recommence with 'Silent Night'. As Mrs Hopkins was led away by the other officers, Phil turned to me and said:

'Sorry if this has ruined the Fayre Dave, but we've had Huw Hopkins and his mob under surveillance for some time. We've received numerous reports of stolen garden ornaments for some months, but despite deploying D.C. Flood to patrol local gardens at night, we've had no luck in catching the culprits. In fact, the only arrest we've made was D.C. Flood; after we received a phone call from an attractive divorcée at 23 Church Close reporting that a suspicious and shadowy figure had fallen in her pond.'

'So how did you discover that Horrible Hopkins was responsible?' I enquired.

'Well,' Phil replied, 'W.P.C. Williams had visited Mrs Hopkins to investigate her complaint that she was being harassed by her ex-husband, and while there, she noticed that the back garden was crammed full of garden ornaments; mostly gnomes, and she reported this back at the station yesterday afternoon. When I went round to investigate this morning, the haul was already on the move, being transported here for obvious sale. So we decided to wait, and let her implicate herself as fully as possible, before we moved in to arrest her.

'Well thanks a bunch!' I exclaimed. 'We almost had a full blown riot on our hands.'

'Yes,' he agreed, 'but it'll be worth it if we can get this female Fagin for handling stolen goods.'

'What'll she be charged with then?' I asked.

'Oh, being a garden fence I should think.' He responded, with a wink and a broad grin as he shook my hand, and said he'd be in touch on Monday to tie up any loose ends.

As I returned to the hall to try and rescue what remained of the Christmas Fayre, I reflected ruefully on my earlier premonition that this was going to be a perfect day. It might not have been a perfect day, but if it resulted in real and meaningful punishment of Horrible Hopkins and his mind-dead mates, then it may yet turn out to have been a day with perfect consequences.

Chapter 6

The School Inspection

Despite the debacle of Mrs Hopkins' knocked-off gnome stall, the Christmas Fayre still managed to raise £830 for the P.T.A's. minibus fund. This was over £200 more than the previous year's total, so, even though the Fayre had been the subject of a somewhat negative article in the Abercwmtwerp Tribune, it was judged an unqualified success by the P.T.A. and the School Governors.

I think that the Tribune's headline of: 'CHAOS AT COMP'S CHRISTMAS FAYRE' was a slight exaggeration, and unfortunately, the event received more coverage than was warranted, due probably, to Mrs Hopkins' very public arrest and the anger and indignation of the paper's valued readers, when they discovered that their treasured and much loved garden gnomes were being flogged off cheaply at the local school.

Still, the first and most welcome consequence of the incident was that, the intense anger of many parents put such pressure on the normally weak-willed Dr Douglas that, he was forced to ask the Governors to approve a permanent exclusion for Horrible Hopkins.

This was an action to which the Governors readily agreed, and which was endorsed by all the staff. It was even reported on favourably by the Tribune, due no doubt, to the clamour of its readers to see all the culprits responsible for this violation of the sanctity of their gardens, suitably punished.

So it was that Horrible Hopkins was permanently excluded, and instead of returning to school in January, he was found a place at the same local charitable trust farm that had accommodated Jamie Fisher. It was subsequently rumoured that the only creatures to be disadvantaged by Hopkins' permanent exclusion were the farm's unfortunate pigs, which were forced to suffer his incompetent ministrations when he was put in charge of their welfare.

By the time Mrs Hopkins appeared before the local magistrates, it was the beginning of February, and the entire school was in a state of nervous paranoia, anticipating the imminent school inspection. I was looking forward to this unhelpful event, but I was also very disappointed when the local magistrates only imposed a fifty hour community service sentence on Mrs Hopkins, and Horrible only received a supervision order, forcing him to report to a local community centre once a week to atone for his crimes. It's no coincidence that such comfortable consequences, and anti-social and criminal behaviour, have flourished under the same weak and ineffectual liberal regime, which views the perpetrators of crime as more deserving than their victims. We are, without doubt, often very poorly served by our judiciary. However, before we had the opportunity to feel grateful for Hopkins' absence, the school inspection was upon us!

The inspection occurred prior to the new regime of 'light touch' inspections and featured the full panoply of thirty-eight inspectors ensconced in the school for a whole week.

We had received some eight months notice of the event, which had resulted in the unedifying spectacle of the Head and other members of the S.M.T. suddenly having to take an interest in the working of the school and its staff, an interest, which unfortunately, had the effect of seriously disrupting the normal teaching and learning regime of all departments.

In the months long run-up to the inspection, the S.M.T. were busy reviewing, amending and delegating the writing of policy documents covering every conceivable aspect of school life. There were policies on everything, from the use of welding equipment by the partially-sighted, to the nature of the sanctions to be imposed upon pupils who told staff to 'fuck off!'. All this frenzied and mostly senseless activity, resulted in almost all staff being diverted from their primary task of teaching, to write pointless policy statements and to prepare massive quantities of jargon filled documentation, which, once passed to the inspectors, would not be viewed again until they were discarded as totally out-of-date and no longer relevant, prior to the next inevitable visitation, by some future team of inspectors possessed of a new and different agenda.

Pupils of all ages quickly sensed that the staff were massively distracted and were now so busy preparing for the inspection, that they were no longer properly focussed upon teaching, or upon the rigorous delivery of the syllabus. Consequently, the quality of teaching and learning severely declined and both standards of behaviour and academic performance deteriorated; thus, making the achievement of a favourable inspection report increasingly unlikely.

As the time for the inspection drew closer, the tension mounted, and the pace and intensity of the preparations accelerated. Many staff were now arriving at school more than two hours before the pupils and staying late into the evening; struggling to ensure that all their extensive departmental documentation was complete, and that their individual teaching rooms were an artistic shrine to the variety and excellence of the pupils' work. Huge displays of pupils' artwork were being erected in the foyer, the main hall and – in a desperate attempt to hide the damage and graffiti – in the normally filthy and ill-maintained corridors. Even 'Free Fall Evans', who usually took months to effect even the simplest repair, was pressured into a doomed attempt to remedy the results of years of neglect and lack of maintenance.

Fortunately, Evans was only one man, and thank God, a lazy, incompetent and scruffy one; whose idea of a clean and well ordered environment was forged in the bosom of a family, who would have considered Worzel Gummidge an example of fashionable elegance, and who viewed knee-high grass, abandoned caravans, rusting prams, discarded lavatory bowls and flea infested underfed dogs, as the last word in garden accessories.

I certainly did not want 'Free Fall Evans' papering over the cracks of neglect, and fooling the inspectors into believing that we worked in an acceptable and well cared for environment. Of course, I was fully aware that the school's physical environment would not figure large on the inspectors' agenda, but it certainly figured large on mine, and like it, or not they were going to listen, as well as judge.

Two weeks prior to the Monday chosen for the commencement of the inspection Dr Douglas called all staff together after school for a pre-inspection meeting; the main purpose of which appeared to be an attempt to cajole us all into pretending that we all worked together as a dedicated team of skilled professionals, who strove in an atmosphere of harmonious partnership, to achieve the best possible results for our highly valued and respected pupils. As a reflection of the truth, this was about as accurate as all the members of the S.M.T. donning black stockings and erotic underwear and trying to persuade senior executives of the Playboy organisation that they were all genuine exotic dancers from an exclusive Parisian lap-dancing club!

His other, less welcome purpose, was a request that – due to the limited parking available on the school site – we all try to find alternative parking during the week of the inspection, so that the inspectors would not be inconvenienced, or annoyed, by having to drive the surrounding residential streets, searching for somewhere to park.

There was, understandably, a universal outcry of indignation at this request, with muttered threats of union involvement and of not turning up for work. I couldn't resist adding fuel to this dissent by pointing out that, in any event, we would be ill-advised to trust, or accept, the critical judgement of individuals who couldn't even manage to park their cars! My observation was quickly endorsed by Chris Reed, who said that we were all being massively inconvenienced by the inspectors' presence and that it was only just, that they should experience a tiny bit of inconvenience themselves. Sophie Miller, the astute Head of Year 11 added to this, by commenting that forcing the inspectors to search for a parking space would be an excellent test of their initiative, and would give us all more reason to respect their skill and tenacity if they succeeded in finding a space. Steve Regan suggested that, as the government spent over one hundred million a year on school inspections, they could easily afford to ferry the inspectors to the site in chauffer driven limousines.

It quickly became apparent, even to the usually unperceptive Dr Douglas that his desire to place the comfort and convenience of the inspectors above that of his own staff, was a desire which was going to be thwarted.

Lofty Lewis, who, in addition to his ineffectual role within the S.E.N. department, was also the very militant union representative for most of the staff, finally buried the request by calling for a show of hands. So that he could better assess the wishes of the staff Lofty moved to the front of the Hall, and said.

'Please raise your hand if you are prepared to give up your parking space to make room for one of the inspectors.'

The only hands to be raised were those of Dr Douglas, Vic Davies and Bert Bowen. Frank Baldwin, the first Deputy Head and the final member of the Senior Management Team failed to raise his hand, and stated later that this omission only occurred because his hearing-aid was on the blink and he'd not heard the proposal.

In any event, this unanimous refusal to relinquish our parking spaces represented a rare moment of solidarity and defiance; taken I'm sure, in frustration at not being able to influence, or escape the inspection itself; nor to have our views as to its worth, or value listened to, or considered. It was a very small triumph, but a very satisfying one. In the absence of genuine influence people are often forced into small acts of sabotage.

Exactly a week after the defeat of the S.M.T. on the parking issue we were once again summoned to an after school meeting in the main hall. This time, it was to listen to Mr Clive Selwyn, the registered inspector leading the team which had been selected to undertake our inspection the following week.

By this stage, the normal life of the school had been so seriously disrupted and staff morale was at such low ebb that, when Dr Douglas introduced Clive Selwyn – the perceived author of our collective anxiety – the atmosphere in the hall crackled with an almost tangible air of suspicion and hostility.

The entire teaching, administrative and ancillary staff sat, arms folded defensively and facial expressions rigid with the rictus of resentment as we were forced to endure yet another session filled with statements of self-aggrandisement and sentiments of insincere reassurance.

In truth, this situation was not the fault of the unwelcome Mr Selwyn, who was as much a victim of this unsound and ill-judged educational insanity as the rest of us. For he, like us, was merely a small player in a farcical game, designed to persuade the educational mafia and the tax paying public that the government was serious about school improvement.

Any thinking person of intelligence and perception must inevitably conclude that an inspection system which discouraged debate, denied dissent, promoted anxiety, instilled fear, fostered resentment, increased stress and significantly expanded administration at the expense of teaching and learning, was not one designed to raise pupils' standards of achievement. The entire system, being based upon American models of monitoring, measuring and control, was one which alienated all sensitive and concerned teachers, and consequently, did nothing to assist any genuinely effective strategy for educational success.

As we all listened to Mr Clive Selwyn promise a fair and even-handed inspection, conducted in a spirit of enlightened concern, I was struck by the cant and hypocrisy of the educational double-speak we were all expected to ingest. What was apparent was that we were all about to be assessed against criteria we had no part in shaping, using categories of attainment we had not agreed, and by people whose intelligence, judgement and skills we had had no opportunity to evaluate or approve. It was no wonder therefore, that most staff awaited the inspection with a mixture of animosity, cynicism and contempt. In such an atmosphere of suspicion, mistrust and anxiety, it was obviously impossible for anyone to make an accurate assessment regarding the normal working of the school.

Dr Douglas had certainly done *his* part, to ensure that what the inspectors saw would be far from normal. Firstly, some thirty or so of the most disruptive and troublesome pupils from Years 10 and 11 had suddenly been found places with various local firms to undertake valuable 'work experience'. Places, which previously, we had been assured by Bert Bowen, would not be appropriate, or desirable. Secondly, others, likely to make effective teaching impossible, had been temporarily excluded, for breaches of the rules, which usually, would have attracted no more than an impatient frown of disapproval.

Other departures from 'the norm' were the switching off of the junk-food vending machines, which were responsible for ninety percent of the mountains of litter which was usually scattered across the school site. Also, there was a sudden and quite disconcerting enforcement of the school rules on uniform and jewellery, with pupils having to face the totally new experience of being challenged by the Senior Management regarding the infringement of rules, which they quite understandably imagined, had long since been abandoned and forgotten. This led to some very interesting confrontations, which, in many cases, due no doubt to their lack of experience in pupil management, the S.M.T. totally failed to win. One such incident occurred, when Dr Douglas unfortunately challenged Carly Devine, Crystal's older, street-wise and vastly more experienced sister regarding her appearance, as she entered the main hall for morning assembly. The resultant battle of wills and words was one, which all who witnessed it, declared that Carly had won hands-down.

He apparently, made his first error by pulling her out from a group of her malevolent mates, as they shuffled sulkily past to take their usual seats at the back of the hall. As he couldn't recall who she was, he inadvisedly requested her name; to which Carly replied, loudly enough for the entire four hundred plus Year 10 and 11 pupils to hear, that she was 'the Bleedin' Virgin Mary,' who the hell did he think she was. He stupidly responded to this piece of sarcastic insolence by asking her if she was looking for a detention, which of course, gave a girl as feisty and quick-witted as Carly the opportunity to say no, but that if he'd lost one she'd be happy to help him search for it.

By now the hall had fallen silent, as all present realised they were witnessing an unequal contest, between the inept and ill-equipped voice of imagined authority, and the immense forces of teenage girl-power, honed to deadly sharpness in a street culture of defiance and contempt. It was really no contest at all!

For a start, the unfortunate Douglas had chosen an arena where Carly's supporters outnumbered his, by at least fifty-to-one. They were also more vocal and enthusiastic in their support, and fired by the same blood-lust that had demanded the death of gladiators. Even the few teachers present, whom he might have hoped were loyal allies, were mainly too fascinated by the contest and too anxious to witness his humiliation, to willingly intervene.

Now, obviously apoplectic with anger and lost for an effective strategy to extricate himself from the situation, he focussed finally, upon Carly's appearance, and began to jabber incoherently about her lack of the correct uniform, her make-up, jewellery and her designer hairstyle. Carly, who was a respected upper school fashion icon of considerable expertise, was fully aware that her attire and appearance, although not conforming in any recognisable way to the school rules, was, nonetheless, far smarter, cleaner and better cared for, than the crumpled, ill-fitting and dirty suit that was sported by Douglas. When she calmly made this comparison, laying particular emphasis upon his scuffed and grease stained 'Hush-Puppies' there was no real escape route from his inevitable defeat.

He finally made one last desperate attempt to inflict damage upon his opponent, by threatening her with 'serious consequences,' a threat which elicited Carly's – still discussed – victory riposte of:

'Serious consequences? In *this* school? You must be bleedin' joking!!!'

This coup-de-grâce was apparently uttered with a contemptuous toss of her blonde curls and to rapturous applause, as she sauntered triumphantly, to the back row of seats to rejoin her cheering companions. Leaving the nonplussed Dr Douglas to be led away supported on the tattooed forearm of 'Free Fall Evans' and to the sound of four hundred jeering kids ringing in his ears.

This was, if any were needed, a salutary lesson in the truth of the statement that, in the absence of fear, we can only ever govern by consent. It was also a microcosm of the similar contempt of the young for authority within the wider community, where 'serious consequences' were equally absent and where the most appalling behaviour frequently attracted no more than a police caution, or, in cases of the most serious nature, a police caution accompanied by the wagging finger of authoritarian disapproval. The newly launched 'respect agenda' was going to require considerably more than pious platitudes and lessons in citizenship.

Finally, the Monday of the week of the inspection arrived. It was probably the wettest day of the winter, with the rain descending like stair-rods and forced into a horizontal wall of water whipped to power-hose intensity by an almost hurricane-force wind. The drive to work was a journey of epic proportions, with hazardous detours to avoid floods, fallen trees and blown down fences.

Most of the staff, who lived anywhere other than in close proximity to the school, arrived late, as did most of the inspectors, whose journeys were made even more unpleasant, by the added inconvenience of having to try and find a parking space close enough to the school to avoid arriving for their first day completely soaked. Those who did manage to park, even within a reasonable walking distance, immediately discovered that their umbrellas were a useless encumbrance, and that only a full set of trawler-man's waterproofs, with waist high rubber boots and sou'westers would be any use in their vain attempts to stay dry. It was only Clive Selwyn the Chief Inspector, and three of his most senior colleagues, who'd been allocated the parking spaces usually occupied by Dr Douglas and the other members of the S.M.T. who had gained the shelter of the school without being thoroughly drenched.

Of course, Douglas and the remainder of the S.M.T. all arrived late and like drowned rats, and with, I'm sure, a deep and very damp reflection upon the toadying stupidity of their decision to relinquish the best and closest parking spaces to the four most fortunate inspectors. Sacrifice is seldom without consequence and rarely without regret.

So many staff had arrived late that the school could not begin as usual at 8.45am. Staff, who had managed to arrive prior to this, had shepherded Years 7, 8 and 9 into the canteen and Years 10, 11, 12 and 13 into the main hall to await the arrival of sufficient staff to commence the day's teaching.

By the time this had occurred, it was almost 9.30am and it was decided to start at 9.45am and simply cancel period one. For the pupils, having to wait around in cramped conditions for over an hour in soaking wet clothes and with the minimum of staff supervision had presented them with a welcome opportunity for a rapid descent into chaos and barbarism.

The floors in both the canteen and the hall very quickly became covered in water from hundreds of dripping coats and bags, and as the heat from the fearsomely hot radiators and their tightly packed bodies raised the temperature, the atmosphere was swiftly transformed into an impenetrable mist resembling the interior of a Turkish steam bath.

Whilst one might hope that, adults frequenting such a perspiration inducing environment would have high standards of personal hygiene, the same could not be said of some four-hundred unwashed teenagers, whose ideas of cleanliness were, as yet, sketchy and unformed. Consequently, not only was the atmosphere as misty and dank as the depths of a tropical rain forest, it also stank like the armpit of a sweat soaked wrestler, and, due to the absence of adult control, was as noisy and riotous as a compound full of drug-crazed baboons.

Although bad, the situation became considerably worse, when due to fatigue and finally boredom, hunger set in. Kids' first response when faced with excitement, boredom, or stress is to eat, and so, abandoned by staff and denied their familiar routine they resorted to the comfort of their crisps, cokes and smelly sandwiches, which, once half consumed, were thrown at their companions with shrill cries of disgust and shouted comments about whose mother made the most revolting food.

It was unfortunately, this hellish scene of a massive food fight, conducted in a setting of unimaginable stench, noise and litter soaked squalor, which was, for many of the late arriving inspectors, their first impression of life at Gruffudd ap Cynan Comp.

Their second, and even less welcome impression, was formed later that morning, when, at exactly 11.14am, some malicious saboteur pressed one of the school's many fire alarm buttons and sent the entire school population of pupils, teachers, secretaries, caretakers, dinner-ladies and most unfortunately, the only just dried out thirty-eight inspectors on to the rain and wind-lashed quagmire of the school field, there to await the arrival of the local Fire Brigade.

This was, an event which had been dreaded by most staff, and certainly, by the S.M.T. who'd been increasingly angered and frustrated by the number of false fire alarms which had been occurring during the last several weeks. Despite their best efforts, the culprit, or culprits had not been apprehended, and the threats, which the S.M.T. had issued in school assemblies and in letters home to parents specifying the dire consequences which would face the perpetrators had been totally ineffective in preventing the problem.

When the deafening clanging of the fire bells erupted in my room I was attempting to teach the rudiments of some of the most common poetic forms employed by the Romantic poets to a bottom set Year 10 G.C.S.E. group, who were as bright as winter in Alaska, and whose idea of great poetry had been formed by the rap-crap currently heard in some of the more anarchic and tuneless examples of mind-numbing popular music. Had it not been for the high wind and torrential rain, most of the class would have been delighted by this opportunity to escape from their exposure to the talents of Byron, Keats and Shelley. However, the weather was so atrocious that, many of them moaned and whinged about this thoughtless interruption to their poetical education.

Due to its recent regularity the routine of fire drill was well practised and the pupils only paused to don their coats, before leading out to join all the other kids in their noisy procession out of the building and towards their designated assembly points on the school field.

Fortunately, I'd not had the presence of an inspector to worry about, and so, when the room was empty, I retrieved my wellington-boots, waterproof Australian drovers coat and bush-hat with chinstrap from my stock cupboard, and once suitably attired to face the elements, I made my way slowly to the field, where the seven forms in Year 8 were supposed to be lined-up in an orderly and patient fashion with their Form Tutors awaiting my arrival. Instead of order, I found *them*, and the rest of the pupil population, in a state of almost uncontrollable disorder and excitement.

The situation was not helped by the wet and windswept figure of Dr Douglas, dressed in a wildly flapping, flimsy black plastic pac-amac, and standing precariously on an upturned milk-crate, supported on one side by a struggling Vic Davies and shouting unintelligible instructions through a malfunctioning megaphone. When the megaphone had one of its intermittent moments of electronic clarity, Douglas' words were instantly whipped away, to be lost forever in the roar of noise generated by twelve hundred shrieking kids and the incessant howling of the gale-force wind.

Matters deteriorated further, when, in his frustration and anger at being ignored, he foolishly leaned forward to try and grasp the whistle, which Bert Bowen, having appreciated the inadequacy of the megaphone, was desperately thrusting towards him, in an effort to rescue him from yet another humiliating disaster. Just as it seemed as if he would succeed, the megaphone, which was hanging from his neck on a wide tape, was caught by an exceptionally powerful gust of wind, and turned his already acute forward motion into an athletic dive of momentary elegance. The moment however, was very fleeting and all that most observers witnessed was him crashing into Bert and dragging the unfortunate Vic Davies, who was still loyally gripping his left arm, down into the sodden mud, so recently churned to its now squelchy consistency, by the trampling march of hundreds of hyperactive school-kids. Bert, who'd landed on his arse with Douglas' knees either side of his now prostrate body, looked like a wrestler in a submission hold as Douglas tried to get to his feet, by pushing Bert's head deeper into the mud. Vic, who'd managed to prevent his own total immersion in the water-logged earth by briefly landing on top of Douglas, was the first of the ill-fated trio to stand-up, and he gallantly assisted the hapless Douglas and the mud-caked and winded Bert to regain their feet.

You may imagine the effect which this widely observed incident had upon the attempted establishment of good order among the pupils. If there was chaos before, there was now, a concerted and mass tribal dance of crazed abandon, as they whooped and splashed about in a frenzy of unbridled approval. As Douglas, Davies and Bowen were no longer in a fit, or proper state to influence events, they retreated from the field, to try and recover their composure and regain their vainly imagined authority.

Some semblance of order was eventually restored, when Steve Regan and I, who were the only members of staff, dressed to withstand the ferocity of the weather, threatened to keep everyone standing out in the rain until they calmed down and formed orderly lines, so that their presence could be checked against the class registers. Needless to say, this was not a popular strategy with the inspectors, or other members of staff, who felt obligated to remain until the check on attendance could be satisfactorily completed.

There was a further slight delay, as the office staff had failed to bring on to the field a list of the inspectors, who, as they were 'on site' at the time of the alarm, were also supposed to be subject to a proper attendance check. Finally, this list was obtained and a roll call of all the inspectors taken and by the time this was achieved, the Chief Fire Officer had issued the 'all clear' and we were all allowed to return to the very welcome warmth and dryness of the various school buildings.

As Steve and I oversaw the relatively ordered dismissal of the now completely soaked and wind-buffeted kids, I couldn't resist acknowledging – with a cheery smile and an encouraging comment regarding the benefit of regular fire drills – a small group of about fifteen drenched and bedraggled inspectors, as they waded past to join the rest of their demoralised colleagues, to no doubt, plan their offensive for their afternoon sessions of lesson observations.

By the time everyone had regained the comforting shelter of their classrooms and offices it was 12.00 noon and almost time for lunch. Unfortunately, the serving of hot food had been understandably delayed, due to the fact that all the cooks had been standing out in the pouring rain for the last forty minutes, waiting with the rest of us, the all clear from the Fire Brigade. This, had the knock-on effect of making life extremely difficult for the team of local ladies – many of them the mothers of pupils – who were employed as lunch-time supervisors, and who, had the unenviable task of trying to maintain order and discipline in the burger-strewn battleground of the school canteen.

Their task was difficult enough under normal circumstances, but the burden of trying to control hundreds of cold, wet and hungry kids, who'd just been told there was no hot food available, had proven too much for them, and members of the S.M.T. had to be called to try and quell the riot which had ensued, when some of the thugs in Year 10 attempted to monopolise the purchase of the woefully inadequate supply of pre-packed sandwiches, and threatened some of the Year 7 kids with extreme violence, unless they shared the homemade contents of their plastic lunch-boxes.

It was stated later that the event would have been much more damaging to the school's reputation, if the riot had been witnessed by any of the inspectors. It was viewed as fortunate that the inspectors had decided to take their lunch in the secluded isolation of the staff workroom, and old and little used temporary classroom, which inconveniently, housed the staffs' personal photocopying machine, and which was located too far from the canteen for the noise of the riot to be audible.

The only genuine casualty of the event was Bert Bowen, who, already weakened from his recent encounter with the descending Douglas, suffered a sprained wrist and a black-eye, when he unwisely, tried to separate a mob of brawling Year 10 boys, who were apparently, fighting over a deep-filled chicken, bacon, avocado and mayonnaise sandwich, snatched from the trampled on lunch-box of the distraught and sobbing Simon Smallwood, a slightly delicate and sensitive Year 7 pupil, whose mother was a gourmet chef, and who, had already gained the distinction of being the boy with the best stocked lunch-box in Lower School.

It was all most lamentable, and resulted in both Bert and three of the rioting Year 10 boys being sent home; Bert to recover from his injuries and the boys to reflect upon their behaviour. Also, Mrs Smallwood was urgently contacted to request that she provide a replacement lunch for the unfortunate Simon, who was still inconsolable at his loss, and was slumped in one of the armchairs outside Douglas' office being comforted by the school nurse.

One positive aspect of having begun the inspection on such a low note was that, there was a general feeling among staff that things could only improve, and so, there was a noticeable uplift in morale and a more relaxed and fatalistic attitude to the whole inspection process. It wasn't that staff began to accept, or value the process, but that, they just cared less about its outcome, and a calm resignation often results from a relative lack of concern.

Of course, the S.M.T. continued to flap about, asking individual teachers how they thought they did during the lessons where they had been observed teaching, and whether the inspector had given any feedback upon their performance. However, after the first couple of days, most staff simply ignored the inspector's presence and often forgot the clipboard carrying interloper who sat at the rear of their classroom, making copious notes on their lesson.

Inspectors are trained to look for particular features of a lesson and grade them according to a predetermined set of criteria. They also grade the performance of the teacher. The grades which they employ for this purpose are, except in the most exceptional circumstances, ones which anyone of my generation would categorise as, 'damning with faint praise'. This is perhaps, not surprising, since there is no kudos in being complimentary. It is therefore, understandable that, usually, inspectors were almost as sparing with their accolades, as they were with their advice.

One welcome piece of news, which arrived on the Tuesday afternoon, was a memo from Vic Davies, saying that the lay inspector, a Mr Rhys Llewellyn, wished to see me during one of my 'free periods' on Thursday to discuss the school's pastoral system and my role as Head of Year. The inspection teams for secondary schools employed a lay inspector, who was someone with extensive work experience outside of education. The lay inspector was there to provide a token balance to the often myopic and unworldly views of the other inspectors, whose prejudices and opinions had seldom been widened, or modified, by experience of working in 'the real world'. It was a meeting which I relished, for the opportunity it would provide me to discuss matters of concern with someone, whose world view had not been shaped and circumscribed by the narrow confines of the classroom.

In the interim, I endured two visits by inspectors to my English lessons and was aware that my lack of deference and obvious cynicism regarding the value of the whole system may have alienated their goodwill and influenced their judgement. However, I was unconcerned, as I knew that my lessons had been brilliant, a grade not achievable within their limited categories of attainment.

At the allocated time on the Thursday afternoon, the expected Mr Rhys Llewellyn duly arrived. He politely knocked my door before entering, and when, on my barked command of 'come!' he did enter, I was unexpectedly and very pleasantly surprised.

Rhys Llewellyn was a tall, slim, immaculately dressed, well groomed and highly distinguished looking man of around fifty. His hair, which was expertly cut and slightly grey at the temples, framed a clean shaven face, whose countenance immediately inspired confidence. He was wearing an expensive navy-blue suit with matching waistcoat, a fashionable, but not ostentatious tie, a crisp white shirt and his shoes gleamed with an almost mirror like polish. He possessed a reassuringly firm handshake and an engaging smile of considerable charm. As he introduced himself, I noticed that his light-grey eyes betrayed an unmistakeable humour and intelligence, the like of which, one may encounter, only once, or twice, in a lifetime, and when he spoke, his voice was resonant with a lyricism and authority, which was irresistible. I knew instantly that here was a man whom I was going to find it absolutely impossible to dislike.

I responded to his greeting of, 'Hi, you must be Dave Falconer the renowned Head of Year 8. I'm delighted to meet you,' with an invitation to sit. He drew up a chair and sat at the opposite side of my somewhat ancient desk. As he did so, he held my glance with an expression of openness and trust, which seemed to imply that we were co-conspirators of long standing. He continued, smiling with sincerity. 'I hear from very reliable, but anonymous sources that you are an exceptionally popular and effective Head of Year, with some interesting views upon the education of the young and I'd be very grateful, if you would share with me some of your opinions and concerns.'

He was obviously, a flatterer of immense skill and I struggled to maintain my usual shield of cynicism and mistrust as I answered. 'Well, that's one way to describe me I suppose, but there are, I'm sure, many sources which would have a far less favourable view.'

'That indeed, may be so,' he responded, 'but I'm sure you will understand and agree with my description of your talents, when I tell you that my anonymous sources were primarily the pupils in Year 8.'

It was very gratifying to learn that the kids had expressed such a good opinion of me, but it was even more reassuring to realise that, it had not been any members of the S.M.T. who had praised my popularity, or expertise; for it is always depressing to learn that one is held in high regard by people possessed of poor judgement. I guessed that Rhys Llewellyn, even in the few days he'd been here, had already formed a pretty accurate view as to the abilities of Dr Douglas and our Leadership Team.

I spent the next hour or so being expertly probed by him regarding the school, the pastoral system, discipline, issues of teaching and learning, assemblies, our relationships with parents and the wider community, the value of the current inspection regime, the on-going burden of ever increasing paperwork, and the effectiveness of the Senior Management Team. He managed the introduction and pursuit of all these topics with a skill and professionalism, which highlighted his intelligence and experience. It was a hugely refreshing and enjoyable experience to be interviewed by someone of perception and empathy. If he was, at any point, being insincere, then I failed to spot it and he had given a seamless acting performance of consummate skill.

When eventually, I read the full inspection report I was very heartened to realise that my initial judgement of Mr Rhys Llewellyn had been proven accurate. For the report was particularly scathing regarding the school's ineffective and incompetent leadership, and mentioned many of the issues which we had discussed as significant shortcomings.

Before we parted company and I reluctantly returned to the less gratifying company of 11/KG and discussion of the masterpieces of early twentieth century American fiction, I persuaded Rhys Llewellyn to accompany me on a tour of the school to be introduced to some of its unpublicised delights.

I derived great pleasure from taking him to some of the more remote and unsanitary corners of the school, which were far more representative of the normal environment in which we all had to work, than the very recently tarted-up corridors and classrooms of the main teaching block. Together we witnessed examples of putrefaction and neglect, which would never have featured in the pages of the School Prospectus. We saw: filthy windows, stained with rivulets of ancient spit, baked hard during years of zero attention; cracked and broken windows; doors and floor tiles; overflowing and unemptied rubbish-bins; broken and graffiti covered desks; damaged and abandoned cupboards; chairs and computers; litter covered corridors; flickering and humming fluorescent tubes; non-functioning lights; locked and evil smelling lavatories; missing door handles; dirt encrusted and sticky carpets; leaking and water-stained ceilings; puddle-filled lobbies and landings; damp and unheated classrooms; peeling and discoloured paintwork on rotting windows and doors, and, the pièce de résistance: a colony of enormous rats, living among the detritus beneath Lofty Lewis's demountable and seagull-shit covered classroom.

It was a tour of unmitigated wretchedness, which revealed levels of dilapidation and decay, that would have made perfect location shots in a movie detailing the end of civilisation. Indeed, it was, in some-ways, a shame to have exposed the smart and immaculately dressed Mr Llewellyn to such scenes of dirt and squalor, but it was very necessary that someone of influence, and with obviously high personal standards, should be shown the truth about our normal working environment, and I was pleased to have been the instrument of his enlightenment.

When we parted company, outside Lofty's classroom, he once again shook my hand and thanked me for being co-operative and helpful. He made no direct reference to our tour, apart from commenting that he had found it very informative. As he walked back across the school yard towards the distant form of the main teaching block, the kids, who by now had filled the yard for their afternoon break, parted before him like the waters of the Red Sea, proving that, charisma and authority can communicate itself, even on a very brief acquaintance.

Finally, the last day of the inspection was upon us, and by lunchtime on Friday all the inspectors had left the site for the last time. Verbal feedback from the inspectors had been given to the department heads and teachers in each subject and we now had to await the publication of the full inspection report, to discover their judgements and opinions in detail.

All the staff showed visible and noisy signs of the release of tension, and they were all looking forward to celebrating their deliverance from the inspection with a long arranged booze-up down at 'The Lonely Leek', a local hostelry once called 'The Colliers Arms', but which had been re-named, refurbished and extended a few years ago in a desperate attempt to attract a younger and trendier clientele, and to discourage the card and domino playing pensioners who had been its regulars. It now boasted a large function room, a surly and ignorant manager, poorly kept beer, abysmal food and Sunday lunch-time entertainment, usually featuring large plates of almost inedible sausage and mash, and fat, cellulite dimpled strippers, grown too old and saggy for the revealing lights of the city's nightclubs.

I found the idea of spending additional and unpaid time in such a venue, endlessly dissecting and discussing the week's events, about as appealing as stripping-off naked and wallpapering the hall, stairs and landing of a large, unheated house in February. So, instead of attending this depressing 'beano' I spent the evening enjoying a superb meal and an excellent bottle of vintage champagne in a favourite restaurant and in the company of my charming, intelligent and vivacious wife, who perceptively appreciated that school inspection was not a welcome subject of conversation.

Chapter 7

Morning Assemblies

On the Monday following the inspection, it could have been expected that the chief topic of conversation among the staff would be the ordeal of the previous week. It was therefore, surprising to discover upon my arrival at school that, the focus of all the gossip was the Friday night's booze-up at 'The Lonely Leek'.

Apparently, the evening had begun with everyone in good spirits, although all slightly hyper and over-excited that the inspection was finally over. It was this heightened state of receptivity, combined with unusually large quantities of alcohol, which was later blamed for subsequent events.

It was agreed that the meagre and tasteless buffet was a failure, but it was not a sufficient disappointment to dampen the wine-fuelled enthusiasm for having a good time which had insidiously enervated the gathering. With the consumption of alcohol came the lowering of inhibitions and the equally perilous increase in bravado and irresponsibility, an increase which persuaded the over-sexed libido of Mark Collins – the weakest link in my form team – that this was the night to give Bonnie Butler, the recently appointed Head of VI Form, the 'seeing to' which, he fantasised, she so desperately desired.

It was Mark's stated opinion that all single women past a certain age, must be in need of 'a good seeing to'. This was an opinion which he invariably expressed when in male company, and he often stated it in the crudest possible language. Of itself, his opinion may not have been too harmful, but it was accompanied by the even more dangerous delusion that he was just the man to satisfy all the sexual longings of these supposedly sex-starved and frustrated women, and by so doing, release the powerful torrent of their suppressed sexuality, and relieve them of all their all too evident, irritability and stress.

He'd long had Bonnie marked down as a woman in need of exactly the sort of attention which he could provide, and so, in a drink-induced moment of insane optimism, he had requested the DJ to play a slow and smoochy love song, and then, he weaved his way unsteadily between the already entangled bodies of other couples who were hoping for romance, and asked Bonnie, in a slurred and incoherent voice, if she'd like to dance.

Bonnie, being polite and a woman whose considerable bulk made her more immune to the effects of alcohol than most, reluctantly agreed, and led the unfortunate Collins onto the dance floor in a vice like grip of purposeful intent; pulling his slightly balding head forward, to rest upon the ample mound of her enormous breasts.

Unusually, she was wearing slinky, diamante studded stilettos, which elevated her to over six feet, and a loose flowing, diaphanous dress which gave her an unfamiliar allure.

Although excessively large, she was well proportioned, and whilst her years in the P.E. Department had not generated a sylph like figure, they had produced great muscle tone and considerable power. By contrast, Mark Collins was, like many lechers, a scrawny, somewhat insignificant specimen of manhood, whose only attribute of stud-like proportions, was his reputation for being well-endowed in the 'dick department'.

It was obvious, to all who observed them, that they were an ill-matched pair in almost all respects. Theirs was an incompatibility made worse by drink, desperation and uninvited desire.

Mark unfortunately, had taken Bonnie's firm grip and all enveloping breasts to be a strong signal of her sexual frustration and lustful intent. Intoxicated by too much wine, the heady muskiness of her perfume, the closeness of her responsive body he'd badly misread the signs. Taking her gallant attempt to keep him upright and prevent him from sinking to the floor as a longing to possess him, he unwisely, removed his right hand from her waist and slid it up her very accessible dress to caress the warm gusset of her silk knickers.

It was reported that, he'd been heard to murmur 'Oh Bonnie, Oh Bonnie,' in a husky and lust-filled voice only seconds before she responded to his advance by clamping her left hand on his scrotum, lifting him bodily off the floor, and swinging him round in a low arc, causing his head to collide with the gently gyrating backside of Gwen Tulley, the hopelessly drunk Head of Religious Education, and another large unattached woman who had also, often been the butt of his suggestive fantasies.

Gwen, who had been enjoying, with the even more hopelessly drunk Lofty Lewis, her first romantic smooch for years, was, to say the least, startled to have her drunken shuffle so disastrously ended by Collins' head smashing into her arse and sending her and the hapless Lofty crashing to the floor.

Mark, who by now had realised the full extent of his misjudgement, was screaming like a banshee, as Bonnie, who still had a very firm grip on his gonads, continued to revolve like a professional pairs skating champion, with him spinning in an almost perfect 'death-spiral' worthy of a score of at least 5.9. Although graceful, Bonnie's movements were unfortunately not conducted in the vast arena of a championship ice-rink, but on a small and exceedingly crowded dance floor. The result therefore, was catastrophic, with couples being toppled like ninepins in a skittle alley. The carnage continued until Bonnie finally released her grip upon the now limp and still screaming Collins, to send him soaring above the writhing mass of mown down dancers to crash into the DJ's kaleidoscopic light show, destroying his new twin-deck and speakers and effectively bringing the whole celebration to an unexpected and premature end.

Many absent spouses and partners had to be contacted early to collect a number of the drunk and injured. Chief among these was Brenda Collins, who was advised that due to a very unfortunate accident her husband could no longer walk and would need to be taken to the casualty department of the local hospital for urgent treatment. The unconscious DJ, who had been buried beneath the debris of his demolished equipment, was also dispatched by ambulance to receive much needed medical attention.

However, everyone who had escaped injury stated that, despite its untimely and chaotic conclusion, the evening had been a great success, and suggested 'The Lonely Leek' as an ideal venue for the staff outing held each year to celebrate the end of the summer term. The only dissenting voices were those of Gwen Tulley, who'd seriously twisted her knee and ankle, and of course, Mark Collins, who had had a month off work, and was currently being sued by the DJ for the loss of his equipment and livelihood and divorced by his wife for his attempted infidelity and for no longer being able to fulfil his marital responsibilities in the bedroom. He was also under threat from Bonnie Butler that, if he ever made unwelcome advances again, she would inflict upon him considerably worse damage than the mere crushing of his testicles.

It took until the Thursday of the week following the Friday night fracas at 'The Lonely Leek' for things to begin to return to some semblance of normality. It was this Thursday which saw the publication of the final 'Inspection Report', and this took everyone's interest and attention away from other events.

It was amazing to me that most departments in the school were judged to be satisfactory, or good, and that the general standards achieved in teaching and learning were acceptable. However, it was gratifying to read that the Senior Management Team were judged to have serious shortcomings, and that almost all of the areas identified as requiring significant action, were all areas for which the S.M.T. were directly responsible. There was, surprisingly, also mention of the appalling lack of maintenance and proper cleaning of the site, with specific mention of many of the items I had shown Rhys Llewellyn on our school tour.

Overall, the 'Inspection Report' was, for most staff, a reassuring endorsement of their own professionalism, and a ringing condemnation of the leadership qualities of the S.M.T. Generally therefore, they judged it to be a fair and balanced report, whilst the S.M.T. thought it to be extraordinarily partial and excessively biased. As a Head of Year, and therefore a key member of the pastoral team, I viewed the report as a very useful tool in our efforts to persuade the S.M.T. to acknowledge and remedy their many and glaring

96

inadequacies. Not least among which, was the talent they possessed for appointing teachers with quite obvious deficiencies, to posts of significant responsibility.

A perfect example of this was the elevation of Gwen Tulley to the position of Head of Religious Education, a job which required organisational and pupil management skills of a high order. This was made necessary by one of the major defined roles of the position, which was to organise the content and delivery of morning assemblies for all year groups in the school, a task of considerable importance and challenge.

Like most schools, we had been censured in the 'Inspection Report' for totally failing to deliver a key requirement of the 1944 Education Act that: 'the school day in every county school and in every voluntary school shall begin with collective worship on the part of all the pupils in attendance'. This requirement was incorporated into law at a time when schools were much smaller and religious (Christian) belief was more universally accepted and approved of. Our censure therefore, was no surprise, and also, no longer any cause for concern; for all intelligent people realise the difficulty, impracticability and inappropriateness of this aspect of the 1944 Act.

Unlike many schools, we did not have to consider the religious sensibilities of our pupils in any significant way. Our school intake was almost exclusively white, Welsh and without any deeply held religious convictions. We did not therefore; have to deal with any of the multi-cultural and multi-faith minefields which afflict so many British schools. I had long held the opinion that the removal of all religious content from the curriculum of all schools would be of enormous benefit in helping to create a more cohesive and tolerant society.

It would also assist all pupils in their quest for knowledge and enlightenment, if we did not present them with contradictory and incompatible messages regarding the criteria required to judge the validity of arguments. For, on the one hand, we teach them the value of logic, reason and scientific methodology, we instruct them to accept nothing without rigorous investigation and irrefutable evidence, we teach them the necessity for critical thinking, and even in law, we expect them to subject 'truth' to the test of 'reasonable doubt'; and yet, on the other hand, we ask them to accept belief systems, which are ludicrous in their implausibility, illogical and inconsistent in their doctrines, and divisive and dangerous in their practice. It is little wonder we produce adults who find the exercise of reason and sound judgement exceedingly difficult.

The cauldron of bigotry, intolerance and hatred which characterises so much of our society can be largely blamed upon our failure to completely separate education from religion. I firmly believe that strongly held religious convictions, of any and all faiths, are, and always have been, the enemy of reason, and the greatest breeding ground for cruelty and contempt ever to impede our doomed attempts to create a rational, tolerant and civilised world. Fanatically held beliefs represent an intellectual failure of potentially cataclysmic proportions, which could yet see humanity destroyed in a maelstrom of irrationality and violence.

It was, however, fair to say that the cult of unreason which occasionally characterised life at Gruffudd ap Cynan Comp owed nothing to religious bigotry. The battles, which we were daily forced to wage against the forces of yobbishness and disrespect, could in no way be blamed upon religious prejudice. Our battles were, invariably, against the anti-learning culture evident among the parents of society's underclass, who, having received no inspiration, or perceived benefit from their own education, saw no reason to value it for their offspring. It is a dreadful indictment upon our educational system, that we have managed to produce an entire generation, who see no worth in learning, or value in any of its outcomes, unless they generate large amounts of cash. For many of our children, their lives have, blessedly, not been blighted by religious bigotry, but they have been just as effectively destroyed by a culture which denigrates sensitivity, applauds ignorance and rewards mediocrity.

It was in this atmosphere, of often callous disregard for life's finer feelings, that the ill-equipped Head of Religious Education was expected to be effective. It was a task which would have challenged the talents of Jesus Christ himself; it was certainly not an arena in which to expose the meagre expertise and confused beliefs of Gwen Tully.

Gwen, who as Head of R.E. bore the responsibility for whatever worship did occur in the school, was a divorcee of long standing. She had long ago lost her burning conviction in the truth of Christianity and the divinity of Christ, and had not had a religious experience since making the wings for her son Damien, when he featured as the Archangel Gabriel in his primary school's nativity play, some sixteen years previously. She was bitter at the early failure of her marriage and viewed most men as opportunistic liars, who were only interested in 'one thing'. Never an attractive woman, she had become a menopausal moaner, who masked her loss of faith by passionately embracing all the new-age crackpot alternative beliefs, which were the current vogue. She dressed like a middle-aged hippy, and lately, had taken to wearing hair extensions, multiple silver bangles and ankle chains. School assemblies, which had never been particularly orthodox, had unfortunately, become the platform for the propagation of her increasingly eclectic and weird enthusiasms. Over the last few months in morning assemblies, she had lectured on: the magical and healing properties of crystals and magnetic bracelets, the meaning of stone circles and Druidic rites, the religious practices of obscure tribes in Mongolia, Borneo and the Amazon rain forest, the benefits of transcendental meditation, and, most worrying of all, the theological significance of 'The Simpsons'.

Apart from Gwen's lack of interest in the main tenants of Christian doctrine, the other major factor preventing the fulfilment of the 1944 Education Act's requirement to commence each school day with a 'collective act of worship', was the fact that our main hall could only comfortably hold around four hundred pupils. It was therefore necessary to ration morning assemblies to a maximum of two per week for any particular year group. Even the achievement of this compromise entailed having two year groups in the hall together. This arrangement was less than satisfactory, as it meant the hall was always packed beyond its capacity during assemblies, and this was never helpful in our efforts to maintain good order.

Gwen was always complaining to Dr Douglas, asking him how she could possibly be expected to deliver interesting and thought-provoking assemblies when, due to overcrowding and pupil inattention, she could hardly be heard, let alone understood. Douglas, whose own appearances in assembly had declined dramatically since the preparations for inspection and his humiliation at the hands of Carly Devine, was of little help, since his own skills in pupil control were lamentably inadequate, and even less effective than Gwen's.

Vic Davies, who very occasionally took an assembly, was little better, as he had the unfortunate habit of telling the kids interminably boring anecdotes regarding his own schooldays. These stories were so mind-numbingly dull, the kids level of attention dropped to the point where many nodded off, or blocked their ears to deaden the impact of his latest tedious tale concerning some incomprehensible event, which had occurred when he had been a model pupil at St Cuthbert's, a minor Catholic public school somewhere in West Wales.

Even less frequent than Vic's rare forays into the bear-pit of morning assemblies, were the appearances of Frank Baldwin, our seldom seen first deputy. Being almost totally deaf was an immense advantage for Frank when taking assembly. He was, unlike others, never distracted from the delivery of his message by loud noises, or laughter, or sudden cries of pain when some juvenile thug in the back row pulled somebody's hair, or punched some other unfortunate victim. The kids of course, were all very aware of Frank's disability, and were therefore always careful to remain relatively still when shouting, giggling and whistling through one of his moralistic monologues. Frank, who possessed excellent vision, was in consequence, always impressed by how attentive everyone seemed during his very occasional appearances as the main speaker in a morning assembly.

It was evident that most staff considered the morning assemblies to be an absolute waste of time, and most resented having to accompany their form across an often rain-and-wind lashed yard, to sit for twenty minutes with four hundred-plus bored and disinterested kids, listening to stories from Vic's uninspiring past, or much more frequently, another of Gwen's sermons on some unlikely topic, such as the sacred significance of tree worship among some archaic tribe of East African pygmies.

It grew increasingly clear to most staff that Gwen was 'losing the plot'. This became apparent to all during her doomed attempt to give assemblies a spiritual 'make-over'. The first intimation of her proposed plans to civilise assemblies came when she asked to address all the Heads of Year at one of our regular Thursday evening pastoral meetings. This was duly agreed, and so, at our next meeting, we had the usual bunch of attendees, plus Gwen and minus Bruce Lloyd, the current Head of Year 10, who continued to treat all pastoral meetings as optional.

Bert Bowen, passed out his latest miss-spelled agenda as he welcomed Gwen to the meeting, and introduced her with, what I felt, was uncalled for obsequiousness, as though she were a person of influence and power. Bert had always been deferential when in Gwen's presence, probably because her increasing weirdness was disconcerting and her noticeable interest in the esoteric was un-nerving. Gwen, who I noticed had recently developed a pronounced facial tick, was rarely challenged or contradicted by the S.M.T., who seemed to fear her eccentricity with the kind of medieval superstition often reserved for those whose madness was thought to be a sign of approval from God. I, and most other staff, possessed a much less reverential view of her condition and, quite simply, judged her to be 'nuts'!

She had obviously been reading the more trendy R.E. journals, and had latched on to a series of proposals for improving the pupils' behaviour and attention during assemblies. She began the introduction of these ideas by saying that she thought that, when pupils were quiet and attentive in assembly, this was achieved by 'enforced silence'; when what she wished to experience was the pupils being well behaved and quiet due to 'voluntary stillness'. She argued that the contrast between these two states was significant, and it was our inability to achieve the latter which was largely responsible for our failure to generate the desired atmosphere of calm and tranquillity.

I said that, our failure to achieve the desired state of calm and tranquillity, owed more to the irrelevant and poorly delivered subject

101

matter of most assemblies and the lack of charisma and personal charm of most of the speakers. Bert, who obviously thought my observation unhelpful, and tried to shush me by tapping his lips with his index finger, was, immediately silenced himself in the clamour of vocal support for my comments. I further asked Gwen to explain how – if I were to enter an assembly where all the pupils were quiet – I would know whether their state of rapt attention had been achieved through 'enforced silence', or 'voluntary stillness', and why should I bloody well care!

There then followed a long, and mainly meaningless discussion of the qualitative differences between the two states, and whether 'voluntary stillness' could ever be achieved, and how we would recognise it, if it ever were.

Gwen came up with several ideas to aid its achievement. These included: not shouting at the kids to obtain silence; playing calming music as they entered the hall, closing the blinds and dimming the lights to create an atmosphere of religiosity and mystery; projecting serene images of tranquillity onto a large screen at the front of the hall; ensuring that all form tutors were made aware of the new regime and did not shush the kids, or disturb their concentration with negative comments about unacceptable noise and behaviour. Finally, despite mine and other staff's misgivings, Gwen was given the green light by the S.M.T. to implement her desired changes and commence her quest for 'voluntary stillness'.

This began the following Monday, with Years 8 and 9 as the unfortunate guinea-pigs. As all four-hundred plus of them shuffled into the hall from the glare of the brightly lit space outside, and passed through the newly curtained double doors, they entered a completely unfamiliar world of almost total darkness, where the only helpful light was the flickering glow of the projection beam as it flashed eerie green pulsing images of imagined serenity onto a large screen mounted on the stage. Further confusion was added by the supposedly calming sound of mystical music by Enya being piped through the P.A. system. To complete this atmosphere intended to promote calm, Gwen had placed burning incense-sticks at strategic points throughout the hall. These gave off tiny pin-pricks of light like glow-worms, and infused the air with the heady aroma of an Arabian brothel.

Blinking furiously, to dispel the stinging sensation caused by hundreds of smoking joss-sticks, and desperately trying to accustom their eyes to the unexpected darkness, the kids began to babble in suppressed excitement. With no one to yell at them to shut-up, the noise gradually increased, as they blindly pushed forward in a doomed attempt to find their way to their usual places. In an ill-judged move to increase the calming influence of Enya's music, someone in the control room at the rear of the hall significantly increased the volume, which had quite the opposite of the intended effect, and caused the kids to raise their voices ever louder in their efforts to be heard.

The general chaos and cacophony was greatly enhanced, as those who had entered the hall first, encountered the front row of chairs. Pressure built as more and more kids, by now, an uncontrolled and ill-disciplined mob, continued to push forward in an unsupervised attempt to locate their accustomed seats.

I, and other staff, who had promised not to subvert the quest for 'voluntary stillness', by insisting upon 'enforced silence' stood quietly by the doors, as the disastrous consequences of the quest became evermore apparent.

Gwen, who had been largely obscured by the darkness and the smoke which had issued from the excessive number of burning incense-sticks which she had placed upon the barely visible grand-piano, slowly emerged from the gloom to try and restore order. Not wishing to be the first to fall back upon 'enforced silence' and negate her own experiment, she performed a strange, dimly perceived ghostlike dance, where she floated among the confused and increasingly panicked kids, flapping her arms like a distressed swan. As the kids fell over chairs and each other, she was eventually lost to sight in the general melee of collapsing bodies and screams of agony, as an increasing number of kids succumbed to the results of her menopausal madness.

Finally, unable to endure the insanity any longer, I switched on the main lights to reveal the true cost of the doomed quest for 'voluntary stillness'. At least fifty moaning kids were on the floor, chairs were overturned and scattered, some kids, knowing they were unobserved, had set up a den beneath the grand-piano, where they were attempting to smoke the still smouldering joss-sticks. Others, who had managed to reach the back of the Hall, were involved in experimenting with some of the more challenging techniques of sexual foreplay they had recently been learning about in their P.S.H.E. lessons. Gwen, who had been forced to the floor by the sheer number of kids who were pushing and shoving in panic, was desperately struggling to extricate herself from the tenacious grip of two Year 9 girls, who were begging her to save them.

The scene of unmitigated carnage, together with the numerous letters and phone calls of parental complaint regarding the unexpected injuries suffered, during what should have been a well ordered assembly, spelled the inevitable end of the quest for 'voluntary stillness', and reinstated 'enforced silence' to its rightful place, as the preferred method of command and control.

A week later, Gwen was admitted to St. Bartholomew's, a small private hospital, specialising in 'post traumatic stress disorder', where she apparently rediscovered her faith in God, eventually leaving the hospital, to run a second-hand Christian bookstall in the local market.

She never returned to school, and took early retirement on health grounds. Her place as Head of R.E. was filled by Steve Regan, who had recently joined the ranks of The Salvation Army, and who, was so desperate to leave the P.E. Department that he'd convinced Douglas and the easily swayed governors that what the R.E Department required was a more authoritarian and militaristic approach to religion, with zero tolerance of alternative belief systems. With the recriminations of the failed experiment in 'voluntary stillness' still firmly in their minds, the interviewing panel could perceive the wisdom of Steve's more orthodox vision, and so, he was rescued from his expected fate of having to end his teaching career in the Special Needs Department, and took up his new duties with evangelical zeal.

Gwen's departure from the School went largely unremarked, apart from a short poem marking her quest for 'voluntary stillness', which some budding satirist had pinned to the notice-board in the Staffroom.

104

It read:

MORNING ASSEMBLY AND THE QUEST FOR VOLUNTARY STILLNESS

It's rumoured that God and Gwen Tulley
Have shared the odd meaningful thought,
He'd advised her on voluntary stillness,
But not upon how it is taught.

On that, God was woefully silent
And wouldn't say what he believed,
He'd told Gwen that stillness was welcome,
But failed to say how it's achieved!

Chapter 8

Sports Day

With Steve's departure from the P.E. Department there was a vacancy for a new teacher of boys' P.E. There being no applicant from the existing staff, the S.M.T. were forced to appoint an outsider. This turned out to be a sallow, skinny and sick looking, newly qualified teacher who had recently graduated from a P.E. college in West Hartlepool. His name was Wendel Wilson, and it wasn't long before the kids renamed him 'Weedy'. He was at the opposite end of the physical spectrum from Steve and was no doubt, a godsend to Greg Butcher, the brash, bombastic, bullying Head of Boys' P.E. who ran his department like a military martinet, and who had always resented Steve's superior size and strength, and was grateful to at last have a member of department, whom he could domineer and terrify.

Greg, a barrel-chested ex-army P.T.I., was, like Dr Douglas and Frank Baldwin, a renegade northerner, who was proud of his reputation for blunt speaking and insensitive opinions. He saw little value in any branch of education other than the physical, and thought anyone, who didn't appreciate the benefits of intense physical pain, a first division wimp. He particularly enjoyed putting the newly arrived Year 7 boys through their paces by having them run the perimeter of the school field, until they collapsed from exhaustion. He would supervise these endurance events through a megaphone from the front seat of the school minibus, screaming threats and insults at the steadily dwindling number still able to trot, until most of the runners had dropped out. Any boys still standing at the end of this ordeal would be earmarked by him as potential future champions, and they would be invited to join the strict training regime of his after school sports clubs, where he further developed and honed their fitness with painful tasks of unbelievable cruelty.

His favourite sports were those with a very high degree of physical contact, where he argued that danger and the ever present threat of serious injury sharpened the senses, and built a valuable team spirit. I personally felt that the only thing it built, had been the sports injury unit at Abercwmtwerp General Hospital, recently constructed to accommodate the very high number of boys who sustained sprains and fractures during their games lessons.

The arrival of 'Weedy Wilson' gave the boys another teacher whom they could insult and intimidate. Caught between a Head of Department who viewed being abusive as a manly virtue, and some of the worst thugs in upper school, Weedy was soon taking time off with stress, wondering why his dedication and enthusiasm had failed to endear him to his classes. What he did not appreciate was that Greg Butcher had given him the most disruptive and insolent boys in the school; an action which Butcher justified, by reference to his belief in the value of 'throwing people in at the deep end', to see if they would sink or swim. As a teaching method this is not to be recommended, as it presents the exam prior to giving the lesson, and therefore has an extremely low success rate. Butcher always argued he didn't have the time to featherbed new recruits, and consequently he ended with no recruits at all. This of course, left the rest of us to fill the gap caused by his failure to protect Weedy from the most difficult pupils, or the harmful effects of his own insensitive and damaging philosophy.

At the time of Weedy's appointment, the overall Head of the P.E. Department was Janice Newman, a twenty-nine year old fitness fanatic who used extreme exercise as a substitute for extreme sex, an activity in which she was far more interested, but much less successful. She had been appointed as a replacement for Bonnie Butler when Bonnie had moved from the P.E. Department to take over as Head of VI Form.

Janice, who had come from an inner-city school in Bristol, had been appointed to her position over the head of Greg Butcher, who had also been a candidate for the position. His failure to land a job, which he thought was his by right and length of service, had caused him immense hurt, which he was determined to assuage by making Janice's task of running the department as difficult as possible. He was therefore resentful and unco-operative, and did everything he could to undermine her authority and thwart her plans for improving the department. One consequence of his truculent and unpleasant attitude towards her was that she crossed him off her list of potential lovers. She had already dismissed Weedy as an unsuitable candidate in her search for a long term and totally fulfilling sexual relationship, and she had latterly latched on to Chris Reed, the teacher in charge of the Pupil Referral Unit, as the most promising prospect in her hunt for a husband.

I'm convinced the reason so many female teachers remain single, is because the pool of men whom they encounter at work, (the most popular place for finding a partner) is not only exceedingly small, it is also stocked with some of the least attractive specimens of masculinity it is possible to imagine. As eighty percent of teachers are female, it is obviously not the ideal profession in which to find an available male, particularly if your preference is for an attractive, talented, charismatic, intelligent and sexy one. The number of male teachers who would fit that description are as rare as nuns in the navy and, therefore, not readily available. The result of this dearth of marriageable men is an army of unattached, unloved and unfulfilled females stalking the corridors of schools in a more or less permanent state of desire and disappointment, and a much smaller number of largely inexperienced men who either fear women, or despise them.

It is this unqualified group of misogynists and sexual misfits to whom we entrust the delivery of sex education to the Nation's children. It's little wonder that some children, caught between the sniggering and inaccurate advice of their mates, and the incompetent, puritanical and repressed views of their teachers, go totally off the sexual rails, and end up pregnant, diseased and sexually misinformed. We would not allow a teacher with no experience, or qualifications in science to teach Physics. Why then, do we allow teachers with no experience or qualifications in human eroticism to teach sex?

It is yet another example of the cowardice and incompetence which characterises the myopic loonies who frame our educational legislation.

Whoever had been responsible for Janice's sexual education had obviously been successful in creating a woman with a voracious sexual appetite and a refreshing lack of inhibitions. She willingly shared her fantasies and talked openly of her interesting selection of erotic toys, which she played with on the nights when she had been unsuccessful in finding a suitable partner to share her bed. She made titillating claims that sometimes, her sexual conquests were female. It was this revelation, made one lunchtime, to a small group in the Staffroom, which sent Mark Collins scurrying to the toilet; only emerging to ask her if her revelations of occasional lesbianism were true, and whether she was aware that he was a talented photographer and that he'd recently purchased a new digital SLR camera, with which, he was anxious to experiment. She told him that she might be depraved and decadent, but she was not desperate, further reminding him that she'd heard that his still discussed encounter with Bonnie at 'The Lonely Leek' had left him somewhat lacking as a legendary lover. He tried to explain that it was his inability any longer to fully participate in sex, which had prompted his interest in observing it. Janice, who was not adverse to indelicate comments, told him that she was only impressed by men who could get it up, keep it up, shove it up and finally clean it up, and that she was interested in lover's dicks, not shutter clicks! Mark, who was already suffering a crisis of confidence since his painful humiliation by Bonnie, and his recent separation from his wife, did not any longer possess his old lecher's contempt for rejection. He was, without doubt, a man robbed of his resolve, and reduced to an uncertain future. Since Brenda had locked him out of the house and dumped two suitcases of his clothes in the garden, he'd been living in one room above 'Bob's Bicycle Shop' in the centre of Abercwmtwerp High Street. It was enough to depress the most resolute of men. It certainly was taking its toll on Mark. So much so, that he'd recently taken to attending Year Assemblies, almost as though he no longer had the will to dream up excuses for his absence, such as an unexpected timber delivery, or urgent repairs to a broken machine.

However grim Mark's current situation, there was general agreement among staff that it was no more than he deserved, and as the weeks passed, interest in his plight, which most saw as the result of his own precipitant action, steadily waned, and other matters came to the fore. The current topics of conversation and speculation were the increasingly obvious feud between Greg Butcher and Janice Newman, and the rumour of an incipient affair between Janice and Chris Reed.

Janice was visiting the Pupil Referral Unit which Chris managed, far more frequently than was necessary to ask about the behavioural progress of the few pupils who would have been her legitimate interest due to their sporting prowess. Some of the difficult and disruptive pupils whom Chris had to deal with, in his vain attempts to improve their behaviour, were members of the school's various sporting teams, but these were few in number, and certainly insufficient to justify, either the number, or the duration, of her visits.

Chris, who had recently become engaged to Sandra, a theatre sister at Abercwmtwerp General Hospital, an attractive woman, who was soon to become his third wife, was very flattered by Janice's attention. He saw her sexual interest as an opportunity for a final fling before settling down, for what he hoped, would be the last time. Janice, on the other hand, saw in his obviously willing response to her advances, the possibility of persuading him to abandon his plans to marry Sandra, and to marry her instead.

I knew all this because they both saw me as some kind of disinterested father figure, in whom they could both confide; and so therefore, unbeknown to each other, they would pop in to my room at different times to keep me updated upon progress, and to seek my opinion upon their plans to achieve their very different, and incompatible objectives. I of course, being impartial, gave them each the advice they most wanted to hear, and so, helped to set in motion a chain of events which would certainly result in a disappointment for someone. Whether this would be Chris, Janice or Sandra, only time would tell.

110

Of more pressing concern was the open hostility between Janice and Greg Butcher, which was becoming more obvious, and was beginning to affect the smooth running of the P.E. Department. Under normal circumstances, this may not have mattered too much, but as the days lengthened into summer, the staff's thoughts turned to the long holiday, and more immediately, to the preparation for the 'School Sports Day'; an event which was always eagerly anticipated, because it came almost at the end of term, and afforded everyone, especially the staff, with an afternoon off in which to laze about in the sunshine, watching the kids expend massive amounts of energy to achieve meaningless points for their even more meaningless Houses.

It was testament to the competitiveness and gullibility of the young that they could be so easily conditioned to identify with artificially created groupings such as the School House system, and that so many of them could be persuaded to participate in pointless and often painful activities, to try to ensure that their House achieved more points than any other. These points were displayed weekly on the House Bulletin Board. Points were awarded for good work, good behaviour, high achievement etc; and were deducted for poor work or ill-discipline. Sports Day afforded an opportunity to accumulate a very high number of points, and was therefore marketed by the P.E. Department as though it were triple points day at Tesco.

At the end of each term, the House with the most points was awarded the House Cup, a badly tarnished and battered goblet in the shape of a Greek urn, and at the end of each year, the House with the most points over the three terms won the Inter House Shield, a huge piece of wood and silver plate, which was so heavy that it took four pupils to carry it, and four pupils over two hours to clean it. It was a monstrous object, which stood for most of the year as the centrepiece in a large, ugly and very dusty display cabinet in the School Foyer. Much was made of the value of winning this worthless and tawdry award, and each year, when it was presented during the final assembly of the summer term, it was carried aloft into the Main Hall, where pupils of the winning House were encouraged to applaud its arrival, and venerate its presentation to the House Captain and Vice Captain, who invariably, staggered under its weight, and attempted to smile, through their obvious discomfort, in triumph at their supposed achievement. It was a manufactured ceremony of the most breathtaking banality, which illustrated perfectly the values of a society which encouraged its young to strive with enthusiasm to win tacky trophies of dubious worth!

The four Houses in competition for the honour of winning the Inter House Shield were named after ancient Welsh saints. They were: St Teilo (Red), St Cadoc (Green), St Dyfrig (Yellow) and St Illtud (Blue). The original reason for selecting these particular saints was long forgotten, as was the rationale for choosing saints at all, since the school had no obviously strong links to Christianity, apart from an unsubstantiated rumour that St Dyfrig and St Illtud had been a couple of medieval monks who'd founded a brewery on the site now occupied by 'The Lonely Leek'. This was as likely as any other explanation, and was partly supported by the fact that a number of the more elderly local residents still referred to the car park at the rear of the pub as St Dyfrig's field.

Whatever their origin, the House system was well established, and was used effectively to promote a spirit of competition and tribalism among the twelve-hundred plus pupils. Members of staff were also assigned to a specific House and helped to reinforce the quite arbitrary loyalty that pupils were encouraged to exhibit towards the success of the House in which they had been placed. Nowhere was this loyalty more apparent, or more forcibly expressed, than among the competitors and spectators at the School Sports Day.

Usually held during the week prior to the end of the summer term, Sports Day was universally enjoyed. Even the loutish non-competitors, who considered themselves far too 'cool' to participate in any activities likely to disturb the sculptured spikes of their gelled hairstyles, were, nonetheless, pleased to have the opportunity to wander the field, buying ice-creams and hot-dogs, and generally making a nuisance of themselves. Most of the non participating boys were content to hang around the periphery of the main event, chatting up equally disinterested girls, who were reluctant to take part in any sport which interfered with their smoking, or their social life.

The younger pupils were the most enthusiastic, and many painted their faces in their House colours and noisily and passionately supported every competitor who represented their particular House.

Most staff, apart from the S.M.T. were allocated specific tasks, such as timekeeping, marshalling, recording, selling drinks and cakes, or worst of all, supervising the hoards of excited kids who were always reluctant to remain in their designated places, and who wandered around, frequently causing mischief and mayhem.

My usual task, which I had first undertaken some years previously, and which I jealously guarded, was to be the teacher in charge of the 'sin-bin'. It was inevitable that, a number of pupils, over excited, or too ill-disciplined to cope with the unfamiliar freedom of the day, would be sent from the field to sit quietly in M12, the ground floor classroom in the Main Teaching Block which was closest to the field, and which had large double doors providing easy access. This room was designated as the 'sin-bin', and it was my responsibility to supervise all the 'sinners' who were dispatched from the field due to their unacceptable behaviour. Needless to say, no pupil accepted their exclusion from the event with good grace, and always had long and ludicrous explanations as to why they'd been unjustly treated. I however, ignored all their pleas to be released back to rejoin the activities, and made them sit quietly copying pages of text from Chaucer's original 'Treatise on the Astrolabe', an obscure and difficult tract in old English upon the workings of an incomprehensible medieval astronomical instrument. It was a task of immense tedium and monumental pointlessness, guaranteed to produce resentment and hand writer's cramp. I loved it; and encouraged my own competition by awarding an excessive number of house points to the pupils who copied the most pages with the fewest mistakes and in the neatest hand. It was a kind of alternative 'Sports Day', which produced a quieter and more sedate version of the meaningless activities occurring outside. It also possessed many of the same elements: concentration, competition, commitment, endurance, irrelevance, and discomfort; and it resulted in similar outcomes, with winners, losers, points, prizes and presentations. I gave the most successful participants, ten, twenty-five, or fifty house points, and presented the winners with Bronze, Silver, and Gold certificates, which marked their skill and effort as award winning copyists. In many ways, they were more significantly and generously rewarded than the individual winners of the athletic events, and the certificates, due to their rarity, were more highly prized than the small plastic badges awarded for success in track and field. It was a con, which kept all but the most truculent pupils focused and fully occupied. It also ensured that I was relatively undisturbed, although closeted in a room with some of the school's most awkward and disruptive pupils, and was therefore able to complete some marking, or other routine, but necessary work.

This year, I managed yet again to secure this assignment, mainly due to its unpopularity with other staff and the fact that I willingly volunteered for this potentially unpleasant duty.

Sports Day was scheduled for the last Wednesday of the summer term and, as usual, we were very fortunate it turned out to be a beautifully warm and sunny day, with only a very slight breeze. The morning was very relaxed and unstressful, as many of the pupils were absent, either participating in various heats, or helping Free Fall Evans and Chesney Winters, our frail and ageing groundsman, to set up chairs for the staff and visiting dignitaries, such as the School Governors and the local Mayoress. Very little work was done on Sports Day and most staff used the morning to tidy their classrooms in anticipation of the imminent end of term. All the members of the P.E. Department, plus a number of the more sporty members of staff, spent the morning either supervising the heats or putting the final touches to the marquee, which stood in the oval in the centre of the running track, and from where the P.A. system boomed out the results of the various events, and kept everyone informed of the relative positions of each House. The P.T.A. had set up their usual stall at the far side of the track selling soft drinks, cakes and strawberries and cream. There was also a local ice-cream van and a mobile burger and hot-dog trailer, both of which were charged a fee by the school to help the on-going P.T.A. minibus fund.

Unusually, I did not have any pressing tasks to complete, and so, at 1.00pm I placed a comfy chair in the doorway of M12 and settled down in the small area of shade provided by the overhanging roof of M Block to await the arrival of the first of the afternoon's candidates for the sin-bin. Papers, pens, copies of Chaucer's treatise were all prepared, and I looked forward to an afternoon of blissful inactivity.

The weather was absolutely glorious, with the temperature in the mid-seventies. The sky was cloudless and there was a very gentle breeze, which made sitting out extremely pleasant. Most of the kids were dressed in their P.E. kit, sporting a wide shoulder band in their House colour. Quite a number of the non-participating girls were in excessively short skirts and were sitting around the edge of the track, waiting for the events to start, or were already queuing at the ice-cream van. It was an idyllic scene, charged with suppressed excitement, as everyone waited in anticipation for the first race of the afternoon.

The long jump pit was quite close to M Block and I noticed Free Fall Evans, dressed in an ex-army khaki string vest and a pair of cropped combats, posing in front of a group of scantily attired VI Form girls, who had sat close to the sand pit, no doubt waiting for the athletic form of Ben Austin to start his run up. Ben was the elder brother of Hannah in 8/MJ and was described by most girls as the fittest boy in the school. Using 'fit' in this context was not simply a reference to his physical condition, but was a popular euphemism for his desirability as a potential mate. Ben himself, was quietly unassuming and gave no indication that he was affected, or overly impressed, by being thought a powerful 'babe magnet'; another expression which teenage girls bestowed upon the boys they most fancied.

Free Fall Evans, who suffered no such false modesty, and who seemed to spend much of his working day counselling the more attractive VI Form girls and no doubt, giving them the benefit of his allegedly, vast experience, had now joined the group of girls by the long jump pit, who were showing an understandable interest in his large number of mildly erotic tattoos, the crudest of which was a naked female figure which did very obscene gyrations whenever be bent his arm and flexed his biceps. Free Fall, who was enjoying the girls' attention, looked understandably annoyed when the group was

115

joined by Mark Collins, who obviously had little awareness of the impression he created in a black 'Nike' baseball cap, black and white quartered rugby shirt, white well worn extremely baggy tennis shorts, calf length grey socks and size ten trainers with flashing red lights in the heels. With the large peak of his cap, his disproportionately small head, voluminous shorts, knobbly knees and skinny legs, he looked like an ageing anorexic ostrich with its feet stuffed into a couple of bumper cars. Why he imagined that he presented a picture of male desirability to a group of intelligent, vivacious and attractive seventeen year old girls was a delusion beyond explanation. Lack of self awareness was, perhaps, a side effect of having his higher intellectual faculties located in his recently damaged testicles. As he began to chat up a couple of girls, who seemed the least interested in Freefall's body art, he was distracted by the arrival of Greg Butcher, who gesticulated at him, obviously indicating that he was wanted to supervise the javelin competition to which he'd been assigned. Butcher had stated a few days previously, when he'd put the Sports Day Duty List on the staff room notice-board, that he'd given Mark the javelin duty in the vain hope that he might, hopefully, be impaled by an over-zealous competitor. Butcher had no time for Mark's sexual obsessions, and thought that anyone who placed the pleasure of sex above the suffering and sacrifice of sport must be some kind of pervert. As Mark scurried off to judge the javelin event and Free fall left the girls to go and collect the hurdles in preparation for the hundred metres, I settled back in my chair, in anticipation of an enjoyable and uneventful afternoon.

The first indication that this was not to be the case came when the first to arrive for time out in the sin-bin were, Stacy Fowler, Tracey-Ann Smith, Crystal Devine and Dixie and Trixie Turner. They'd all been caught smoking round the back of the gym and had been dispatched to M12 moaning and whinging about the injustice of their punishment. I ignored all their complaints and set them all to work diligently copying, after I'd first ensured that the twins sat well apart from each other. Crystal, who'd made a brief improvement in her appearance subsequent to a meeting I'd had with her extensively adorned mother, had now reverted to her previous appearance as 'The

Empress of Bling', so by the time I'd confiscated all her earrings, studs, rings and chains the others had already managed to complete half a page. I'd bribed them all with a promise of House points plus a review of their misdemeanour and a possible early release back on to the field, if they all behaved and worked quietly. Once I was satisfied they all were all fully occupied, I returned to my chair in the doorway, where I could watch both the miscreants in the classroom and the activity on the field.

The races were now fully underway and the kids were noisily screaming their encouragement to the runners, and Steve Regan, who, just for the day, had agreed once again to perform his usual function as 'The Voice of Sports Day' could be heard through the P.A. system, commentating upon the efforts of the competitors and announcing the names of the winners and the relative positions of the Houses.

All seemed fine and the afternoon looked set to become another successful sporting event, until the second indication this was to be a stressful day came when Greg Butcher put in motion the first phase of his plan to humiliate Janice Newman and ensure that her first time in charge of Sports Day would be a memorable disaster, which would reflect poorly upon her competence and reinforce his claim to have been the best candidate for the job of Head of P.E. and expose the S.M.T.'s stupidity and lack of vision for preferring an unknown and untested female over his own obvious ability and undoubted commitment.

His first small, but effective act of sabotage had been to alter the names of all the competitors entered for all the events staged after 2.00pm. This produced absolute chaos, with kids who were supposed to be participating in the high jump being called to the start of the 400 metres. Almost every competitor's chosen sport had been switched, so kids were being sent to far flung corners of the field to participate in events which they had not entered, and for which, they had no aptitude. It is difficult to overstate the unbelievable disorder which this simple, yet very vindictive act, actually caused. There were legions of bemused athletes wandering the field in complete confusion, trying to explain to staff that they were not entered for the

117

events for which they had been called and asking for guidance as to where they should go.

The non-competing kids, who formed the bulk of the spectators, naturally became increasingly frustrated at the lack of action, and their anticipation and excitement slowly turned to restlessness and misbehaviour. From my vantage point in the doorway of M12, I could clearly see several members of staff remonstrating with an increasing number of unruly pupils who, I knew, were being dispatched in my direction, with obvious gestures, indicating their exclusion from the field. My hopes for an enjoyable afternoon were dashed as the numbers sent to the sin-bin steadily increased to the point where Vic Davies was forced to also open and staff M10 and M11, to accommodate this rapidly growing group of disruptive and disobedient pupils.

Sports Day had descended into an irrecoverable disaster, which perfectly illustrated the potential consequences of perceived rejection and thwarted ambition; two of the most powerful, yet sadly, often unwisely ignored motives for revenge.

Janice's first Sports Day was forever after remembered as the only time the event had to be abandoned due to circumstances other than bad weather. Whilst it may have been possible to recover the event after Butcher's first piece of sabotage, it became impossible to rescue anything from the day when a group of Year 10 boys, all in Butcher's Rugby Team, and all bribed by him with threats of losing their coveted first team place, wandered nonchalantly, through the throngs of milling and baffled athletes, towards the central marquee, which housed, not only Janice and senior members of the P.E. Department, the vital P.A. system, the recently polished cups, shields and trophies, the Headteacher, his first Deputy, but also the Chair of the Governors, and most importantly, 'The Right Honourable Cynthia Hammond-Smythe, M.B.E.', the Lady Mayoress and local benefactress of the school.

Whilst this gathering of august personages was struggling to comprehend the depth and scale of the catastrophe which was slowly overtaking them, Butcher's boys, trained and drilled by him to the professionalism of a crack S.A.S. squad, had stationed themselves at each guy-rope which securely tethered the large marquee to the ground, where, at the pre-arranged signal of Butcher flashing the lights of the old school mini-bus, which he'd positioned on a slight rise at the edge of the field, they all whipped out the Stanley knives which he'd provided, and with perfect synchronicity, cut through the ropes. The resulting collapse of the marquee was a heart-stopping vision in slow motion mayhem which moved the event from partial confusion to total panic.

The screams and cries for help from the victims trapped beneath the collapsing canvas and falling tent poles could be heard right across the field, and prompted a swift and concerted response by most staff and several of the more senior and responsible pupils, who, galvanised into action by the unfolding tragedy, gallantly crawled under the edges of the writhing and heaving fabric to effect a rescue of all the trapped and increasingly frantic staff and guests. It was a scene of quite touching and unexpected heroism, in which I had absolutely no intention of becoming involved.

Butcher's gang of well drilled saboteurs, having achieved their objective, quickly melted into the milling crowd of panicking spectators and would be difficult to identify, or apprehend.

My own position as a relaxed observer of the unfolding events was immediately threatened by all the kids in M12, who, upon hearing the screams and commotion from the field, had all rushed to the doorway and windows.

'What's 'appening Sir?' shouted Stacy, as she, and the rest of the detainees attempted to exit the classroom for a better view of the disaster being enacted on the field. It took all my resolve, and the use of my chair as a four pronged cattle prod – a vaguely remembered control strategy used by a lion-tamer in some long forgotten movie – to round them all up and force them back into the room.

'What's 'appening Stacy,' I breathlessly responded, 'is that Sports Day is regrettably over!'

Once I had them all safely corralled, I shut and locked the doors, and then joined them all at the window to watch the progress of the rescue. With our faces pressed eagerly to the glass we clearly witnessed the crouching figure of Free Fall Evans, emerging arse first from the still bucking canvas, displaying the revolting spectacle of his spotty builders bum, and dragging to safety, the prostrate and dishevelled form of the Right Honourable Cynthia Hammond-Smythe, whose worsted tweed skirt had ridden up to reveal the awful sight of her pale green directoire knickers. This scene alone, provided for me, and the whooping kids, a rare moment of shared unity and enthusiasm, where we all felt that if Sports Day had to prematurely end, then this was a beautiful way!

Chapter 9

Year 9
(Choosers and Losers)

Returning to school during the first week of September, after a six
week summer holiday, made the disastrous events of Sports Day
appear a less significant occurrence than they had seemed at the time.
Fortunately, none of those trapped beneath the collapsed marquee –
including the Right Honourable Cynthia Hammond-Smythe – had
suffered any serious injury, and the most that had been sacrificed had
been a little personal dignity on the part of the P.E. Staff and their
invited guests, and a great deal of physical energy on the part of the
participating athletes.

Greg Butcher, who'd quickly been identified as the architect of,
potentially, the most dangerous and irresponsible piece of sabotage the
school had ever suffered, managed to escape the consequences which
he so richly deserved, by persuading his doctor to certify that he'd
acted from intolerable stress, brought about by acute paranoia, which
had been occasioned by the failure of the Senior Management to fully
appreciate the effect which their rejection of his job application would
have upon his mental health. This spirited and quite ludicrous defence
persuaded the S.M.T. to beg all the victims of his attack not to involve
the police, or to press charges. However, the seriousness of his actions
could not go totally unpunished, and so, to calm the anger of his
victims, particularly the vitriolic hatred expressed by Janice Newman,
who had understandably felt the most humiliated and aggrieved as a
result of his actions, he was forced to take an extended period of
absence to regain his mental equilibrium, and cure his dangerous
paranoia. It was further decided that, upon his return, he could no
longer be relied upon to run the Boys' P.E. Department in a proper

and professional manner, and so therefore, he was told that if he wished to return to continue teaching at Gruffudd ap Cynan, he would have to accept a temporary job share with Lofty Lewis, who'd announced at the end of the previous term, his intention to go part-time in preparation for his planned retirement. So it transpired that Butcher moved from his full time position as Head of Boys' P.E. to become a part-time teacher within the Special Educational Needs Department, where, he joined the ranks of the many other ex-teachers of P.E. throughout the country who'd been reluctantly relegated to the educational graveyard of 'Special Needs'. His self-inflicted demotion had also placed him along-side Lofty as another failed male with good reason to detest Pamela Potts, the incompetent and self deluded Head of the S.E.N. Department.

Pam made her resentment of most men quite obvious, and with Greg's appointment she had to deal with two of the most strident misogynists in the school. Things were certainly set-fair for a future crisis in the S.E.N. Department, and I looked forward to the outcome of mixing such competing and incompatible egos.

The commencement of the autumn term meant that I was now the Head of Year 9, an unenviable responsibility, even in a successful and well run school. At Gruffudd ap Cynan, the position was made much less appealing by the large numbers of pupils for whom the narrow and largely academic curriculum offered at Key Stage 4 (14 to 16 year olds) was totally inappropriate.

Year 9 was not only the year when pupils took S.A.T.S. (Standard Assessment Tasks), a series of external examinations designed to assess their progress against national norms, but also, the year when any gullibility, or innocent faith they had in authority, finally vanished. For many of the street hardened kids, with little or no parental support, disillusion with the worth of education, or the importance of teachers, set in long before Year 9. However, even the kids from supportive homes, who were shaped and burdened by concerned and loving parents, began to withdraw into their own private teenage world of mysterious motives and inexplicable values, where all adults were judged against the kids' illogical and constantly changing criteria.

Both teachers and parents suffer a rare period of unaccustomed unity in finding the teenage years between 13 and 16 the most difficult. For, between the onset of puberty and the eventual arrival of sexual maturity, lays the unfathomable minefield of teenage angst and self absorption, which makes logical and meaningful communication between adult and child almost non-existent. It is a time when teachers and parents view adolescent behaviour with a mixture of incomprehension and concern, and adolescents view much adult behaviour with disbelief and acute embarrassment.

This eventful time of hormonal imbalance, intense feelings and desires, coupled with lack of experience and limited knowledge, make teenagers unpredictable and volatile; yet, it is into this cauldron of passionate and unchecked emotion that we throw the first of a quite pointless series of public examinations. These examinations are mainly designed by out-of-touch and myopic professional educators, to test the kids' knowledge of a limited and largely irrelevant national curriculum, which serves up bite-size chunks of unrelated knowledge, unconnected facts and life-inhibiting expectations. Between the ages of 14 to 18, we present our children with: Standard Assessment Tasks in Year 9, internal exams in Year 10, mock and final G.C.S.E. exams in Year 11, AS levels in Year 12 and A2 levels in Year 13, and, unfortunately, like our motor cars, we test some of them to destruction! The ironic truth is that this intense pressure and ill-considered culture of constant assessment still results in a significant number of pupils who leave school without having achieved the much vaunted 5 G.C.S.Es at grades A to C, and even more damning, A level students, who leave school only semi-literate, and totally incapable of writing a coherent and well argued essay.

To compound this folly, we also force this limited academic and restricted curriculum upon pupils for whom it is wholly irrelevant, and then raise our voices in concern and incredulity at the levels of truancy in our secondary schools.

It has always been a matter of complete amazement that the levels of truancy in our secondary schools are not far higher than the current level, especially when I seriously consider what the curriculum actually offers.

123

One of the key responsibilities as the Head of Year 9 was to help pupils choose the most appropriate subjects to study in years 10 and 11 for their G.C.S.E. examinations. These choices are universally known as 'options', and every year, in schools throughout the U.K., pupils must opt to study certain subjects.

The actual choices which the pupils have, are of course, necessarily limited by cash and the availability of teachers in the subjects offered, and therefore, what is available was not such a life changing opportunity as it may sound; since all pupils are compelled to study the 'core' subjects of: English, Maths and Science and, for our pupils, also the terminally ill, but not quite dead language of Welsh, a recently imposed subject, made compulsory and forced upon the vast majority of the non-Welsh speaking pupils by the small yet voluble and powerful Celtic mafia, who control both the Welsh media and Welsh politics. Unfortunately, the victims of these remote and self serving politicians were the bulk of the nation's children, forced to act as an unwilling life support machine in an attempt to revive a language which refused to die.

However, Welsh was not the only subject which failed to engage the enthusiasm of the less able. The whole of the curriculum in Years 10 and 11 needed urgent reform to make it more appropriate and relevant to the very large minority of pupils who were increasingly disaffected and disillusioned with their final years of compulsory schooling.

In an endeavour to assist pupils make the best choices they were subjected to a series of assemblies, in which the various Heads of Department attempted to sell the benefits of their particular subject. These were usually occasions of immense boredom for the kids, but enormous entertainment for me. A typical example of the enlightenment to be gained from these talks came early on in the term, when Geoff Pritchard, the demob happy Head of History, came into a Year 9 assembly to attempt to sell the pupils the benefits of choosing to study History.

He appeared, still wearing the same shabby jacket which he'd reputedly worn since he started teaching forty-plus years ago. He was planning to retire at the end of the summer term, so he would not be around to teach any of the pupils to whom he addressed his sales pitch on the value of taking History as one of their subjects.

His talk, somewhat like his appearance, was a rambling, incoherent and practically incomprehensible account of the doors which would open for them once they had achieved a G.C.S.E. in History. These included: teaching History to the next generation of disinterested and inattentive school pupils, working in local government, cataloguing books in a public library, becoming a museum curator, and, most inexplicably, achieving success as a rock star. I later discovered that this was included because Geoff had read somewhere that Mick Jagger had studied History when he'd been a schoolboy.

Needless to say, apart from the rock star option, which strangely appealed only to those incapable of achieving a G.C.S.E. in anything more challenging than 'corridor studies'; the rest of the potential career suggestions left the majority of the kids hardly able to contain their indifference, or recover from the almost terminal boredom which his talk had induced.

Things livened slightly when, despite his forty odd years teaching experience, he unwisely concluded his talk by inviting questions. An unidentified voice from somewhere close to the back row, which I suspected belonged to Ben Jacobs, loudly asked if it were true that Hitler had only got one ball. As much of the secondary History syllabus was devoted to a study of the Third Reich, it was a question which was not only relevant, but also one which, it was not unreasonable to presume, Geoff knew the answer. However, instead of answering it, he attempted to generate a more acceptable enquiry by ignoring it, and asking if there were any more questions. This attempt to divert the questioner was greeted by noisy complaints from a large number of the audience that he still hadn't answered the first question. This complaint was totally predictable, since his audience consisted of fourteen-year-old boys, for whom testicles were a matter of intense interest and new found fondness, and fourteen-year-old girls, who variously regarded them as objects of disgust, mystery, excitement and, in a few cases, alien objects of recently fondled familiarity. It was not therefore, surprising that they wished an answer, since they had asked a question on a topic of universal teenage interest.

As chants of: 'We Want an Answer! We Want an Answer!' started to spread and grow in volume, I began to move to the front of the Hall to join Geoff, to quell, what looked set to become, a riotous end to his assembly. However, before I reached my goal, the strains of a very familiar ditty, sung to the stirring march tune of 'Colonel Bogey', began to supplant the more monotonous chanting. Like most disruption, it began in the rebel filled back rows, but was quickly taken up by the entire year group. It started tentatively, but rapidly developed into a loud and surprisingly tuneful rendition of:

'Hitler has only got one ball,
Goring, has two, but very small,
Himmler's are somewhat similar,
But poor old Goebbels has no balls at all!'

Unfortunately for Geoff, and before I intervened to stop this unprompted and unexpected community singing, they had substituted 'Goebbels' with 'Pritchard' in the final line, which I could see, was beginning to cause him embarrassment and stress. However, I was so impressed by the unfamiliarity and musical excellence of their vocal efforts that I was slow to react, and instead of putting an immediate end to their subversive song, I stood, momentarily entranced by their newly revealed ability to sing in tune and with such skill and enthusiasm. It suddenly became apparent that their usual reluctance to engage in any kind of collective singing, was not because they were shy, embarrassed, or talentless, it was because they didn't find the content of 'Hymns Ancient and Modern' sufficiently inspiring. I made a silent resolve to exploit their newly revealed talent for comic songs; by teaching them a few other choice examples remembered from the heyday of old time music hall.

That however, was an action plan for the future. The immediate need was to put an end to their enjoyment and Geoff's humiliation. I noticed that the subversive Dr Moore, unable to resist the tribal intoxication of the singing, had joined in, and was enthusiastically

126

leading the most vociferous group in the back few rows. Even Miss Monk, April Summers, the vivacious French teacher, and the hapless Mark Collins had all found the pace and passion irresistible, and were mouthing the words in silent approval as they rocked in their chairs in time to the songs hypnotic rhythm.

If I was to gain the pupils attention, and have any chance of restoring order and silence, I needed an effective diversion. Normally, I could command their attention, simply by standing in front of them with an appropriate expression of weary resignation, until they fell silent. However, on this occasion, that was unlikely to prove a successful strategy, as they were now consumed with the thrill and intoxication of mass insurrection, and were certainly not going to respond to a look; no matter how disapproving! I doubted if they would have responded to a loud shout, or even a shrill whistle. No! What was required was an unmissable distraction of sufficient interest to stop them in their tracks.

All this flashed through my mind as I finally reached the front of the hall, to stand in support next to the dispirited figure of Geoff Pritchard, the by now, totally demoralised Head of History; who must have wished that his eagerly anticipated retirement was already an historical event. As I considered my options, desperately trying to think of an effective strategy to divert their attention from the intoxication of their own subversion, I longed for the sort of divine power which could conjure a miracle.

Eerily, at the precise moment I wished for miraculous intervention, the hall doors were thrust open to reveal the somewhat bemused figure of Steve Regan, the recently appointed Head of Religious Education, who, having propitiously been passing the hall, had heard the unfamiliar sound of mass singing, and, whether or not influenced by his new Christian responsibilities, had mistakenly assumed that what he was hearing, was a spirited rendition of 'All Things Bright and Beautiful'.

It was obvious from his flushed and enthusiastic expression that he failed to immediately realise his error and appreciate the true nature of the song and its unequivocal non-Christian message. What he also failed to realise, was that he'd been followed into the hall by the same large black labrador which had caused him such grief and pain on the rugby field the previous year.

Despite his move from Boys' P.E. to Head of R.E. he had foolishly failed to abandon his familiar tracksuit for more appropriate attire, and the dog, which had obviously remembered their previous fun and games gave a playful bark of recognition, and firmly fastened its teeth onto the flapping left leg of his un-zipped track-suit bottoms. Steve, who also had very good reason to recall their previous encounter, panicked; and struck out at the snarling beast with such violence that, he over-balanced into the first two rows of nonplussed kids, who had, thankfully, now been successfully diverted from their musical insurrection. Even though I experienced momentary concern for the terrified and screaming kids, who'd been pole-axed by Steve's sudden fall, I was also very relieved that my wish for divine intervention had been so effectively answered, and that the obscene community singing, had been totally silenced without the need for any aggressive intervention by me.

After much squealing and general thrashing about, Steve and the still snarling dog were finally separated; blessedly, without any serious injury to him, or to any of the kids whom he had flattened. Geoff Pritchard had taken the opportunity offered by the dog attack to leave the hall and end his unfortunate humiliation. I was just grateful that the latest G.C.S.E. pep talk had ended without a riot, and apart from a few bruised kids, without the need to phone any parents and spend hours completing accident report forms.

As the weeks passed, talk followed talk, until all the non-core departmental heads had been given the opportunity to promote their department, and try to persuade their largely disinterested and disenchanted audience of the value of studying their particular subject. Following these talks came the lengthy process of interviewing each pupil to finalise their option choices, and to endeavour to place them all in the subjects most appropriate to their aspirations and most suited to their abilities.

This was an onerous task of considerable challenge and monumental thanklessness, riven with unhelpful intervention from confused and concerned parents, and by constant complaints from self-interested Heads of Department, who wished, at all costs, to prevent disruptive low achievers from choosing their subjects. The entire system seemed designed to foster frustration, enmity, disaffection and, most serious of all, failure!

It was a perfect example of an inappropriate curriculum, devised by an inadequate committee, and imposed upon an ill-taught cohort of childhood victims of educational mediocrity. It exemplified, with terrifying clarity, the paucity of ideas which characterise our educational thinkers, and exposed the nation's children to the life long consequences of their lack of vision and ability.

In addition to the complex task of selecting their 'options', Year 9 pupils also had to sit a series of external examinations (S.A.T.S.) designed to compare their performance in the 'core' subjects of English, Maths, Science and Welsh with all the other Year 9 pupils throughout the Country. This was supposed to provide an opportunity to benchmark their relative abilities, but unfortunately, what it also provided was an opportunity for Tracey-Ann Smith, the most precocious girl in the year, to artistically carve on her exam desk the skilfully executed statement: '**Doctor Dougless is a Fucking Wanker!**' Apart from the statements veracity, it was also easily attributable, for, in addition to the care with which she had carved the sentiment, she had also carved her name beneath it with equal skill and pride.

Vic Davies, who had the misfortune to be collecting up the English papers at the conclusion of the exam, had arrived at Tracey-Ann's desk, just as she was blowing the wood dust from the final letter of her name, and carefully folding the blade of the small penknife which she always carried to sharpen her frequently used eyebrow pencil. Vic, who – despite his ineffectual qualities as both a leader and a Deputy Head – was not without a sense of humour, commented to Tracey-Ann that, Dr Douglas may or may not be as she had described, but that he *had* achieved the highest possible level of academic qualification; an achievement which Tracey-Ann was extremely unlikely to equal, as she hadn't even managed to correctly spell 'Douglas', and, even allowing for the fact that she had correctly spelled 'fucking and 'wanker', this could not be considered a significant achievement, as these were words to which she had been exposed since an infant, and which she could reasonably have been expected to know how to spell. Noting the expertise of her carving, he also commented that he hoped she had chosen to study art and woodwork as two of her options for G.C.S.E.

Tracey-Ann, who failed to fully appreciate the subtlety of Vic's sarcasm, was bright enough to realise that he was 'taking the piss', immediately responded with:

'He may be a doctor, but he's not a real doctor like they've got up the Health Centre, and he's no bloody good. He can't control us and he don't ever listen to what we say. This school's gone right down the pan since he's been here!'

Vic, although experiencing a feeling of sneaking admiration for the accuracy of Tracey's observation was, nonetheless, obliged to discipline her and bring her offence to the attention of the Head.

I was aware of all this because I was, fortuitously, in a meeting with Dr Douglas in his office, to discuss Year 9 options, when Vic, accompanied by Tracey-Ann and the offending and now folded exam desk, were ushered into the room by Cynthia Richmond, the Head's attractive, and relatively new secretary.

'Sorry to interrupt Headmaster,' said Vic, acknowledging us both, and adopting a tone of feigned respect, delivered no doubt, to impress upon Tracey-Ann, the seriousness of her actions; 'but I've just caught Tracey-Ann Smith carving inappropriate comments on her exam desk, and I think you need to see exactly what she has written.'

I suspected that Vic enjoyed a moment of vicarious pleasure as he unfolded, and displayed the offending desk top to Douglas, allowing Tracey-Ann's artwork to express a sentiment with which he was in total agreement, but was too circumspect to express.

I watched with interest as Douglas took in the full import of Tracey-Ann's opinion of him, and although I felt a slight twinge of responsibility for the fact that she had misspelled his name, I was, basically, in agreement with her views, and more than a little impressed by the skill of her carving. Douglas however, had turned red, with I guess, a mounting mixture of fury and embarrassment, and he turned to me for much needed support.

'Well! Mr Falconer!' he exclaimed, 'it's very fortunate that, as Head of Year, you're here to witness this outrage, committed by one of your insolent and feckless Year 9 pupils. What have you got to say about this piece of obscene and extremely offensive graffiti?'

During this tirade I watched both Vic and Tracey-Ann struggle to suppress their amusement at Douglas' understandable anger, and because of this, I failed to immediately respond to his question. Misconstruing my silence to my not having properly heard, or understood his question, he continued. 'As this crude and offensive young lady's Head of Year, Mr Falconer, I would appreciate your opinion of her totally unacceptable behaviour!'

'Well, Headmaster,' I responded, with what I hoped was sufficient gravity, 'I am, of course, appalled by the sentiments she has expressed, and very disappointed by her failure to correctly spell your name, but I believe that her efforts do demonstrate some small measure of respect.'

Douglas looked at me with annoyance and obvious incomprehension, before he exclaimed.

'And how precisely, do you reach *that* conclusion? Just explain to me how this misspelled, offensive and obscene description of me can possibly demonstrate any kind of respect?'

I made a deliberate show of carefully examining Tracey-Ann's carving, before I straightened, and slowly turned to face Douglas.

'Well,' I answered, in my most serious and considered manner, 'she's called you *Doctor*!'

Tracey-Ann, who by now had realised she was possibly in serious trouble, and who wished to minimise the impact of her offence, immediately nodded vigorously in agreement, as though she wanted it noted in mitigation that, she had fully acknowledged Douglas' academic status. Vic meanwhile, was desperately struggling to suppress an imminent fit of the giggles at my somewhat wry observation.

Douglas, who had completely failed to be impressed by my explanation of Tracey-Ann's respectful intent in acknowledging his qualifications, or to perceive the tongue-in-cheek nature of my comment, was now purple with indignation at her obscene insolence, and obviously, disappointed by my lack of support he began to splutter as he screamed in response,

'She may have called me "Doctor", but that can't possibly compensate for her other crude and totally unacceptable opinions. Take her out of my sight! Give the desk to Mr Evans to clean up or dispose of, and telephone her mother, and tell her to expect a very long period of exclusion!!!'

He was obviously, far too angry to be placated by anything which I, Vic, or Tracey-Ann could have said, and so we, and the offending desk, all quickly retreated, leaving him in the lonely space of his poorly furnished office, shaking and twitching in apoplectic rage.

I gently closed the door and told Tracey-Ann to go and wait outside my room, while I had a word with Mrs Richmond. Vic, having enjoyed presenting Tracey-Ann's thoughts to Dr Douglas, seemed keen to have no further involvement in her punishment, for as he left the small lobby between the Head's and Cynthia Richmond's office, he turned to me and said; 'Stroke of genius Dave, to find some redeeming feature in *that* situation; wound him up like watch spring that has! I'll take the desk to Free Fall and leave the pleasant task of phoning Mrs Smith to you.' And with that, still chuckling over the incident, he left with the now folded desk tucked securely beneath his right arm. I acknowledged his departure and entered Cynthia's office to explain the reason for Douglas' anger. She expressed sympathetic concern at his ordeal, and, like any loyal and efficient P.A., she immediately entered his room to administer support and understanding, whilst I left for my room to convey the news of terrible Tracey-Ann's exclusion, to her equally terrible mother.

Chapter 10

The Trip to Paradise Park

After the difficult conversation I had with the truculent Mrs Smith, patiently explaining the nature and seriousness of Tracey-Ann's offence and that Dr Douglas would be imposing a long period of exclusion, imagine my annoyance when I received a copy of his exclusion letter and noted with dismay and disappointment that he'd only given her a temporary exclusion for five days. Douglas's notion of what constituted 'serious consequences' had obviously not been hardened, even though the offending behaviour in this case had been personally directed towards him. At least it proved that his woolly minded liberalism was deeply ingrained and not simply a device to please his political and educational masters. His idea of proportionate punishment would, I'm sure, have been loudly applauded by our timid and out of touch judiciary, but was totally incomprehensible to all of us who valued responsibilities above rights.

Responsibilities were, however, taken very seriously by any teacher who found themselves in charge of a school trip. Organising these understandably increasingly rare events is a burdensome and thankless task riddled with potential pitfalls. These ranged from the predictable consequences of taking two hundred-plus excited, inexperienced and ill-disciplined teenagers out of school, to the dreadful and career ending possibility of serious injury, or even death!

Unfortunately, we live in a blame and child centred culture, where all harm, tragedy, or personal failure which befalls an individual, must be the fault of someone else. The idea of any kind of personal responsibility for suffering any of life's many hazards seems to be an idea beyond the mental capacity of our law makers, or law enforcers. It is therefore, hardly surprising that the advice of the major teaching unions to their members regarding school trips, is to refuse to organise them, or take part in one as a supervising adult.

This was immensely sensible advice. It was also advice which I unwisely failed to heed, when I was persuaded to organise a Year 9 trip to 'Paradise Park'. Instrumental in this persuasion was Mandy Jones, my young and irrepressible Assistant Head of Year. She argued that after the trial of their exams, the kids deserved a break from their normal routine and would enjoy a trip to somewhere exciting. So, against my better judgement, I was skilfully manipulated by Mandy in agreeing to take them to 'Paradise Park', a recently opened theme and adventure land buried in the remote wilds of West Wales. Apart from a small wild life enclosure, Paradise Park contained very few attractions which could, even loosely, be described as educational. The bulk of the fifty acre site was given over to sick inducing rides and roller-coasters of truly frightening possibilities, where the opportunities for mishaps, serious injury, or death, were all too apparent. Mandy thought my caution and reluctance a sign of my increasing years, and it was probably her implication that I was too old and unadventurous to any longer take risks, that finally convinced me to book the trip.

With just over two hundred pupils and accompanying staff to transport, we needed four large coaches, and so, after a considerable number of unsuccessful phone calls to reputable coach companies, who all said they had no suitable vehicles available on the required date, I finally managed to book four vehicles with a small coach company from a neighbouring valley called, 'Happy Trip Executive Tours', which sounded just the sort of hopelessly optimistic outfit to cater for the needs of our ill-disciplined future executives.

To supervise this jamboree I had all my Form Tutors apart from Mark Collins, who pleaded on-going psychological problems as his reason for not wishing to attend. In addition, I successfully persuaded Chris Reed from the Pupil Referral Unit; Janice Newman, the Head of P.E., who still hoped to lure Chris away from Sandra, his fiancé; Steve Regan, to provide a spiritual dimension; Bonnie Butler, Head of VI Form and Sophie Millar, who having served as Head of Year 11 last year had now been rotated to become the current Head of Year 7.

Sophie was an experienced teacher with an engaging personality and a very high level of competence. I prayed her skills would not be required on this trip. I assigned three teachers to each of the coaches and set about the tricky task of deciding which pupils would travel on each coach. This was not an easy decision, since I had to consider friendships and enmities and ensure that the potential troublemakers did not all end up sitting together in the back rows of the same vehicle.

Finally, all the arrangements had been made, and having endured a sleepless night worrying about all the potential disasters, I arrived at school early on the morning of the trip to await the arrival of the kids and the coaches from 'Happy Trip Executive Tours'.

The day began to fulfil my worst expectations when, after five increasingly desperate telephone calls and the passing of half-an-hour beyond our due departure time, 'Happy Trip Executive Tours' had failed to arrive!

Keeping two hundred-plus kids waiting in the restricted confines of the school hall, was not an easy task, even when they were only anticipating the boredom of a normal morning assembly. Today, dressed in non-school uniform, and awaiting the commencement of their 'day out', it was impossible! Fortunately, just as their understandable restlessness looked set to descend into uncontrollable chaos, a great cry of excitement went up, as they saw, through the grimy and spit-encrusted windows of the hall the first of the four clapped-out coaches, bearing the worn, tarnished and paint-chipped livery of 'Happy Trip Executive Tours' drive into the school car park with a screech of brakes and enveloped in a cloud of foul exhaust fumes. It took all my crowd control skills and considerable behaviour management experience to prevent the entire year group from rushing from the hall as an ill-disciplined and dangerous mob. All of them had been assigned to a specific coach and as I emerged from the fetid atmosphere of the hall I was relieved to see that 'Happy Trip Executive Tours' had done as I requested, and attached a large white numbered card in the windscreen of each coach. The senior driver and the person responsible for transporting and returning us all safely to Abercwmtwerp, was an obese, florid-faced, sweat-soaked ex-miner,

135

who introduced himself as, 'Ivor-the-Driver and coach crash survivor from Happy Trip Tragic Tours'.

'Only joking squire!' he exclaimed when he saw the disbelieving and horrified look which greeted his jocular introduction. 'Sorry we're late Sir', he said, finally acknowledging my status and his failure to arrive on time, 'but the boss sent us out on our normal school runs before we could come and pick up you lot; but don't you worry Sir, once we get them all on board we'll put our foot down and make up for lost time.

The thought of them collectively putting their feet down and propelling these obviously ancient, clapped-out and poorly maintained coaches, at anything faster than twenty miles per hour, filled me with absolute dread. Sensing my apprehension, Ivor continued,

'Don't you worry Sir, Don't you worry! These may look like the last and least loved coaches from hell, but they've been lovingly maintained and expertly tuned by 'Taffy-ton-up-Thomas', the finest mechanic in the valleys and the only man on Earth who could make a Bedford OB outrun a Bugatti Veron. These coaches are not simply wolves in sheep's clothing; they are tigers in tortoise-shell livery. What time did you plan arriving at 'Paradise Park'?

'About 11.00am.' I responded, in amazement at his terrifying confidence.

'No problem!' Ivor exclaimed. 'I'll just have a word with my drivers and then we'll be off.' And with that, he quickly visited each coach in turn to issue his instruction, and we were, as he predicted, finally off!

The kids cheered, as the four coaches, belching smoke, careered out of the school car park to join the traffic heading out of the valley towards the M4 Motorway and our fun-filled destination in the depths of West Wales.

I don't know at what point in their development that children, when embarking on a journey to an unfamiliar destination, stop asking: 'Are we nearly there?'; 'How much further is it?' And, 'Can we eat our sandwiches now?' It certainly happens some time after Year 9, probably, after they've left school and become responsible for their own travel plans. All I do know is that our kids asked these

136

questions repeatedly on the thirty minute journey from the school to the slip-road on to the motorway.

Once on the motorway, Ivor was as good as his word and rapidly moved the lead coach he was driving into the fast lane, where he proved the mechanical skills of Taffy-Ton-up-Thomas by accelerating to a frightening and bone-juddering speed, which, if his speedometer was to be believed, was just a shade over eighty-two miles per hour.

The kids, who were oblivious to the dangers of driving at this speed, found the risk-ridden ride an exhilarating and noise inducing experience, since, to be heard above the deafening vibration of the ancient and rusting bodywork of a coach driven far beyond its natural limits, they were forced to raise the volume of their conversation to the level of a parade ground sergeant-major in the Welsh Guards. The ride was close to the most terrifying and stressful experience of my life, and all my shouted requests to Ivor the driver for him to slow down, were met with a blank stare of incomprehension, as he gesticulated dramatically towards his ears to indicate that, it was far too noisy for him to hear, and as this response seemed to necessitate him removing his hands from the steering wheel, I decided that further protest was not in the best interests of passenger safety.

With all four coaches locked into a bonnet to bumper convoy and travelling at excessive speed in the fast lane, with most of the kids whooping, shouting, eating and throwing objects to attract the attention of their mates, we made up for lost time, and soon passed Swansea, as we hurtled towards our destination. Once on this quieter and slightly less congested stretch of the motorway, the four obviously demented drivers from 'Happy Trip Executive Tours' decided to test the relative performance of their vehicles by staging their own geriatric coach grand-prix. They broke their nose to tail convoy as first one, and then another of these ancient vehicles attempted to pass the others to occupy, the obviously coveted, lead position. As the kids realised they were participating in this suicidal race, they all cheered and shouted encouragement to their respective driver to go ever faster. For the next twenty plus miles we endured this macabre and hazardous contest, as inspired by the kids' enthusiasm, each driver strove to attain the lead. Stretched across all three lanes, and occasionally, also the hard-shoulder, these frustrated Fangeos fought to establish the superiority of their vehicles and the pre-eminence of their driving skills.

My enduring memory of this race will forever be the expression of maniacal glee on the face of each driver as they drew level and passed the current leader. It perfectly illustrated the irresponsible, competitive, and reckless nature of the unenlightened male. It was a journey of immense danger, irrepressible enthusiasm, and ultimately, intense excitement, as I, like everyone else, was caught up in the primitive desire to win. It was exactly the kind of experience which gave meaning to existence and which valued the rush of danger above the comfort of security. It made, for a brief moment, living less of a chore and more a rare affair! The kids loved it, and despite my fear and misgivings, deep down, I knew the value of occasional moments of insanity.

What I didn't know was if anyone actually won this race, but it certainly recovered all of our lost time, and had it not been for the police road block awaiting us at the end of the motorway we would, undoubtedly, have arrived at Paradise Park well before our 11.00am deadline.

The roadblock was effected by five squad cars, striped like tubes of Signal toothpaste, which drove to block the road just as our four coaches reached the roundabout which marked the end of the motorway and the beginning of the twisting and tortuous 'A' road which then snaked its way further West. To avoid a lengthy tail-back the police quickly directed our coaches onto the car park of the 'Happy Eater' restaurant which was conveniently located off the first slip-road. This also provided an ideal landing site for the police helicopter, whose presence became apparent only now that the deafening vibration of our racing coaches had finally ceased. The incident of the road block and the impact of such a large gathering of police, had caused much excitement among the kids, who were already wound-up by the experience of participating in probably, one of the most exhilarating public service vehicle races in history. However, their fervour was just about containable until they heard the whirring rotors of the descending helicopter, and witnessed its dramatic descent to the unoccupied area adjacent to our now stationary coaches, where four officers, in full body armour and carrying assault rifles, exited the 'copter with a zigzag and crouching run, to join a similarly armed force issuing from the rear of an armoured police vehicle, which had screeched to a tyre-smoking stop between our coaches and the five squad cars, which, in a typical display of authoritarian over-enthusiasm, had their sirens screaming and their blue lights flashing like a noon-day disco.

A large officer, who appeared to be in charge, and who was burdened with a flack jacket and considerable hardware, now addressed us through some kind of speaker system mounted on the roof of the armoured van and ordered us to stay in our vehicles. If he imagined that, surrounded by about thirty police with automatic weapons, we were about to make a bid for freedom, he was sorely mistaken, particularly as this considerable force had now been joined by a group of snarling dogs with their police handlers.

I, and I'm sure the teachers on all the other coaches, upon realising the potential seriousness of our situation, had made efforts to calm the kids, as with their anxious faces pressed hard against the coach windows they watched in fascination as the police set about securing the area around our little convoy. A large crowd had emerged from the 'Happy Eater' and they were now being corralled behind police incident tape, which some of the unarmed officers were erecting around our beleaguered site.

Once the area was secured to their satisfaction, several of the armed officers approached each coach, and when they were all in position, with some kneeling, others lying, elbows on the ground and with all their guns directed at strategic points, we received a loud-speaker instruction to remain calm and to open the coach doors. What possessed the officer issuing the instructions to imagine that we were calm was beyond me! My mouth was dry, my skin clammy and my heart racing. Ivor had his hands on his head and was staring fixedly ahead at his insect splattered windscreen.

'Ivor,' I said, 'please open the doors.' When he failed to respond I repeated my request several times, before he eventually reached forward as though in a trance, and flicked the switch which operated the doors. Even before the doors had fully opened, two armed officers had bounded up the steps onto the coach; the first one, covering Ivor with his automatic rifle and the second, pointing a menacing looking black handgun straight at me.

'Nobody move! Nobody move!' was the fiercely barked command from the officer looking directly at me. The last thing I wanted was to antagonise him, so I sat completely immobile in my front seat position and wondered if I should copy Ivor's submissive posture and put my hands on my head, or, even raise them to indicate surrender, but I thought that, as I'd been instructed not to move, any sudden gesture of submission on my part might be my last, and so, I remained perfectly still. The kids though, who'd all been raised on a diet of police action movies, couldn't resist acting out the role of desperate and cornered fugitives, either by raising their hands and pleading not to be shot, or by ducking down behind the seat backs to make themselves less of a target.

'Right, kids!' shouted the same officer. 'No need to panic, we've got everything under control. You're all safe now!'

What did he mean, they were all safe now? They were trapped on a sweltering coach with a suicidally reckless driver, parked in a strange car park miles from home, surrounded by sirens, flashing lights, salivating dogs, the pulsating throb of a whirring helicopter rotor-blade and facing the itchy trigger fingers of a couple of extremely edgy, heavily armed police, dressed in the frightening clothing of a full combat uniform. I found it very difficult to imagine a less safe scenario!

However, before I could contemplate the hazards of our situation any further, Ivor, Mandy, Bonnie Butler and I, were all ordered off the coach and instructed to walk slowly towards the line of armed police waiting like a well disciplined death-squad in front of their armoured personnel carrier.

Crossing the few yards of bare and unyielding tarmac from the coach to the line of police was a truly terrifying experience. I was aware of the bright lights, the dogs, straining against their taut leads, the hushed mutterings of the gathered crowd of on-lookers and the sinister presence of the helmeted and vizored gunmen, who watched

140

our progress with intense concentration. I was genuinely fearful, and as I approached, a tall unarmed, and, judged by the amount of silver decoration on his uniform and hat, a very senior officer, stepped forward from the group to take control now that the situation appeared secure.

I was conscious that the other coaches were also being emptied of their drivers and supervising teachers, and I was desperate to know exactly what the police believed we had done to deserve such a massive and terrifying response. I knew they wouldn't have assembled all this fire power just because we had been speeding, not even because we had staged a dangerous and life threatening race.

Once he had identified me as the person in overall authority, the senior officer – whom it turned out was a Chief Superintendent Donaldson – took me to a waiting car, and, having solicitously opened one of the rear doors, and invited me to enter, swiftly moved to the other side of the vehicle and joined me on the back seat. It was immediately obvious from his placatory and smiling demeanour that somebody, probably him, had made a gigantic cock-up!

'Mr Falconer,' he began in a somewhat hesitant manner, 'it seems as though there's been some kind of mistake.

'Hang on!' I exclaimed. 'How do you know my name?'

'Ah, well,' he replied, 'we've just received a message from Sergeant Jenkins at Abercwmtwerp Police Station confirming your trip, and he's relayed all the details of staff and destination to me just moments ago as you all exited the coaches.'

'What do you mean exited?' I said in amazement. 'We were all forced off at gunpoint!'

'Yes, yes,' he wearily agreed, 'most unfortunate, most unfortunate, but you see Mr Falconer, until I received that call from Sergeant Jenkins, we were all labouring under the impression that what we were dealing with here was the abduction of over two hundred children, possibly by armed terrorists.'

After spending the next ten minutes listening carefully to Superintendent Donaldson's detailed explanation, I was astounded by the chain of events which had led to our current unfortunate situation. It appeared that the police had received a phone call at twelve minutes past ten to report the abduction of some children by a coach driver. This subsequently turned out to be Abdul Hussein, a desperate Iranian mini-cab driver, who had kidnapped his own eight children from the home of his ex-wife Deirdre Hussein (nee Dewhurst), a notorious ex-Abercwmtwerp schoolgirl, who'd recently returned to the area, following a very acrimonious divorce. Abdul, who had borrowed a mini-bus from his brother Omar, had been reported by both a nosy neighbour, who was chairwoman of the local Neighbourhood Watch committee, and by a mobile phone call from a concerned motorist on the M4, who'd seen Abdul's many children, frantically banging on the windows of the speeding mini-bus, in obvious distress and holding up a small, terrified little boy with the word 'HELP!' clearly emblazoned on his small white T-shirt. Coincidentally, a few minutes after these calls, the police received a number of additional calls, reporting our coaches being driven along the motorway at a dangerously reckless speed and full of, what appeared to be, panicking children; who were all signalling their terror, by waving wildly, and gesticulating in a strange manner to the occupants of every vehicle as they overtook them at a dangerous and inexplicable speed.

'Naturally,' explained Superintendent Donaldson, 'we thought we were caught up in a major terrorist incident, and when our own surveillance cameras and some of our patrolling officers confirmed your speeding coaches, we feared the worst, and in today's climate we just couldn't afford to take any risks; so we mobilised all the resources at our command to try to avert what looked like turning into a very tragic incident. I'm sorry that you have all been subjected to what must have been a frightening ordeal, but we acted in good faith, on what we thought was reliable information.'

Personally, I was relieved that we had all escaped their well intentioned, but mistaken actions, without loss of life, and was grateful to have survived, to hopefully reach retirement. When I finally emerged from the police car, all the kids and other staff were sitting on a grass bank at the side of the 'Happy Eater' restaurant, eating their lovingly prepared lunches and trying to persuade the many police to demonstrate their arrest techniques by handcuffing some of them and showing them various capture and restraint strategies using

CS gas canisters and their extendable riot batons. It was a commendable example of community policing, but it was not helping us to achieve arrival at our planned destination.

However, once the police had breathalysed all four drivers – which thankfully they all passed – and issued them with speeding tickets and a severe caution, we were all allowed to re-board our coaches, and continue our intended journey to Paradise Park. As we drove slowly out of the 'Happy Eater' car park we were waved on our way by a large group of grinning police officers and cheering crowds of spectators, who all seemed to have enjoyed the unexpected and dramatic interruption to their stop-off for a quick snack. The helicopter, which had ascended to a clearly visible position directly in front of us, dipped its nose and raised its tail in a graceful aerial salute, and the police dogs, sensing the dissipation of tension, were all wagging their tails with enjoyment, and finally, the tall and dignified figure of Superintendent Donaldson, touched the silvered peak of his impressive cap with his black, silver topped swagger-stick, in a silent and respectful tribute to our departure. It was a deeply emotional and memorable send off!

The rest of our journey was, in comparison, relatively uneventful, with a very subdued and chastened Ivor leading the convoy with restrained caution and ensuring that they all stayed well within the prescribed speed limits. It was just after 12.30pm by the time we finally pulled into the coach parking area of Paradise Park. I'd already telephoned their reception office to inform them of our unexpected delay, although I didn't detail the reason. Everyone had to remain on the coaches until I had presented the school cheque in payment for our entry and confirmed our total number of visitors. Once inside the park, apart from a couple of very special attractions, the rides were all free, even though many of them, like the big roller-coaster, were frequently subject to long queues. The perimeter of the park was secured by a very high metal fence, which prevented the general public from either deliberately or accidentally, gaining access, or wandering off into the surrounding countryside. This made it a very safe venue, especially for children, who, unless they were very young, could be allowed to explore the park without adult supervision. So, after I'd told our kids our planned departure time and issued instructions for them all to be back by the main entrance in good time, I allowed them all to head off to enjoy the attractions and to join the crowds of excited pupils who had already arrived from many other schools.

I, and the rest of our staff, made our way to a few recently vacated tables, located on a raised area outside a brightly painted cafeteria, which served drinks, snacks and even full meals. The day was glorious, and I was grateful for the large multi-coloured umbrellas placed above each table. Once we were all settled and had equipped ourselves with food and drink, the conversation inevitably turned to the morning's terrifying, yet strangely exhilarating events. I'd already briefly outlined to the staff the explanation provided by Chief Superintendent Donaldson and I now expanded on this, by telling them the full story. Once I'd concluded, we were all surprised I think, to learn from Sophie Millar, who'd been on the staff of Gruffudd ap Cynan Comp for many years, that she remembered Deirdre Hussein (nee Dewhurst) and that Deirdre's first pregnancy had occurred, some fifteen years previously, when she had been a pupil in Year 10. We further learned that the unfortunate father had been a boy in Year 9 called Tyrone Thomas, who'd been expelled for making improper sexual advances to Zoë Merryweather, who at that time, had been a young, extremely attractive and newly qualified teacher in the R.E. Department.

Another unfortunate consequence of the premature sexual encounter between young Deirdre and the even younger Tyrone, was that Deirdre's mother, Irene, a voluptuous and formidable bleached blonde with a fiery temper, had – the moment she learned of Deirdre's condition – rushed around to confront Tyrone's parents to have a very serious discussion regarding the whole sorry mess. When she arrived at the Thomas's household, she discovered to her annoyance that, Sally Thomas, Tyrone's long suffering mother, was temporarily away from the family home nursing her sick father, who had only recently been discharged from hospital after a serious operation. However, Mr Thomas, a muscular, unemployed window-cleaner and part-time all-in-wrestler, was at home, and invited the irate Irene Dewhurst in, so they could discuss the situation in private, away from the prying eyes and ears of his inquisitive neighbours. All that anyone knows about their subsequent discussions concerning their sexually precocious children, was that they continued throughout the night, and only concluded, when Mrs Dewhurst returned home early the following morning to inform her husband Gordon that she was leaving him to set up home with Mr Thomas. Mr Dewhurst apparently wasn't too upset by the news, since he'd been enjoying a secret and torrid love affair with Sandra Thomas ever since he had telephoned her some months previously to inform her that he'd caught Tyrone and Deirdre in bed together, and wondered if they could meet to discuss things. So it was that, by the time Deirdre gave birth to Morgan, the first of her nine children, both sets of his grandparents had swapped respective spouses, and since Deirdre and Tyrone were judged far too young and irresponsible to rear a child, they shared Morgan's upbringing between them, each pair of exchanged grandparents having him for a month at a time. Eventually, Mr Thomas and Mrs Dewhurst and Mr Dewhurst and Mrs Thomas went on to have several more children, so Morgan enjoyed some local notoriety, for being one of the few children whose brothers and sisters were also his uncles and aunties!

After Morgan's birth, Deirdre returned to school for a few weeks before she met Abdul in a Cardiff nightclub and ran away with him to meet his family in Iran, eventually arriving back in the U.K. with three children, and a fourth on the way. She and Abdul then settled in London, where Abdul worked for his brother in his coach and taxi business. Finally however, cultural and religious differences, coupled with sexual boredom and disillusionment, drove them apart, with Abdul insisting that they all return to Iran and join the holy war against the Western infidels. Deirdre, who found Western infidels infinitely preferable to Abdul's fanatic and fundamentalist mates, left him, and returned to her childhood home, taking their eight children with her. The rest as they say is history, but I hoped that the police managed to rescue her children before Abdul left the Country.

Sophie's recounting of Deirdre Hussein's early life had certainly kept us all entertained, and when Bonnie Butler said that she had to go because she'd left something important on the coach, and returned, carrying a large ice-box containing six perfectly chilled bottles of Chablis, we were all entertained even more!

The wine was immensely welcome, but it did have the predictable effect of lowering everyone's inhibitions, none so dramatically as those of Chris Reed and Janice Newman, who had travelled together on the same coach, and who, after a few glasses of Bonnie's excellent wine, began to view their survival of the morning's events as a sign that they were destined to be together. As the wine went down, so their opinion of each other's courage, character, and sexual attractiveness went up, until finally, they could contain their passion no longer, and left our company to stroll arm in arm towards a nearby boating lake, all the time gazing into each other's eyes, with what appeared to be expressions of intense and mutual sexual desire. Their short journey to the lake took quite a long time, as they paused every few yards to embrace, kiss and writhe together in a sickening display of over-eager and ill-advised lust. It's amazing what sunshine, alcohol and the stimulating effect of shared danger can achieve. Still, I couldn't help but feel that desire built upon such transitory foundations, was likely to collapse in tears and recriminations.

It was also setting a poor example of restraint to the several thousand school kids present, many of them from our own school, who passed by from time to time, often with their own newly acquired admirers in tow, and trying to deal with their own blossoming desires. At least, any newly formed liaisons were likely to be very short lived, since our departure time was 6.00pm, and many potential teenage love affairs would be prematurely nipped-in-the-bud by the even earlier departure of coaches heading home to schools in far distant, unfamiliar towns with intriguing and evocative sounding names. It's remarkable how a brief and chance encounter with some stranger from an unknown place, can leave a fierce memory, formed by the power of unrealised dreams. It is such moments where kids feel the sweet intensity of loss, and learn that life rarely rewards our deepest desires with fulfilment. It is thankfully, in the momentary and unguarded responses of the young, that we are sometimes privileged to glimpse, and perhaps also remember, emotions which lie beyond the reach of words.

Finally, Chris and Janice reached the boating lake and managed to disentangle themselves long enough to embark upon their voyage of discovery in a brightly painted Indian canoe. The last I saw of them that afternoon, was as they paddled away in what could have been perfect unison, but for their inability to focus upon anything other than their newly discovered passion.

The wine had relaxed everyone, and the afternoon passed in growing contentment. Eventually, I wandered off to explore the park and to make some show of concern that the kids were all enjoying themselves without causing grief and annoyance to other visitors. Every time I encountered a group of our kids, they appeared to be having a great time and they excitedly related the thrills they'd just experienced on their most recent ride. Also, they all seemed to be behaving themselves, and justifying Mandy's desire to give them a good time by acting like model pupils. I'm sure it was the wine I'd consumed, coupled with their positive and polite attitude which temporarily lulled me into the hopeful belief that, despite the earlier disaster, the trip had been a relative success, and that the kids obvious pleasure, had made all my efforts worthwhile. As I walked back to rejoin my colleagues I experienced a warm rush of unfamiliar euphoria as I anticipated a pleasant and incident free journey back to school.

With our departure time fast approaching, I asked some of the staff to tour the park to begin to round up all our kids, and send them towards the designated meeting point by the main entrance. There was a large paved marshalling area adjacent to the entrance gates, which was an ideal place to undertake a thorough headcount, before leading all the assembled kids through onto the coach park, to board their respective coaches. They had all been instructed to sit in exactly the same seat and on the same coach which had delivered them. This minimised the risk of inadvertently leaving someone behind; and had become doubly necessary, since last year's memorable Year 10 G.C.S.E. History trip to Hampton Court Palace had ended in panic, embarrassment, tears, recriminations and national scandal, when it was discovered, an hour and a half after departure that, Darren Dinsdale and Melanie Applethorp had both been left behind. This in itself was bad enough, but at about the same time that their absence was discovered on board the coach, their presence was being uncovered beneath a large, elaborately embroidered quilt adorning a solid oak, four-poster bed, in the very bedroom reputedly used by Henry VIII to deflower Anne Boleyn. Such sacrilege against the alleged royal conception, might have been forgiven, had it not been for the fact that Darren and Melanie were caught attempting to re-create this historical event, and would probably have succeeded, had it not been for the new hearing-aid worn by Ivy Painswick, the alert, slightly arthritic seventy-eight year old housekeeper and part-time tour guide, who'd said, when interviewed about the incident later that, she'd been drawn to the bed by moaning and the tortured sound of a female voice shouting 'Yes! Yes! Yes! I'm coming! I'm coming!' It wasn't until she went to investigate, that she discovered the source of the shouting, and managed to interrupt the proceedings just before Darren was able to achieve the first impregnation in the infamous royal bed since 1533.

Due to these events of last year, I was, understandably, acutely aware of the potential consequences of departing without a full compliment of pupils, and counted everyone five times, before I allowed them to move into the coach park to board their assigned coach. I was surprised and slightly disconcerted by their behaviour however, as they boarded the coach on which I was travelling. They were all uncharacteristically quiet, with hardly any sound, apart from when I detected, what I thought, were a few suspicious giggles.

I may have discovered exactly what they were up to, had I not been suddenly called away to deal with an incident on coach 3, where Dixie and Trixie Turner had trapped the unfortunate Lance Morris on the back seat, where they were insisting that he bought kisses off them both, or suffer the unspeakable consequences of spurning their advances. By the time I'd managed to rescue Lance from their deadly embrace and returned to my own coach, all the kids were aboard and sitting quietly in their seats.

'Everything OK?' I enquired of Mandy, who was just completing a final head count.

'Yes,' she replied, 'they're all here, but they're strangely subdued, I think they're up to something.'

'Like what?'

'I dunno, but Stacy Fowler and her mates were all trying hard not to giggle as they got on, and Nathan Hyde was unusually quiet.'

'Right,' I said. 'You're sure everyone's present and that they're all in the correct seats.

'Yes,' she confirmed, 'but they're not behaving normally; they're all so compliant.'

'They're most likely really exhausted after all the day's excitement.'

'Yes, that's probably it,' agreed Mandy, but without any great conviction.

'I'll just go and see that the other coaches have a full compliment and then we can be off,' and with that, I left to make the vital last checks to ensure that all the pupils were present. I still experienced a feeling of cold panic when I recalled the consequences of last year's History trip. Having satisfied myself that all were accounted for, I returned, and gave Ivor the driver the all clear to lead the convoy out of the coach park and head back on the journey home.

I'd expected, that once we were underway, the kids disconcerting quietness would quickly dissipate, to be replaced by their more normal noise and chatter, but when, after we'd travelled about ten miles, they still remained unusually subdued, my vague suspicion that they were up to something, became a raging certainty. Unable to endure my doubts any longer, I stood, and holding each seat-back in a firm grip, I wobbled my way towards the rear of the coach, where I could now detect the unmistakeable sound of suppressed hysteria. As I drew closer to the rear seat I clearly heard: 'Quick, Sir's coming! Sir's coming!' frantically whispered, as all the kids swivelled in their seats to face the back, where Stacy Fowler and her gang, unable to cope with the mounting tension any longer, all rolled around in a fit of uncontrollable giggles.

'Right!' I shouted, once I'd firmly anchored myself a few seats from the back. 'What's going on back here? And don't tell me "nothing". I know you lot, and you're definitely up to something!' I focused all my attention upon the heavily made-up and grinning face of Crystal Devine, who, of all Stacy's notorious mates, was the least able to keep a secret. 'Well!' I growled, staring directly at Crystal with what I hoped was my most intimidating look, 'I asked you what was going on?'

Crystal, who was obviously bursting to disclose exactly what was going on, and unable to contain herself any longer, blurted out: 'Nathan's nicked a duck! And with that, she collapsed in hysterics.

It took a moment before the full import of Crystal's unexpected revelation hit home, and even then, a desire to disbelieve what I'd heard, prompted me to request confirmation.

'What do you mean, Nathan's nicked a duck?' I asked, still focussed upon Crystal, who was alternately, giggling and gasping like a fish out of water. Apart from Nathan, all the occupants of the rear seat, plus all the kids in the back few rows, were now gripped by a mass fit of the giggles, and were incapable of giving me any kind of sensible answer. The only one not totally caught up in the hysteria, was the accused perpetrator of the theft, Nathan Hyde, who was sitting in the centre of the rear seat, with the quaking figures of Stacy and Crystal flanking him on either side.

'Nathan!' I shouted above the raucous sound of mass laughter, 'have you nicked a duck?'

He locked and held my stare with a malevolent expression of pure evil, which would have been worthy of Lucifer himself. Without answering, or lowering his gaze, he allowed a slow triumphant grin to reveal a row of very neat, very white, very pointed teeth, before he reached beneath his seat to retrieve from under his red 'Niké' jacket, a large, somewhat bewildered Mallard drake, with its beak held fast shut by a green hair-elastic, more usually employed to secure Stacy's ponytail. The duck took a few faltering steps towards me before its sudden exposure to the light and the noise of a coach full of baying kids, caused it to panic and try to escape by attempting to take off down the coach's central aisle. To avoid a collision, I threw myself to one side, landing heavily on Ben Jacobs and Kyle Bowman, who'd been whooping and shouting encouragement to the duck as it flapped its way frantically down the coach, causing fear and excitement as girls screamed and cowered and some of the braver boys tried in vain to capture the terrified bird.

Finally, and just before the duck crashed into the coach windscreen, Bonnie Butler, who after her encounter with Mark Collins at The Lonely Leek, was well used to dealing with out of control males, rose from her seat, and like a skilled player in a rugby line-out, caught the bird on the wing. There was much cheering, whistling and clapping from the kids, many of whom were relieved that the incident was over. Ivor the driver had surprised us all, by staying calm and fully focussed, as all hell had broken loose. I was very grateful that he'd managed to successfully concentrate on his driving, despite the potential distraction of the chaos occurring behind him.

Bonnie calmed the duck and removed the elastic from its beak, before covering it with a pink towel from her backpack. By the time I'd staggered my way back down the aisle of the swaying coach, Bonnie had everything under control, and was concerned about how we were going to return the duck to its home on the lake at Paradise Park. Having, by this time, travelled some twenty plus miles, I was extremely reluctant to turn around and drive the duck back home, but I realised that I couldn't take it back to school, so I telephoned the number given to me earlier by Superintendent Donaldson, and was surprised and relieved when he answered personally. I explained the entire situation and he promised to send a patrol car to intercept us and to take the unfortunate duck back to Paradise Park. So, for the second time that day we were stopped by the police, but this time, the officers were helpful and friendly.

As they carried the duck, still securely wrapped in Bonnie's pink towel, from the coach to their waiting squad car, the kids all broke into spontaneous applause, and I thanked the officers for their help and understanding. However, I was unfortunately, unable to persuade them to arrest Nathan Hyde, as they seemed to consider his actions as a harmless boyhood prank, and that any punishment should be left to my discretion. Knowing that my discretion did not extend to summary execution, I was thrown back on the wholly inadequate justice, likely to be administered by the jelly-livered Dr Douglas.

Still, at least the remainder of our journey was, blessedly, without further incident, and I managed to return all the pupils safe and unharmed to their naturally anxious parents, many of whom, had learned of our potential death at the hands of suspected terrorists on the six o'clock news, and had bombarded Dr Douglas at home, plus the School governors, the press, the politicians and the police with incessant and unremitting enquiries concerning our safety. Some parents, unable to stand the tension and uncertainty, despite police assurances that we were all safe and well, had set off for Paradise Park to discover the truth for themselves. Fortunately, they had all arrived too late to delay our departure, but apparently, just in time to witness the return of the distressed and traumatised duck.

All in all it had been a very interesting and eventful day, and a salutary lesson in exactly why it's not advisable to ignore sensible advice and organise a school trip!

Chapter 11

The P.R.U.

The repercussions of our eventful trip to Paradise Park were many and varied. Ivor and the other three drivers from Happy Trip Executive Tours were all fired for speeding and for endangering the lives of both the children in their care and other road users. Abdul Hussein was apprehended and arrested at Heathrow Airport with his eight children, who were thankfully, all safely returned to Deirdre, their very anxious mother. Chief Superintendent Donaldson was promoted to Assistant Chief Constable for his skilful and sensitive handling of, what could have been, a major national disaster. Nathan Hyde was given an A.S.B.O. by the local magistrates and a good talking to by Dr Douglas, who banned him from any and all future school trips. The duck, and Bonnie's pink towel, both enjoyed a fleeting moment of fame when a picture of them being presented to Walter Whitney the Operations Manager of Paradise Park by two beaming police officers, was printed on page three of *The West Wales Gazette*; and I was undeservedly portrayed as the calm and resourceful trip organiser, who'd managed, not only to return all the children safely to their worried parents, but had also ensured that they all enjoyed their day out. The greatest praise however, was reserved for the action I had taken to ensure the rescue and safe return of the abducted duck. It was, on balance, quite a result, both personally and for the school, which despite Nathan's actions, had been congratulated by the police for the calm and responsible attitude of both the staff and the pupils, when they'd found themselves facing the awesome fire power of a highly trained armed response unit. However, the last and perhaps the most enduring consequence of the trip was the passion kindled between Chris Reed and Janice Newman, which, rather than abating when they

153

returned to the mundane routine of their normal lives, took on an even greater intensity.

After the long summer holiday and the commencement of the autumn term I fully expected the passion generated by their intense shared experience on the trip would have cooled, but apparently, they had managed to keep their smouldering relationship alive with phone calls and the occasional clandestine meeting when Chris's fiancée Sandra was at work in the operating theatre of the local hospital, blissfully unaware of his infidelity and dreaming of their planned nuptials. Consequently, upon their return to work in September, they were once again in daily contact, and their growing mutual desire was able to fully blossom.

There are few situations in life more cringe makingly nauseous, than having to witness two mature and usually sensible people experiencing romantic emotions more appropriately exhibited by a pair of love struck teenagers. There is something quite sad about this triumph of desire over reason. It is invariably, a victory which destroys families, alienates friends, and ultimately, turns to ashes in the fire of its own intensity.

For Chris and Janice though, the onset of disillusionment lay some time in the future, as their relationship entered its most exciting phase, where desire is undiminished by familiarity and discovery, ecstasy and possession form an intoxicating cocktail of raw emotion. One sign of their new found passion was their need to be constantly together. This was evident from the increasing number of visits which Janice now made to the Pupil Referral Unit, where Chris was supposed to be employed in trying to contain, and hopefully modify, the behaviour of the school's most disruptive and ill-disciplined pupils.

This was an extremely difficult and challenging task, even without external emotional distractions. To be successful in motivating disaffected and often disturbed children to change their behaviour and achieve success was a challenge which required concentration, consistency and commitment, and while, prior to his romance with Janice, Chris had possessed these attributes in some small measure, after the onset of their love affair, he totally lost his

154

focus and good judgement, allowing his passion to undermine his performance.

Due to the inappropriate behaviour of the pupils who regularly attended the Pupil Referral Unit, Chris was instructed to never leave them on their own, or leave the unit unsupervised. Consequently, he was unable to visit Janice during the school day, and was therefore, totally dependent upon her visits to the unit to satisfy their overpowering need for regular physical contact. Fortunately, the Pupil Referral Unit was a remote outpost, tucked away behind an old and obsolete P.E. storage hut. It had once been the outside P.E. changing rooms and was constructed in the shape of the letter 'E'. There were stone steps up to central double doors and the three changing rooms, for staff, boys and girls, had been converted into a central office, with one of the former pupils changing areas now being utilised as a classroom and the other as an isolation room, where particularly disruptive pupils could be segregated when they had been excluded from mainstream lessons. All the rooms were excessively dark and dingy, due to the very small high windows, originally constructed at such a height to protect the privacy of the pupils when they were changing. This feature now proved useful in giving the rooms a suitably penal atmosphere, with no distracting views of the outside world and a dank and oppressive interior, which Chris argued, provided excellent acclimatisation for the real prisons awaiting many of his regular clients when they left school.

Like many who deal exclusively with low achieving and disruptive pupils, Chris had become a cynical pessimist, whose lack of faith in the futures of the most disadvantaged pupils had been fashioned by his extensive experience of their persistent failure. The pupils who were usually sent to the unit were the regular offenders against the school rules. These pupils came from all year groups, and from my year, these commonly included Nathan Hyde, Kyle Bowman, Jack Reynolds, Stacy Fowler, Tracy-Ann Smith, Crystal Devine and the increasingly weird and scary Turner twins, Dixie and Trixie. In addition, Chris also dealt with a few very low achievers from Years 7 and 8, who spent a term at a time in the classroom of the unit on a catch-up programme, designed to increase their abilities in the basic skills of literacy and numeracy.

Constant exposure to this depressing environment in the company of kids whose main reasons for attending school was to socialise with their mates and to avoid the wrath of their often violent and abusive parents, was the prime explanation for Chris's cynicism and disillusionment. It was also viewed by some as the reason why he was a loner, with a healthy distrust of authority and an intense dislike of pomposity and cant.

In many ways it was exactly those attributes which made him liked and generally well respected by the majority of the very difficult pupils who spent much of their school time in the P.R.U. The fact that he had to man the unit over the lunch period made it a popular drop in centre for many of the school's most disruptive pupils. This was especially true of a group of disaffected girls from Years 10 and 11, who welcomed Chris's tolerance of their flexible interpretation of the rules concerning jewellery and make-up, and who felt that he understood their occasional lapses into insolence and aggression.

Assisting him in the unit and acting as a teachers' aid, part-time secretary and unofficial counsellor, was Sharon Hardy; a stunningly attractive blond thirty-five year old ex-pupil and local divorced mother of three, who related well to the pupils, due to her often intimate knowledge of their family circumstances and her own reputation as a woman with a mysterious and intriguing sexual history. She was well acquainted with the intensity and potential consequences of teenage emotions, and it was well known that she was still an object of sexual fantasy among the fathers of many of the current pupils, who were all very well aware of her iconic status as the most desirable female ever to have attended Gruffudd ap Cynan Comp.

Reputedly, prior to her failed marriage to a wealthy local motor trader and ex-night club bouncer called Barry (Beefy) Bullock, she'd been tantalisingly selective with her sexual favours, and although many men had persistently attempted to add her as a notch on the bedpost of their sexual conquests, very few had actually succeeded. This of course, increased her allure and desirability, and left the fathers of many current pupils, nostalgically regretful that she'd been so reluctant to bestow her sexual favours more widely. When she'd first become engaged to Barry Bullock, many of her unsuccessful suitors viewed her involvement with him as a tragic and bitterly resented waste. When therefore, after twelve years of marriage she unexpectedly left him to return to a single and unattached existence, she was, despite her three kids, hotly pursued by many of her old admirers, who felt excited by the possibility of finally realising their long held fantasies of occupying her bed. However, she proved as resistant to their clumsy advances at thirty-five, as she had been as a teenager, and only added to their frustration, desire and regret, by her continued unavailability.

Chris, who despite his present infatuation with Janice, had many times declared to me his own intense desire for Sharon, was, like many others, skilfully resisted, and left feeling strangely honoured that their advances had been so graciously rejected. He always said that failing to seduce Sharon was like being denied sexual intimacy by Aphrodite, who valued the worship and attention of her mortal admirers, but was reluctant to grant them the life threatening gratification of sexual congress. I tried to remind him that Sharon was simply an extremely attractive, and unfortunately, mortal woman, who, despite her obvious desirability, was an ex-pupil of an obscure Welsh comprehensive school, who'd chosen as a husband an ill-educated, if wealthy philistine, whose career had included violence and vehicle misrepresentation on a grand scale. This was undoubtedly, a history and set of circumstances which hardly qualified her to be elevated to the divine status of the Greek goddess of love. Unfortunately, Chris failed to acknowledge the essential truth of my argument and continued to regard Sharon as a desirable, but unobtainable deity. Yet it was, surprisingly difficult, when in Sharon's company for anything longer than a few moments, not to experience the feeling that one was in the presence of a powerful sexual divinity. She was, unquestionably, desirable beyond the experience and expectations of most ordinary men.

Sharon was delighted by Chris's newly discovered infatuation with Janice, since it provided her with a welcome respite from his unsuccessful attempts at seduction. Even though he was still officially engaged to Sandra, the vivacious theatre sister from Abercwmtwerp Hospital, and conducting a passionate and still secret affair with Janice, it did not prevent him from still longing for a sign from Sharon that his advances were welcome. However, the fact that Janice now made numerous unannounced visits to the unit, prevented him from continuing to show such an intense interest in Sharon, and she encouraged his new affair as a means of deflecting his attentions.

The pupils, who regularly attended the unit, quickly became aware of the newly charged atmosphere of sexual desire and tension, which now permeated the place like the sweaty smell of a seedy sex club. Their vague awareness of sexual intrigue and innuendo was, unfortunately, confirmed when Stacy Fowler, Tracey-Ann Smith and Crystal Devine visited the unit one evening in late October after providing vocal support for the school's Year 10 Girls' Hockey Team, by shouting obscenities and throwing clods of mud at their opponents from the touch line. Growing bored and disenchanted by their failure to prevent the opposition from taking an eight goal lead, and noticing that Chris's car was still in the school car park, they'd decided to leave the match and visit the unit, to see if he was still there, and to try to persuade him to provide them with tea and chocolate biscuits, while they moaned about their latest perceived injustice.

Chris and Janice's affair was, by this time, a well known fact among staff and pupils. Janice's regular visits to the P.R.U. were common knowledge and several VI Form students, had run into them in a couple of the more remote local pubs, where according to reports, they had been acutely embarrassed by their discovery.

On the evening of the visit to the unit the girls must have suspected that Janice and Chris were together, for they all later admitted that, they'd noticed her car was also still in the school car park; and, they did not adopt their usual brash approach of running up the steps of the unit to bang insistently for admittance on the double doors, until someone appeared to let them in. By the time they arrived it was quite dark, and there was already an autumnal chill in the evening air. The light in the central office wing of the unit shone brightly through the high window, which, since the building's conversion, had been fitted with steel bars to prevent break-ins by enterprising pupils to steal valuable items such as computers and printers. The windows were far too high to enable anyone to see in, but ever resourceful, the girls knew a means to access the flat roof, from where they could hang over the roof's edge and gain a perfect view of the office's interior.

Anticipating the thrill of perhaps witnessing the consequences of Chris and Janice's passion, and excited by the possibility of discovering two of their teachers in a compromising position, they suppressed their nervous giggles, and silently signalled to each other their intention to climb onto the roof. They crouched low and carefully circled the building, taking great care to be quiet. Once they reached the unit's entrance they first climbed effortlessly on to the hand rails which flanked the front steps, and with a feline grace worthy of Cat Woman, they swiftly pulled themselves up onto the roof. They were all wearing their highly prized designer trainers and were conscious of the need for extreme silence and stealth if they were to achieve their objective without discovery.

Keeping to the roof's edge to minimise any noise, they slowly made their way to where the brightly lit office window cast a narrow beam of light, illuminating the graffiti daubed wall of the nearby P.E. storage hut. Like a crack S.A.S. squad they were extremely quiet and cautious as they slowly lowered themselves, to lay full length, on the felt covered roof. The office window was now directly beneath them, only a few inches from the narrow facia-board which ran around the roof's perimeter. In perfect unison they silently wriggled forward, until their upper bodies were extended out over the edge. With the toes of their beloved trainers anchored in the roof's rough surface they gripped the facia-board with their hands, and, as one, lowered their heads and shoulders so they could see directly into the office window.

What they saw exactly will never be fully known, for whatever activity Chris and Janice were engaged in had caused the top part of the window to mist up with condensation, effectively obscuring the girls' view of the interior. They could apparently make out two entwined and inverted human shapes in some kind of rapid movement, but the figures could not be clearly identified. They felt disappointed and frustrated that, having risked so much to gain definite confirmation of the school's most discussed scandal; they'd been thwarted at the final hurdle. Although unable to obtain a clear view of the proceedings inside the office, they could hear the unmistakable sounds of moaning, interspersed with muffled speech and occasional loud female screams, which due to their relative inexperience, they were unable to categorise as signs of ecstasy, or agony. However, despite their lack of intimate knowledge of all the possible vocal expressions of impending orgasm, they were nonetheless, very aware that whatever was occurring only a few feet beneath their prostrate bodies, was likely to be of immense interest. Stacy, who was lying between Crystal and Tracey-Ann had noticed that lower down and directly beneath her, towards the bottom of the window, was a small area free of condensation, which was bound to offer a much better view of events. Foolishly, and without indicating her intentions to Crystal, or Tracey-Ann, she wriggled further out over the edge of the roof, and, releasing her hands from the facia, she lowered her entire upper body to try and peer through the lowest part of the window.

Even if she had paid close attention during her Physics lessons, any knowledge gained concerning the force of gravity, would not now have helped her to counter its effect. For, no longer anchored by her fingers, and with the tenuous grip from the toes of her trainers now seriously failing, she began to slide headfirst down the wall towards the concrete base some fourteen feet below.

Had she not screamed, it's doubtful whether Crystal, or Tracey-Ann, would have realised her predicament in time to have saved her from a very serious injury. As it was, they only just managed to each grasp a leg of her regulation black school uniform trousers, as she accelerated downwards. Unfortunately, the firm grip they had on the bottoms of her trousers, combined with the inexorable force of gravity, caused her trousers to slide down her descending legs, exposing her quite inappropriate choice of a pink satin thong, as suitable school underwear, and, had Crystal not realised her plight, and quickly switched her grip to Stacy's left ankle, things would have been much worse. By the time Tracey-Ann had also managed to grab her other ankle, Stacy's trousers were almost off, and she was left dangling down with her scantily covered crotch, pressed firmly against the Office window. This, coupled with her terrified screams and Crystal and Tracey-Ann's shouted advice not to panic, immediately halted the passionate proceedings in the office and caused both Chris and Janice to abandon their activities with a rapidity which must have come close to a new world speed record for coitus-interruptus. Galvanised with unspoken terror at the thought of what might be occurring outside, and fearful of what may have been witnessed of their illicit passion inside, they both hurriedly dressed and rushed from the building to investigate the cause of their anxieties. By the time they'd circled the building, Crystal and Tracey-Ann were struggling to retain their grip on the still screaming Stacy, and were both loudly shouting for help; as they too, were now in imminent danger of being dragged over the edge.

Quickly assessing the situation, Chris shouted to them to hold on, and positioning himself beneath the trouserless and terrified Stacy, he stretched upwards to try and help her to descend in safety. However, even on tip-toe he was only just able to touch her fingers. Realising his difficulty, Janice shouted that she'd go and fetch something for him to stand on, and she rushed back into the building, leaving him trying to calm the girls and encouraging them to hold on. Within moments, she returned with a sturdy wooden chair and steadied it for Chris to stand on. He was now able to grasp Stacy's shoulders, and, once he had a firm grip, he instructed the girls to release her ankles. As they did so, Stacy slid slowly down, until he was able to circle her torso with his arms and gently lower her, keeping her body between his and the wall. Once she'd reached the level of his knees, Janice helped to turn her the right way up. Fortunately, her trousers had remained around her ankles, and, to save her further embarrassment, Janice quickly assisted her to pull them back up. Now she was no longer in danger, Chris left her with Janice and instructing Crystal and Tracey-Ann to make their way towards the steps at the front, he went to assist them. Once all of them were safely down, Chris and Janice took them all into the unit, where finally, they all received their tea and biscuits. They also struck a mutual bargain, that their dangerous and irresponsible escapade would not be reported, providing no

161

mention was ever made concerning what they may, or may not, have witnessed through the office window.

I learned all this from Chris the following Friday, when we went for our usual lunchtime drink in the lounge bar of The Lonely Leek. He'd been keeping me up to speed with the progress of his affair with Janice, and as Stacy, Crystal and Tracey-Ann were all in my year, he was anxious that, just in case one of them broke their promise and told someone, I would be forewarned, and therefore, able to minimise any potential damage. What he didn't know was that the girls had already broken their vow of silence, for, on the morning following the incident, they had all been waiting outside my room, bursting to tell me that they'd heard him and Janice shagging when they went to the unit after watching the Year 10 hockey match. Of course, I didn't tell him this, but I did feel strangely honoured that three of the most notorious girls in my year trusted me enough to take me into their confidence and reveal their totally reprehensible behaviour. After I'd established that they'd not actually seen anything, and that they had not told anyone else of their activities, I strongly advised them to maintain their silence from now on, both to protect Chris and Janice's careers and to prevent their own certain punishment. Chris and Janice were, I reflected, both very fortunate that the kids really liked and respected them and had no wish to be the cause of their dismissal. I did however, tell him that I thought the girls all liked him and Janice far too much to knowingly get either of them into trouble and I reminded him of the wisdom of conducting his affair off-site in the future.

His other, and yet to be resolved, concern was how he was going to break the news of his affair to Sandra, with whom he was still living, and whom, as far as she was concerned, he still intended to marry. I advised him to be honest, to tell her the truth, and, if he was now genuinely committed to Janice, to do the honourable thing and end their relationship. Unfortunately, before he summoned the courage to follow my advice, Sandra learned of his unfaithfulness from one of her fellow nurses, who had apparently witnessed him and Janice booking a room in a motel close to where her parents lived, and which she herself was coincidentally visiting to arrange a silver wedding celebration for their forthcoming anniversary. Her discovery coincided with the one occasion when Sandra was away, attending an overnight nurses conference in London, so had the ring of authenticity. After confirming the story by means of a swiftly hired private investigator, Sandra planned her own very special brand of revenge.

Her position as a trusted theatre sister at Abercwmtwerp General Hospital, had given her a profound knowledge of male anatomy, advanced surgical procedures, effective pain management, and provided her with unfettered access to powerful anaesthetic drugs. This was a combination of skills and opportunity, blessedly, rarely afforded to women who feel cheated and deceived. Men should perhaps always be careful when being unfaithful to women to whom they have declared their undying love and fidelity. They certainly should be especially careful when the woman in question is in possession of specialist medical skills, the key to a secure drugs cabinet and a vindictive nature. For, as her gift to bless his and Janice's new relationship, she waited until the Friday following her discovery of his infidelity, and then cooked him a splendid meal, accompanied by soft candle light, romantic music, pre-dinner cocktails, two bottles of expensive wine, and rounded it all off with a couple of large glasses of his favourite late night brandy, to which she added a powerful, but tasteless anaesthetic.

Once he was deeply unconscious, she carefully undressed him, and being well used to moving inert bodies, she dragged him into the bedroom and put him carefully to bed. She then inserted a catheter down the flaccid length of his usually responsive penis and passed it skilfully through his urethra and into his urine-filled bladder. She was particularly careful to fully inflate the small balloon at the end of the catheter, which ensured that it was securely anchored and could not easily be removed. With this achieved, and a bag correctly attached to contain his dripping urine, she settled down next to him to enjoy a restful night's sleep.

The following morning, being a Saturday, she rose unusually early, and checked that he was still in a deep sleep, before packing all his clothes, his beloved CD jazz collection and his treasured stamp albums into large black refuse sacks. She then drove to the local council rubbish dump and disposed of all the bags into a large yellow skip. Returning to their shared rented flat, she packed all her own possessions, and made three journeys to deposit them with her best friend Julie, with whom she had arranged to stay. By the time this was achieved, it was mid-morning, and when she arrived back at the flat, Chris was still deeply unconscious. She checked his urine bag, which was now three quarters full and to ensure he stayed sedated, she injected him with sufficient anaesthetic to keep him under for a few more hours. Next, she calmly wrote him a goodbye and good-riddance card, in which she told him to consider himself fortunate, to have only been catheterised, since her first impulse had been to perform a penile amputation. To be certain that he would find the card and read her parting message she expertly sutured it to his left testicle, using a complex embroidery stitch, which was notoriously difficult to unpick. Finally, she dialled a premium-rate sex line, and, leaving the phone off the hook, she took one last regretful look around the flat, before she quietly departed to commence her new life.

Chris did not regain consciousness and discover his predicament until after 8.00pm. It took him a further forty-five minutes to assess its seriousness, end the premium rate call, and telephone his brother Roger for help. By the time he was finally seen in the A and E department of his local hospital it was almost 1.00am, and it was past noon on the following Wednesday before he was finally discharged, free of both his catheter and Sandra's farewell card.

The hospital staff had been extremely concerned regarding the whole incident and despite Chris's protestations they had wanted to call the police. Chris's reluctance to have his situation publicly investigated was not because he wanted to protect Sandra from her deserved prosecution, but because he wished to avoid becoming a national laughing stock. Consequently, he had insisted that the obvious cruel and humiliating assault upon his person had been perpetrated by unknown assailants during a wild stag night to celebrate his forthcoming nuptials. It seemed as though his request not to have the incident reported was going to be unsuccessful, until his treatment at the hospital unexpectedly provided him with a powerful bargaining chip. For, although he was undoubtedly fortunate to have retained his manhood during Sandra's recent revenge, he was extremely unfortunate in having been attended in Casualty by student nurse Kylie-Jayne Evans, a tired, acne blemished and myopic teenager, whose medical skills were about as sharp as her eyesight. Having never inserted a catheter, let alone removed one, her understanding of the procedure was sadly limited, for, not only did she fail to properly deflate the balloon which anchored it in his bladder, she also failed to cease pulling when the tube refused to move and his agonised screams should have alerted her to the fact that things were going badly wrong. The resulting damage to his urethra only became fully apparent, when finally, due to her persistent tugging; the balloon at the end of the tube exited the top of his penis with an audible pop, to be followed a millisecond later by a fountain of blood, which drenched her glasses and splattered her crisply starched uniform.

As a result of this very unfortunate example of medical incompetence Chris was able to negotiate a deal, whereby, providing the police were not informed, he would not pursue his justified claim for negligence. So it was that he finally left hospital with his urethra in tatters, but his dignity and reputation intact.

One further outcome of his injury was it effectively brought a temporary end to his and Janice's sex life, while they waited for his pain and discomfort to subside. It also resulted in making Janice's visits to the P.R.U. for extra-curricular sex no longer necessary, or desirable, and he was therefore, once again able to focus upon all the unfortunate pupils who depended upon his skills and commitment to enhance their education.

Chapter 12

The Talent Show

Gradually, life in the P.R.U. returned to normal. Subsequent to his very traumatic and painful split from Sandra, Chris took a few days sick leave, before resuming his usual depressing duties, attempting to modify the behaviour of the school's most disaffected pupils. Janice adopted a much lower profile and ceased her regular visits, being content to pursue their affair out of school hours. Unfortunately, due to the extensive damage to Chris's urethra their ardour was, temporarily at least, confined to the relative passionless activity of holding hands and fleeting, chaste kisses on the cheek. This was necessary to avoid the possibility of Chris experiencing an uncontrollable erection, which certainly would have arisen, if they had continued to indulge in their accustomed levels of intense eroticism. Whilst their relationship languished on the plateau of platonic disappointment, I was forced to focus upon the pressing need to undertake various fundraising activities to meet the considerable cost of producing the Year 11 Year Book.

This time-consuming and largely unappreciated publishing activity had been initiated some years previously, by an over zealous and gung-ho twenty five year old American female teacher called Davina-May Dallas, who'd been briefly employed in the R.E. Department, and who, even more briefly, had occupied the position as temporary Head of Year, whilst Sophie Millar was absent on maternity leave. Davina-May had moved to the U.K. to be with her new Welsh husband, Dafydd-ap-Pritchard-Davies, a short, swarthy, animated media mogul and professional Welshman, whom she'd met in her native Texas, when he'd been the producer of a B.B.C. Wales television documentary featuring a disparate group of media studies students from Aberystwyth, traversing America in an up-market camper van. The programme was called 'The Winnebago Welsh'. It was, as I recall, a resounding flop, but failure, being no bar to advancement within the ranks of the Welsh media, Dafydd went on to greater heights, and was assigned the task of producing a new political programme entitled 'Welsh Winners at Westminster', which featured the political achievements of Welsh M.P.s throughout the twentieth century. However, once he'd covered Lloyd George and Aneurin Bevan the series sadly went downhill, as it successively attempted to highlight the achievements of less accomplished candidates and, like 'The Winnebago Welsh' it faltered, and finally failed upon the dreadful mediocrity of its own subject matter.

Despite Dafydd-ap-Pritchard-Davies's unfortunate employment with the B.B.C. the one significant and lasting legacy of his brief sojourn in the Lone Star State was his marriage to, and subsequent import into Wales of, Davina-May Dallas, to join the staff of Gruffudd ap Cynan Comp and act as Head of Year. She brought to the job naïvety, energy, optimism and lunacy in almost equal measure. She was an inspirational disaster of the first magnitude. The kids adored her, the staff, mostly detested her, and the Senior Management Team totally failed to perceive, either her considerable weaknesses, or her formidable strengths!

When I first met her at a school staff meeting at the beginning of the autumn term of her appointment, I was captivated by her attractiveness, and impressed by her vivacity, confidence and rampant enthusiasm. She was a twenty-five year old American dynamo, with an almost total lack of inhibition, or natural reserve. She believed in the rightness of her own ideas with a certainty beyond arrogance. She also had an unshakeable conviction that all the kids of Gruffudd ap Cynan Comp really needed was a huge injection of modern American educational practice to transform them from disenchanted losers, into high school achievers of the highest order. It was a laudable conviction, but unfortunately, doomed to fail upon the altar of Anglo-Welsh apathy, and the staff's hostility to, and intense mistrust of, 'The American Dream'.

167

Davina-May's first and least successful innovation was her attempt to introduce American style high school fraternities and sororities. These, she hoped, would provide a meaningful alternative to our moribund and largely discredited house system. Regrettably, the concept was so alien to the culture of indifference and contempt endemic in most of our kids, that they were suspicious of the entire enterprise and viewed it as no more than just another ruse to persuade them to value the school and identify with its aims and objectives. A few of the more disruptive elements did show some mild interest when they thought that fraternity, or sorority membership, might confer some power and authority to allow them to bully and intimidate the weak, but their enthusiasm quickly waned, once they were told that the constitution and activities of the scheme would be overseen by a governing senate, comprised of: members of staff, pupils from the School Council and representatives from the P.T.A. and Governors.

She had much greater success with the promotion of baseball, which at first the kids viewed as simply a more robust form of rounders, but they took to the baseball dress code with a rare enthusiasm. They liked the much larger and more dangerous bat and they adored the shirts and genuine baseball caps, which Davina-May had specially imported from Texas. They also developed a passion for the finely crafted leather catcher's mitts and, it took no time before the sights witnessed upon the school field could easily have been mistaken for a games lesson in a Fort Worth high school.

Within a few short weeks of Davina-May's arrival there was a huge upsurge of interest in all things American. In classrooms and corridors throughout the school, posters began to appear; these mainly depicted steer roping and bull riding contests at various rodeos, portraits of sporting stars from the world of American football, basketball and baseball, and advertisements for Broadway shows. Much to the approval of the boys there were also pictures of the entrants in the current Miss America Pageant and photos of high kicking high school cheer leaders. During the next few months the school was in the grip of a rampant American fever, and even in the main hall, the unfamiliar strains of country music became the usual introduction to morning assemblies.

Fortunately, very few of these imports had any lasting, or significant impact, upon school life. Most of them faded almost as quickly as Davina-May when she returned to Texas at the end of her brief spell as Head of Year 11.

Apparently, she had not found life in the depressing dampness of South Wales nearly as stimulating as she had hoped. Also, her marriage to Dafydd-ap-Pritchard-Davies had been a major disappointment, due partly to his Welsh speaking family and work colleagues, whom she said had made her feel as welcome as an outbreak of genital herpes at a lesbian gay rights convention in California. In addition, she was massively depressed when she learned that her new husband's interest in physical activities tended towards a passion for Rugby Union, rather than sexual union. She also claimed that the less than enthusiastic reception to most of her suggestions by the school staff had added to her disillusion, and that she'd rather be a short order waitress in Waco, than spend another winter in Wales.

Thus it was that, after her short but dynamic sojourn as our very own 'Calamity Jane', she returned to the warmth and familiarity of her Texas homeland. However, during her brief stay she introduced two American high school customs, which left a valued and lasting legacy for all the future generations of our Year 11 pupils. These were the production of a Year Book, to mark their time at Gruffudd ap Cynan Comp, and the organising of a Year 11 Prom to celebrate the end of their compulsory schooling.

Although laudable, both these enterprises cost large sums of money. The Prom, being a highly desirable, if fleeting event, was much easier to finance, since the pupils were immensely excited by the prospect of dressing–up and attending their first real formal function, so they willingly paid the individual ticket price. The Year Book however, although a more durable memento of their school life, was a very expensive item of less obvious immediate interest, and so, it became necessary to raise considerable funds to ensure the production of a high quality book.

This was achieved by organising various events, such as a sponsored silence, an event which was always immensely popular with the staff, a parents' cheese and wine evening, manning a bring and buy stall at the Christmas Fayre and running an evening disco for the kids in Years 7 and 8. All of this was moderately successful, but by far the most profitable and the most stressful fundraising event was the Year 11 Talent Show. This was yet another innovation introduced by Davina-May, and it had, over the few years since her departure, grown into a mammoth event, involving a huge number of pupils and a great many of the more exhibitionist staff. There were teams of backstage helpers, stagehands, scenery designers and producers, lighting and sound engineers, front of house personnel, ushers and programme sellers, refreshment staff, musical and artistic directors and last, but certainly not least, the performers!

These were comprised of the few Year 11 pupils with some genuine talent, plus other sadly deluded fame junkies, who fancied themselves, usually, as either future pop stars, TV presenters, or fashion icons; most of whom, if they ever managed to achieve their fifteen minutes of allotted fame, would only do so as humiliated audition freaks in some future edition of The X Factor. Also on the bill were a motley collection of teachers, who wished to enhance their street-cred and lacklustre reputations by attempting to impress the kids in the audience, with often cringe-making exhibitions of their musical, or theatrical, mediocrity.

Just occasionally, there were truly memorable moments, of high excitement; like when, during the first ever show, Davina-May, dressed as a cheerleader for 'The Dallas Cowboys,' had performed a high-kicking, tassel-waving dance routine while miming to a pre-recoded tape of herself singing, 'Nothing could be finer than to be in Carolina' in a sexy southern drawl, which hit occasional notes of such high and ear-splitting falsetto that she sounded like a cat impaled by the business end of a Texas longhorn. As she high-kicked her way across the stage, revealing the tight stretched gusset of her white panties the male members of the front row, which consisted mainly of the S.M.T., Governors and key members of the P.T.A., all suddenly showed a marked increase in attention and nodded and smiled in a quite transparent display of approval. They all remarked after the show, how much they had appreciated her performance, and commented upon the uniqueness of her singing and the energy of her dancing. It was obvious however, that their unbridled enthusiasm, owed more to the many revealing views they'd enjoyed of her underwear, than to any genuine emotion aroused by her vocal talents.

Last year's show had also produced a moment of high drama, when, during an absolutely appalling, hip-swivelling impersonation of Elvis, singing 'All Shook Up', Mark Collins split his skin-tight faux-leather trousers, as he attempted the splits at the conclusion of the final verse. All shook up was certainly an accurate description of the many females, who were close enough to the stage to receive a full frontal view of his limp dick and swinging gonads, before they were unfortunately crushed by the careless placement of his guitar-effects pedal, which he failed to avoid as he descended to yet another ball-crushing finale. Things would not have been quite so revealing, had his trousers been loose enough to allow for underpants, but yet again, his misplaced vanity had been the cause of his misfortune. The kids of course, had rated his performance very highly, and it became the topic of many jokes and comments in the following weeks.

Knowing that the Year Book would be one of the final tasks I would undertake for the benefit of the kids, I was determined that it would be a high quality publication in full colour and with a gold blocked hard cover. Such a production was going to be very expensive and it was important therefore, that the talent show was a financial success.

This was almost guaranteed, as most parents would willingly spend money to watch their offspring take centre-stage, but I was concerned to put on a memorable event, which would reflect well upon the pupils and the school. So, a couple of months prior to the planned date for the show, I called an after school meeting in the main hall, of all the interested parties, to discuss the event and obtain a commitment from the kids to organise themselves into some credible acts. Apart from the usual desire to imitate the song and dance routines of the latest girl and boy bands, many of those attending made some interesting proposals.

A group of Dr Moore's boys from 11/SM wanted to gargle a medley of Welsh songs dressed as daffodils to give their performance a certain Celtic authenticity. Stacy, Crystal and Tracey-Ann said they, and others, would perform a female full-monty, but promised it would be decent, as they would retain their bras and knickers. The Turner twins, frighteningly, offered to stage a magic act, which involved sawing Lance Morris in half and then, when he emerged unharmed, tying and handcuffing him in a sack full of rats; submerging him and the rats in a large water filled tank, from which they would all miraculously emerge just prior to death by drowning. Not to be outdone, Lance said he and his dad could play 'Men of Harlech' and famous show songs on a row of suspended bottles, filled with varying amounts of water. John Griffiths, Matt Thomas and Ben Jacobs suggested that they could perform an armpit farting accompaniment to 'Three Blind Mice'. Jack Reynolds proposed that it would be more entertaining if they ignited real farts, to end the show in a spectacular climax of noise and light. Concepta O'Conner, a newly qualified teacher, and an extremely sexy, raven haired, blue eyed twenty-two year old Irish stunner from Galway, who'd recently been appointed to the R.E. Department said she was willing to sing 'The Lord's Prayer' in Gaelic dressed as the Virgin Mary, or, if that was not thought appropriate, a nun. Lofty Lewis boasted he could play 'Swanee River' on a kazoo attached to a neck-brace, whilst he accompanied himself by banging on his skinny thighs with a couple of dessert spoons. Vic Davies, who never minded dispensing with his dignity, volunteered to yet again recreate his infamous Shirley Bassey impersonation; an act he had been performing at each talent show since the very first. To achieve the required transformation from a sallow faced, balding, slightly over-weight and immensely unattractive Welshman, to a believable facsimile of Wales' premier female diva of song, was nothing short of miraculous.

He was first, forced into an industrial strength corset, which pushed the ample flesh covering his hairy chest into a 42D bra; then, he donned fishnet tights, a pair of five inch platform stilettos, a sequin covered, gold lamé split skirt evening gown, and a large black afro-wig. The whole ensemble was finished with an awesome make-up job, topped by crimson painted toe and finger nails, but by far the most impressive part of his entire performance, was the uncanny accuracy of his voice, movements and facial expressions. Witnessing him singing 'Goldfinger', in all its awful splendour, it was almost impossible to believe that this was not Dame Shirley herself, who had deigned to honour us with her presence. In fact, Vic's appearance always ensured a full house, since his act alone more than justified the ticket price. I was, like all previous organisers of the Year 11 Talent Show, immensely grateful for his contribution; even though I suspected that his interest in female impersonation probably went far deeper than his annual opportunity to dress up and strut his stuff as Shirley Bassey.

After several other bizarre suggestions, such as an offer by Angus Paisley the Head of the Art Department to perform a musical comedy routine, with his wife Moira, in which they yodelled a Frank Ifield medley dressed in penguin costumes, whilst shuffling through a line dancing number they'd recently learned at the American country dance lessons they'd been attending at their local leisure centre; and, after Luke Lowe said that Spot, his Jack Russell terrier could bark an accompaniment to 'How much is that doggie in the window?' whilst standing upright on his hind legs, I reluctantly realised it was time to call a halt to the proceedings. I ended this first meeting, by saying that I would be holding auditions each Monday after school for the next few weeks, to select the acts for final inclusion in the show.

With Karen Owen's and Mandy Jones' much appreciated help, the auditions proceeded with ruthless candour and efficiency. Karen, with her extensive music and drama experience gradually rejected the more esoteric and weird contributions, and also told Stacy Fowler and her gang of aspiring strippers that she was quite happy for them to perform a dance routine, but there would be no female full-monty, not even if they did promise to retain their bras and knickers.

Over the next several weeks, involving much work and many hours of after school commitment the Year 11 Talent Show slowly began to take shape and offer the possibility for a really impressive and enjoyable evening. Scenery was prepared, costumes designed and made, props obtained, labelled and stored, lights and sound levels checked, programmes designed and printed, refreshments ordered, running order decided, tickets sold, acts rehearsed, until all was ready, and the entire cast and crew were as eager for the off as thoroughbreds at Epsom. So, finally, the evening of the show arrived. The audience were all in their seats by 7.00pm, eagerly anticipating 'curtain-up' and the appearance of the opening act. The show was definitely for one night only, and so, the front couple of rows had been reserved for the S.M.T. and their guests, the School Governors, and specially invited local big-wigs and councillors. The rest of the audience comprised parents, plus many younger siblings of the Year 11 pupils appearing in the show. The hall was packed, with all the seats taken and many standing at the rear and down the side aisles.

An undercurrent of excited, whispered conversation permeated the Hall, as Karen struck up the orchestra and choir to announce the show's commencement with her own rousing arrangement of Queen's 'Let Me Entertain You'. As the music filled the hall the general low hubbub subsided, and I, as the unfortunate organiser of the event, felt temporarily relieved that the show was finally underway!

As the opening number ended and the thunderous applause died away, the curtains slowly parted, to reveal the flamboyant figure of Lance Morris, who'd eagerly volunteered to act as Master of Ceremonies for the evening, and who obviously relished his role, presenting the performers and filling in between the acts. He was dressed in a pinstripe black suit with matching waistcoat, black shirt, white bowtie, white gloves and a wide brimmed black felt fedora, and was carrying a silver topped cane with remarkable aplomb for such an untutored teen. He certainly looked the part, and, not unexpectedly, proved to be a natural in the role. He had, after all, had many years practise as the class clown, a role which he had assiduously developed, ever since he discovered his performance potential, as an infant. For when, many years previously, he had failed to achieve his burning ambition to star as Joseph in the School nativity play, and was cast as a sheep, he decided to express his disappointment, by pulling the white, blue edged tea-towel from the head of the Virgin Mary, mounting the back of the luckless child dressed as a donkey, and, using the crook he'd snatched from the grasp of a distressed and weeping shepherd, had hooked the unfortunate doll playing the baby Jesus from the comfort of its manger, and flung it high above the upraised heads of his disbelieving audience, who followed its trajectory towards the rear wall, where it was neatly decapitated by an unused row of metal clothes hooks next to the boys' toilets. Immediately, the audience fell silent as they turned on mass to witness the doll's tragic fate. For the briefest of moments, the head remained perilously impaled on a hook, before falling to the floor. There was the sharp crack of breaking porcelain as it rolled beneath the seats in the back row, leaving the now headless body hanging grotesquely, with its legs twisted, and its arms outstretched on the hooks in a monstrous parody of the crucifixion.

Despite being seriously admonished for his vindictive and dangerous action by the Headteacher, his parents and the mothers of the Virgin Mary, the injured donkey, the traumatised shepherd and the distraught owner of the decapitated doll, what Lance remembered most from this childhood incident, was the absolute and indissoluble thrill of, for once, being 'centre-stage'! It was an experience which fuelled his desire for attention and moulded forever his dream of becoming a world class entertainer. Judged by his witty and well polished performance as compere of the Year 11 Talent Show, he was already well on his way to achieving his ambition.

After warming up the audience with a couple of well chosen gags about Dr Douglas's disastrous descent into the mud during the school inspection, he introduced the first act, which was, the irrepressible Mark Collins and his mixed group of press-ganged technology teachers and impressionable VI formers, which he'd immodestly called 'Mark Collins and the Collinsmen'. Following his show stopping and ball crushing performance the previous year, he'd been instructed to stage a less vigorous routine. Thankfully, he'd chosen a ballad as his opening number, and what he, and his under-rehearsed band lacked in musical ability, they more than made up for in cringe-making incompetence. It was obvious however, that many of the kids were disappointed that the act had been toned down, and that they were unlikely to witness another embarrassing exposure of his battered love tackle.

Next up, and after he'd managed a lightning change of costume, was Lance Morris and his dad Len, with their water-tuned 'Bottlephone'. This remarkable instrument consisted of a couple of portable metal clothes racks on wheels, from which a large number of wine bottles were suspended on strings. Each bottle was filled with a different amount of water, which, when struck by what looked like tablespoons, emitted a pre-determined note. Potentially, this could have produced a quite pleasing sound, particularly if any of the notes had conformed to any recognisable musical scale. Their first number, which I was assured, was 'The Flower Drum Song' in b-flat, sounded more like 'Bing, Bang, Bong' in b-awful. Things went from bad to worse in the next number, when Lance became completely carried away during the final crescendo, and gave his bottles such a forceful whack that two of them completely shattered, sending water and shards of flying glass into the first couple of rows. Fortunately, the ensuing pandemonium lasted long enough for Sue Williams to fetch the first aid kit from the office and for the crew to clear the stage of glass and water. The most seriously injured was Frank Baldwin's wife, Betty, who'd suffered a cut lip, and she was helped from the hall to receive attention in the brightly lit foyer.

Once calm was restored and Lance had recovered his composure and changed back into his role as compere, the show thankfully recommenced. There was a hushed and expectant atmosphere in the hall as, after telling another successful joke at the expense of Dr Douglas, Lance introduced Concepta O'Connor as Sister Dominique, our very own singing nun. Concepta had been advised by Karen Owen that appearing as the Virgin Mary might offend some people, especially those who would find it difficult to reconcile their belief in Mary's divinity with her appearance in a school talent show. However, in a moment of theatrical mischievousness of sheer genius, Karen did persuade Concepta that the overall impact of her singing nun act would be vastly enhanced if she spiced it up a little by drastically shortening the skirt of her habit. Then, in a final master-stroke of pure inspiration, she suggested the addition of a male backing group to add interest and musical depth to the performance. To provide the required touch of religious authenticity Karen bribed four of her most talented male pupils from the school choir to dress as Dominican friars and to appear with Concepta as 'Sister Dominique and the Dominicans'. It was inspirational, and transformed what could have been a dour and depressing religious experience into a glorious moment of high farce.

Never had a rendering of the Lord's Prayer sounded, or looked, so suggestively erotic, as Concepta, in high heels, sheer black tights and the shortest habit in history, perched cross legged upon a high stool, and sang in the unfamiliar strains of Gaelic; which only served to add to the exotic and sensual impact of her performance. She sang in a husky Irish mezzo-soprano, and swayed provocatively, in unison with the four hooded Dominican Monks, who moved and warbled behind her like a bunch of love-sick apostles. It was brilliant, and nearly brought the house down, with all the clapping, whistling and stamping which greeted the coquettish curtsy with which she concluded her performance. It was a moment which would forever live in the memory, like a vision of how Heaven could have been portrayed, had the authors of the Bible only possessed more interesting and fertile imaginations.

It was perhaps a weakness in the running order that Stacy Fowler and her wannabe teen temptresses, had the misfortune to follow such a highly charged performance of sacred eroticism. For, despite the best efforts and undoubted attractiveness of her troop of teenage totty, they failed to arouse quite the same intensity of response as the myth making sexuality of the delectable Miss O'Conner. However, it was very encouraging to see some of our most obdurate and wayward girls willing to work hard, even if it was only to practise skills usually reserved for the more exotic stages of inner city nightclubs. It was understandable that Karen had absolutely refused to allow them to perform 'The Full Monty', but it was quite clear from their appearance that her prohibition was only a pyrrhic victory; since they had obviously taken her instruction that, under no circumstances were they allowed to remove any clothes, as an excuse to wear very few to begin with. In fact, dressed as they were, in what looked like red lurex bikinis and tight knee high white leather boots, they seemed to have fulfilled their initial promise not to strip off beyond their bras and knickers, by the simple expedient of commencing their act in the same undressed state, in which they'd originally promised to finish. The boys of course, absolutely adored them. It was no doubt, a rare treat

177

for them to see what was normally hidden beneath the sexless anonymity of the girls' school uniforms. And I'm sure, caused many to re-evaluate the images they had of their female classmates.

As act followed act, the audience retained its undiminished enthusiasm and gave every performer a rapturous welcome and a rousing send-off. It was a very successful evening, which was finally crowned by Vic Davies, when he yet again ended the show with his legendary impersonation of Shirley Bassey singing 'Goldfinger'.

As I stood in the school foyer thanking departing guests and parents, and receiving their congratulations, I was struck, not for the first time, by just how much genuine talent and enthusiasm managed to survive society's best efforts to stultify the creativity of the young.

Chapter 13

P.S.H.E.

There was always a slight sense of deflation after the euphoria of a successful event, and everyone involved in the Talent Show found it somewhat depressing to return to the humdrum normality of the ordinary school day. My own feelings of dejection were partly alleviated by the fact that the show had raised sufficient money to enable me to fully fund the Year Book and pay for both the disco and photographer for the Year 11 Prom. As it would be my 'swan-song' and practically the last thing I would ever organise for my year group, I was determined would be the most memorable Prom ever! For the vast majority of our kids the Prom would be their very first formal event at which they could dress up and demonstrate their social skills in a real life setting. It was very much part of their education, and allowed them to practise an important range of unfamiliar behaviours. Unfortunately, for a few, it was also an opportunity to get pissed and exhibit a range of more familiar, though less attractive skills.

It has always seemed inexplicable to me that we metaphorically wring our hands in despair at the anti-social and impolite behaviour of our school children, and yet, do so very little to effectively teach them social and inter-personal skills. What small acknowledgement we do make to the importance of these skills is, within schools at least, totally inadequate, and poorly taught.

Like most schools we had a couple of time-tabled lessons each week to deliver P.S.H.E. (Personal Social and Health Education). There was little prescription as to what should be taught during these lessons and even less attention paid to the qualifications, or expertise of the staff selected to teach such an important subject. It is unthinkable that, we would ask a newly qualified R.E. or History

179

teacher to teach 'A' Level Physics, yet we appear to have no objection to them teaching the most fundamental and important aspects of personal and social relationships. It is hardly surprising, under such circumstances of inadequate provision, that P.S.H.E. is a sadly neglected and grossly under-valued part of the curriculum, and for those who would argue that, in a very full school day, we cannot afford the time to teach these skills, I would say that given the appalling ill-manners and disrespect shown by many of our young people, we cannot afford not to!

It was certainly indicative of the very low priority given to P.S.H.E. at Gruffudd ap Cynan that the staff cajoled and bullied into teaching it were either naïve newcomers, or those with the least command of their own specialist subjects, or control of their pupils. Thus it was, that, the teacher placed in charge of P.S.H.E., was the notoriously weak and disorganised Angus Paisley, the school's ineffectual and slightly loopy Head of Art. Angus was a red headed, forty-year-old Edinburgh Scot, who was so far up his own artistic backside that such trivial issues as effective teaching, or classroom organisation and management, played no discernable part in his educational philosophy. He was forever attempting new and innovative educational initiatives, which could only have had their origin in the secure ward of a high security asylum for the criminally insane.

I clearly recall, one wet and stormy Monday afternoon, when I was telephoned by Nesta Braithwaite, a junior member of the Art Department, to report that a large gang of my year group were rampaging and splashing about on the field outside her art-room, throwing clods of mud at each other, and generally causing mayhem. By the time I'd donned my wet weather gear, traipsed across the yard and rounded the prefabs which housed the Art Department, the mayhem had descended into outright war. The scene which greeted me as I walked out onto the school field resembled film footage I'd recently watched on 'The Battle of the Somme'. There were a group of mud splattered kids bunkered down in the long-jump sandpit, attempting to defend their position from another, equally mud covered group, who were mounting a frontal assault across the no-man's-land

180

between the sandpit and a row of dustbins outside Miss Braithwaite's art-room. As they advanced, using the dustbin lids as shields against a barrage of mud-bombs, I debated with myself the wisdom of intervening, and reluctantly decided that caution was required if I didn't wish to end up flattened under a deluge of squelchy missiles. So, I wisely retreated and settled back under the roof overhang of the art-room and watched, as the advancing troop finally reached their objective and routed the defenders of the sandpit, surrounding the courageous few who'd not retreated and rubbing mud into their hair and faces. I was however, forced to finally mount a rescue mission, when the conquerors began to bury the vanquished face down in the sand, and stand on the backs their heads to try and prevent them from squirming in protest.

Once I'd succeeded in quelling the violence and rounding up the combatants, I questioned the leading protagonists, and discovered that they were on the field because Mark Plowman had asked Angus Paisley if he, and a couple of his innovative mates, could go outside to make some avant-garde sculptures out of mud. Angus, who was obsessed with the notion of using locally obtained materials in the furtherance of creativity, readily agreed, and naturally, once those who'd remained in the art-room saw Mark and his mates messing about outside in the mud, they also quickly discovered an intense desire to express themselves artistically through the same medium. Angus, who was naïve to the point of idiocy, and reluctant to stifle any child's creative impulse, readily acceded to their requests to join the experimental endeavours of the mud artists outside.

On another occasion, when I'd been passing Angus's room and had been interested to see the progress of a sculpture which had been slowly evolving from items of scavenged and abandoned junk, I'd found his room almost empty of kids. Angus was perched precariously on top of this huge scrapheap sculpture trying to creatively place a broken white plastic bicycle pump in the bent lid of an inverted 'Hostess' warming trolley, which was itself supported by, and welded to, an enormous industrial chest freezer and several old bed and motor-cycle frames. It was a monstrous and nightmare construction, of dubious artistic merit, which over the months, had grown to a gigantic size, and which was now so large that all the kid's desks were of necessity pushed up close to the classroom walls.

When I'd asked Angus where his class was, he said that he was trying out a new system of trust and mutual respect, in which the kids no longer had to ask permission to visit the toilet, but could just go whenever they felt the need. I caustically observed that it was an odd coincidence that, apart from Hannah Austin, who was wedged in the far corner, quietly painting a still-life of flowers and fruit, they'd all felt the need at precisely the same time! Angus thought this was simply due to the unfamiliarity of his new liberal regime, and that things would improve once they became used to the new and more relaxed arrangement.

Whether his theory would have proved true, I never discovered, for once I'd kicked them all out of the toilets, confiscated their cigarettes, separated two ardent potential lovers hiding in the entrance to the Boiler House and escorted them all back to Angus's art-room; I told him that his new liberal experiment was at an end, and that, if I discovered any further migrations from cubism to cubicles I'd place all the kids in detention and would report him for gross negligence and the contravention of health and safety regulations. Although I experienced an authoritative rush of power at the sternness of my instruction, I possessed no real hope that any of my dictates would be obeyed, or that Angus would cease his constant quest for educational and artistic lunacy.

In his role as Head of P.S.H.E. Angus was given free rein to devise the curriculum and implement many of his more ill-advised educational innovations. As P.S.H.E. was given a very low priority by the Senior Management Team they paid scant attention to what was actually taught, and even less to the skills and experience of those whom they'd dragooned into teaching it! Consequently, as a subject, it became fertile ground for insolence, poor behaviour and misinformation.

Unfortunately, I discovered just how much misinformation when, due to Nesta Braithwaite's nervous breakdown and subsequent six months paid leave, I was asked by Vic Davies to cover her Year 8 P.H.S.E. class for the duration of her absence. Although I was not keen to tackle the minefield of teaching P.S.H.E., which included sex education, to a bunch of precocious and puberty afflicted thirteen year olds, I was reminded that I did owe Vic a favour, ever since he'd so ably supported my Year 11 Talent Show, and so therefore, I reluctantly agreed. When I made this commitment I was unaware that Nesta's P.S.H.E. class was 8/BB, a wayward and challenging form more familiarly known as 'Beelzebub's Babies,' a passing reference to both their hellish behaviour and to their strange, amulet wearing, crystal worshipping form tutor, Belinda Babcock, a fifty-five year old spinster who dressed as a geriatric Goth, and who expressed an intense interest in the black arts and was a self-professed witch and follower of 'Wicca,' the ancient religion of Celtic pagans. Many felt that, Belinda was only saved from her own complete nervous breakdown from her regular daily contact with the members of her disruptive form, by her strong identification with, and sympathy for, their innate evil. She viewed many of her pupils as embodying living proof that Satan's kingdom was in the ascendance and that his demonic influence was still a powerful influence in the world and on her form's behaviour. It was difficult to say if her attitude to them was a contributory factor in their dreadful resentment of authority, or whether she was correct, and they actually were the spawn of Satan.

My first encounter with this class of pubescent reprobates was the last lesson on a wet and miserable Tuesday afternoon, when I took over as their P.S.H.E. teacher. They arrived at Nesta's art room after afternoon break, damp, bedraggled and smelling faintly of brimstone, sweat and stale urine. A more unprepossessing bunch of future mature and valued citizens it would be difficult to imagine. Not only were they wet, they were also whinging about my appointment as Miss Braithwaite's replacement. It was obvious from their behaviour and Nesta's stress-induced absence that they were going to require a few lessons in attitude realignment, if they were to gain any benefit from my care, and the content of their P.H.S.E. syllabus.

It took me very little time to learn that this nightmare class of 32 thirteen-year-olds comprised, two bright and sensible girls called Fiona Garrity and Rhia Osborne, three able, but depressed and defeated boys called, Jason Wallace, Peter Dibley, and Malcolm

Mountjoy, and the easily led remainder, who were, to a greater or lesser extent, the brain dead disciples of the six feared and influential class ringleaders, who dictated the daily agenda, and who between them, caused or instigated ninety-nine percent of all the trouble and disruption. This small clique of embryonic gangsters consisted of three boys and three girls. They were, in no particular order of evil, Giovanni Demarco, Onslow Jones, Tyrone Price, Aimie-Lee Harris, Chelsea Reynolds and, undoubtedly the Devil's handmaiden, Layla Moon.

Giovanni was a third generation Italian immigrant, whose family still owned and ran a local Italian restaurant, originally founded by his grandfather. Giovanni was a small, swarthy, dark and gelled-haired evil charmer who, due to his grandparents emigration, had been denied the opportunity to join the ranks of the Neapolitan Mafia, which his innate ruthlessness and cruelty indicated was his natural home.

Onslow Jones was that all too common manifestation of modern parenting, a wilful, selfish, moronic, low browed thug, who, due to having always achieved his immediate desires by displays of uncontrollable temper, had learned the temporary effectiveness of the ultimately doomed life skill strategy of hitting anyone who opposed his will.

Completing this trio of trouble was Tyrone Price, a small, ginger-haired, ferret-faced failure, whose idea of meaningful discourse with his teachers and fellow pupils was to shout and spit at them. If he felt especially expressive, he frequently added scratching and biting to his severely limited repertoire of communication skills.

It was unusual in any class to have an equal number of girls who exhibited evil to the same degree as the worst of the boys, yet in 8/BB the three female examples of Old Nick's naughty nymphets, were in every way the equal of their maladjusted male classmates.

The first and most devious of this bunch of budding harpies was Aimie-Lee Harris, another of the hyphenated harridans which make regular unwelcome appearances in teachers' nightmares. She was a tall, angular and somewhat gawky girl, whose physical development had already outstripped her intellectual development by several years.

She had a wild shock of dark curly hair, and potentially, a very pretty face, which was unfortunately, frequently disfigured by her twin demons of anger and resentment.

Aimie-Lee's faithful lieutenant was the stunningly attractive Chelsea Reynolds, whose name was not a tribute to her place of conception, since most of her mother Zoë's illicit affairs had been consummated behind the waste-bins in the car park of the Lonely Leek, where she had, and still was, employed as a part-time barmaid. Allegedly a fabulous beauty in her youth, she was now the prematurely aged single mother of six separately fathered children, ranging from six to sixteen. Chelsea, who had just turned thirteen, was the second of this disparate group, and had, reputedly, been fathered by a travelling shoe salesman, who, due to his company's meagre expense allowance had been forced, in the bleak winter of 1992, to book one of the four letting bedrooms which exemplified the Lonely Leek's conception of comfort and sophistication. His brief sojourn as a guest had allowed Zoë very little opportunity to discover much concerning his personality and interests. The second of the only two hard facts she discovered during their passionate one night stand, was that he was a fanatical football supporter, and so, unable to bestow upon Chelsea the honour of her father's true identity, she had forever marked his contribution to her existence with the name of his favourite club.

It was, perhaps unfairly rumoured that, due to the extremely complex nature of Zoë's claims for child maintenance, she had, single handedly, been responsible for the failure and eventual collapse of the Child Support Agency, that costly and disastrous government attempt to extract money from feckless fathers. Whatever the truth of the rumour, it was definitely true that she had never received a penny of child support from any of the six men, who at various times in her chequered progress from tantalising teen to tired tart, had enjoyed the fleeting ecstasy of her sexual favours. One certainty was, whoever's long spent semen had been responsible for Chelsea's existence, had combined in her, his genetic genius for irresponsibility, with her mother's predisposition for promiscuity.

185

The final female enfant-terrible in this triumvirate of terror, was Lucifer's lovely herself, the lost and completely lunatic, Layla Moon; a gorgeous girlie grotesque, whose conception of high achievement consisted in maximising the suffering of others, especially her luckless teachers. She was an amazingly beautiful, perfectly formed, diminutive blond imp, whose angelic countenance was totally undermined by her cruel and vindictive nature. She was an unsurpassed vision of childhood innocence, whose delicate features, golden hair, disarming smile and obviously cultured background, belied the malevolence of her blackened soul. She could change in an instant from a divine example of the consummate nativity play virgin, to the degenerate daughter of the Prince of Darkness himself. She was living proof of the corruptibility of the young and inherent evil latent in many apparently guileless coquets, and had been such an unexpected challenge to her parents that they'd abandoned her early in life to be cared for by her American maternal grandparents, Chuck and Charlene Sherman. When this arrangement also eventually broke down, Layla was sent back to the U.K. to once again be cared for by her father, Joseph, as her mother had long since lost interest in her and had divorced her father to marry an obscenely wealthy aristocrat with a large country estate in Northumberland. However, despite her father's best efforts, he was unable to tame her demons, or influence her increasingly disruptive and wayward behaviour and so; she was placed in therapy with a series of expensively trained psychiatrists who diagnosed everything from A.D.H.D. to manic depression.

Although these highly skilled professionals tried every therapy from psychoanalysis to acupuncture, nothing seemed to work and Layla simply failed to respond.

As she grew older, they gradually abandoned their more idealistic treatments for her serious misbehaviour, and fell back upon ever increasing doses of powerful tranquilising drugs. At first these were mildly effective in controlling the worst manifestations of her increasing maladjustment, but whatever demons possessed her, slowly developed a resistance to Ritalin and all the other chemical soporifics tried with decreasing success. Finally, like many children presenting intractable problems she was placed in the tender hands of those who were paid to care, and who made their living from trying to pick up the pieces left when love and good intentions fail! Currently she was living in 'Prospect House', a local Social Services childrens' home, housing the detritus of our civilised and caring society. I too was among the professionals paid to try and provide some stability and hope for kids like Layla. It was always a challenging and unenviable task, which was constantly demanding, but very rarely successful.

I was forcibly reminded of this low success rate by the attitude and demeanour of 8/BB as I welcomed them to their first, and massively resented, P.S.H.E. lesson in Miss Braithwaite's paint-daubed and disorganised art room. Although I had never previously taught them, my reputation as a no-nonsense enforcer of rules had obviously preceded me, for their response to my presence as their P.S.H.E. teacher, was one of almost total hostility and dismay. Only Fiona Garrity and Rhia Osborne showed any sign of acceptance and seemed pleased, when I signalled my intention to bring a new and unfamiliar sense of order and purpose to their lessons.

I began this process by splitting up the six identified trouble-makers and sitting them on different tables. I also ensured that the seating at each table was arranged boy-girl, boy-girl, to provide some steadying influence, and prevent the risks posed by same sex tables. After much complaining, which I totally ignored, they finally settled down and I was able to walk around and briefly look at a selection of their exercise books, which quickly established that all they seemed to have covered during last term was drugs and their attendant social problems, which Giovanni Demarco's book clearly indicated, he felt, were the huge cost of the high speed power boats required to out-run the vessels supplied to the Italian customs marine division, and the excessively long and unjust jail sentences handed down to many of his Neapolitan cousins for drug trafficking across heavily policed international borders. In Aimie-Lee Harris's book I learned that she thought that, on the whole, drugs were a good thing, since they helped people to be happy, and also prevented her mum from becoming depressed and suicidal. Chelsea Reynolds thought that, generally, drugs were a bad thing, except for alcohol, tobacco, the contraceptive pill and those prescribed to Aimie-Lee's mum to stop her from killing herself. Onslow Jones had attempted to express his opinion that, drugs should never be given to children, because they stopped them wanting to fight and kill people, and Tyrone Price had filled his book with crudely executed drawings of cigarettes, whisky bottles and hypodermic needles, plus a grossly incompetent representation of an erect penis, which more closely resembled the nozzle on a watering can, since the supposed spray of semen issuing from the top looked exactly like water exiting a fine meshed rose. Only Rhia Osborne's book gave me any idea of the ground which Miss Braithwaite had attempted to cover with this bunch of unruly and untutored terrors.

'Right!' I exclaimed, having established the pitiful state of their knowledge and motivation, 'We are going to move on to the next very important topic on the syllabus. Can anyone guess what that topic might be?'

After a few moments of blank incomprehension, during which no-one was prepared to hazard a guess as to the next riveting subject for study, I dropped my attention getting bombshell.

'Sex!' I shouted, 'that's what we're going to study! Sex! Sex, in all its forms and manifestations. Sex, with all its excitements, ecstasies, desires and disappointments. We are going to have the best, the most interesting, the most exciting, the most honest, the most open, the most truthful and the most informative sex lessons ever to have been taught, in this, or any other school! That, as I knew it would, grabbed their attention and transformed their resentful lethargy and inattention into a bright-eyed willingness to learn.

Before they'd recovered sufficiently to make any kind of response, and whilst I still had them gaping in stunned silence from my totally unexpected introduction, I removed my jacket, cleared a space on Nesta's extremely untidy desk, which I then sat on, and confronted them with my best and well practised persona of polished professionalism. I surveyed their upturned and expectant faces, and waited exactly six seconds, the time required before the impact of my statements wore off and would begin to prompt questions and comments, and then, just before the spell was broken, I continued.

'You are going to learn about one of the most important and most exciting subjects in the world. I am going to tell you everything you ever wanted to know about how babies are made, and about how to prevent babies being made. You, for the first time in your short lives, are going to have the opportunity to learn everything about sex that you ever wanted to know, and many things that you don't yet know you want to know. You are going to learn about the basics of how men and women, and sometimes unintentionally, boys and girls, produce babies. You are going to learn about the excitement of sex, the dangers of sex and most importantly, the responsibility of sex. There will be no taboos, or banned subjects. You will be able to ask me about any aspect of sex you wish. I intend to take you all on such a journey of discovery and exploration that, after your P.S.H.E. lessons with me, you'll be wondering why all your subjects aren't taught like this.'

Now, and only now that I had their full and undivided attention, did I relax enough to ask if there were any questions.

Usually, asking a class with the reputation of 'Beelzebub's Babies' if they had any questions was an ill-advised tactic, since it presented the class comics with an irresistible invitation to make irrelevant and often disruptive observations. However, on this occasion I was fairly confident that they were all too interested to discover what was about to happen next, for them to try and compete with me in gaining their class-mates attention. So, before they recovered sufficiently to sieze the initiative, I pressed the play button on the VCR and started the sex education video, which I'd previously forwarded to the point where Pat, the very attractive actress playing a pregnant wife, was explaining, with relevant filmed inserts of her with her partner Bob, the mechanics and magic of sexual intercourse, together with graphic footage of foreplay, the process of sexual arousal and the nature of the male and female orgasm. As the very explicit full colour images on the large screen TV grabbed their full attention I quietly crossed to the classroom door and switched off the overhead lights. I then made my way to the chair I'd strategically placed at the rear of the room and sat down to watch the programme, as Pat revealed the position and sensitivity of her clitoris and the visually dramatic effect of her erotic stimulation of Bob's flaccid penis.

189

The atmosphere in the room had, in the matter of a few minutes, been transformed from one of hostility, suspicion and resentment to a palpable mixture of excitement, uncertainty and embarrassment. It was a powerful cocktail of disruption-suppressing emotions, which held 8/BB in its grip until the bell signalled the end of the school day, and thankfully, the end of my first encounter with Gruffudd ap Cynan's most feared and sinister form. Probably, for the first time in their school life, they groaned in disappointment at the end of a lesson. I switched on the lights, stopped the video and told them it was home time. Before I dismissed them however, I prepared the ground for a trouble free lesson next week, by promising to show them the remainder of the programme and telling them we would be continuing to explore the fascinating topic of sex education.

During the following week I was reminded of the impact of the lesson by the large number of staff who enquired what I'd done to make 8/BB so keen to continue their P.S.H.E. lessons. I did not fully enlighten them, but was gratified to have sparked 8/BB's interest, and selected an approach and subject which had fired their curiosity and primed their willingness to learn.

On the following Tuesday it was a very different 8/BB that arrived for their P.S.H.E. lesson. Gone was the sullen, whining and resentful mob which had turned up the previous week. Now, they arrived with a flushed eagerness and took their seats with a quiet and suppressed anticipation.

I quickly reinforced my enthusiastic message of the last lesson, and, without any further preamble, I restarted the video from where it had finished, and settled back to watch, as Pat and Bob resumed their demonstration of the startling changes which their bodies underwent during orgasm. Over the next forty minutes, the kids were given the visually explicit story of Pat and Bob's sex life, from foreplay to the eventual birth of their baby daughter Rachel. As the programme concluded, with a very self-satisfied Pat and Bob propped up on fluffy pillows, cradling a contented and gurgling Rachel and smiling smugly into each others adoring faces, I just had time to tell the class that next week we would be discussing the video and exploring any issues which it raised.

So far, so good, that was two lessons I'd managed to survive without disruption, or major incident. I feared however, that the following week, without the distraction of the video and with the promise of a discussion, things just might prove a little more challenging. I knew that next Tuesday, the lesson would have to be tightly structured and very well planned to have any chance of continuing to fully engage their attention. For even though sex was an interesting subject, it was also a potential minefield, full of pitfalls and possible career ending errors of judgement.

It had only been a couple of years previously, when Sarah Jennings, a young, enthusiastic, sexually liberated and cannabis smoking member of the Music department, had been inadvertently, but expertly sidetracked by a few of the more sexually precocious boys in her Year 9 P.S.H.E. lesson into a discussion about the prevalence of bestiality among Welsh sheep farmers and whether it was in fact true that they prevented the prettiest and least willing ewes from escaping by stuffing their back legs down the front of their Wellingtons. Such speculations quickly lead on to questions about which other members of the animal kingdom were possible partners in humanity's search for sexual gratification. Unusually and undoubtedly, partly due to her lack of teaching experience, Sarah allowed herself to be drawn into an inappropriate and complex area, which, unless you're a trained vet with an extensive knowledge of animal genitalia, can easily lead to some pretty wild and inaccurate speculation.

For, a month or so later, during his court appearance for seriously injuring one of his neighbours hens while trying, unsuccessfully, to locate an orifice suitable for his lustful intentions, Jason Moody's legal-aid lawyer, pleaded in mitigation, for his attempted buggery, the misinformation he'd been subjected to during his P.S.H.E. lessons at school.

It was extremely unfortunate for Sarah that in court that particular morning was Danny Fenton, an ambitious cub reporter for the Abercwmtwerp Tribune, who saw in these revelations an opportunity to significantly advance his parochial and languishing career. This he attempted to achieve, by phoning the story through to a high flying ex-student mate of his, who now occupied an influential position as an investigative journalist with *The News of the World.*

To give credit to Sarah's trade union, they succeeded in persuading the school governors and parents not to bow to the demands of the incensed national media for her instant dismissal, but, unable to cope with the pressure of the scrum of reporters permanently camped outside her flat and the school, she reluctantly resigned, changed her name and emigrated to New Zealand, to open a music store in Auckland with her partner Melvin.

This regrettable incident was a forceful reminder to all P.S.H.E. teachers, of the need for both circumspection and accuracy, particularly when teaching sexual matters to impressionable and easily aroused young boys, whose sexual appetites, unfortunately, develop well in advance of their ability to appeal to the equally young girls, who should be the more appropriate recipients of their ardour.

There was of course, as Jason's defence council pointed out, a case to be argued that the unfortunate chicken may have been spared Jason's sexual assault, had it not been for the speculation in his P.S.H.E. lessons concerning the suitability of alternate species as potential sexual partners. I was very conscious of the importance of not allowing a group of lust driven boys, to set the agenda for the topics to be covered in their Sex Education lessons.

My third lesson with 8/BB therefore, commenced with a structured discussion of the Pat and Bob video, with no deviation allowed from any of the information presented by the programme. Thanks to the easy availability of pornography on the internet, most kids are now very aware of the mechanics of sex, and know far more than previous generations concerning what are its physical possibilities. However, no matter how informative pornography may be in certain areas, it still fails to answer many of the questions which occur to the young and inexperienced. For example, the first question prompted by the video was Onslow Jones' concern that the pain from the groin strain he recently sustained in his P.E. lesson was a sign that his ovaries and fallopian tubes were seriously damaged, and that this would prevent him from being able to make babies. It was to be hoped that far more likely as a cause for him failing to achieve fatherhood, would be his revolting personality, coupled with his extreme lack of charisma, intelligence, or physical attractiveness; but judging from the frequency of babies born to such charmless thugs, my hope would probably prove overly optimistic. Of more immediate concern was the sneering derision which greeted Onslow's ignorance of male anatomy, which very nearly resulted in him inflicting serious damage on his tormentors, and I had to quickly defuse the situation and move swiftly on to the next question.

Before the question and answer session had progressed very far, I became acutely aware that a considerable number of kids had not asked any questions, or participated in any of the discussions. It occurred to me that this was because they were terrified to ask any question which may have exposed their sexual ignorance, since this would have seriously damaged their street-cred and lost them the respect of their mates. As it was nearly home time I quickly rounded the lesson off with a very brief explanation of the major methods of contraception, and when I dismissed them, I asked Onslow to stay behind, so that I could reassure him about his concerns, without the embarrassment of a scornful audience.

The next Tuesday I was determined not to repeat the error of continuing with open questions, which presented the ever present risk of public humiliation, and so, I gave out sheets of paper and asked them to all to secretly write down any questions about sex, which they wished me to answer and discuss. I promised that I would put all the papers, suitably folded, into a box, and then draw them out one at a time and read the question to the class and then answer them. To further protect their privacy, I told them to print their questions in block capitals, so I could not identify their handwriting. I reluctantly took the risk of sitting Giovanni Demarco with Onslow and Tyrone, so he could act as a scribe and print out any questions, which I said they could whisper quietly to him.

I told them all they could ask any questions they wished, no matter how strange they thought them. I said that I could not be embarrassed or shocked, and so there was no point in simply using this as an opportunity to ask obscene questions in the hope that I would be too outraged or upset to answer. I told them I would answer each question honestly, and not tell them half truths, or fairy stories.

I was surprised by the eagerness with which they undertook the task. For several minutes there was hushed concentration as they wrote their questions, whilst carefully shielding their paper, from their equally secretive mates. There would have been complete silence had it not been for Giovanni asking how to spell 'transvestite' and Chelsea coming up to check the syntax of her question about mothers' responsibility for telling their children the truth about their fathers.

It was with some trepidation, that sometime later, I reached into the box to retrieve the first question, particularly as Layla Moon had come up three times to request extra sheets of paper. I slowly opened the first sheet to reveal my first question, which surprisingly was correctly spelled and punctuated. 'HOW AND WHY DO GIRLS MASTURBATE?' For the briefest of moments, I doubted the wisdom of my promise to provide complete and truthful answers to anything they may ask, and felt a slight misgiving at having to cover the magic of masturbation this early, but I'd made a commitment which absolutely had to be honoured, and so in a clear and steady voice, I read the question to the class.

The effect was electric, and a little like the trauma caused some years previously, when Gwen Tully, our one time head of R.E. during an assembly she was taking on the subject of the importance of addressing people in respectful and appropriate language, forcibly made her point, by calling all the kids in Years 10 and 11 'a bunch of fucking brain-dead retards'. She certainly succeeded in causing a controversy, since her remarks almost resulted in her dismissal, and was yet another occasion when Dr Douglas had to be assisted from the hall on the tattooed arm of Free Fall Evans.

It's not that kids are unfamiliar with obscene language or crude and offensive insults. The shock factor comes from hearing such language issue from the lips of a trusted teacher. Equally, my willingness to talk openly and honestly about masturbation was a novelty, and its unexpected setting had prompted the kids' stunned reaction.

Gradually however, as question followed question, and they began to trust my willingness to treat each question seriously, and to address every topic in an honest and open manner, they began to lose their inhibitions and reluctance to talk, and started to ask follow-up questions without the need to remain anonymous.

Over the next few weeks we covered almost every aspect of human sexuality, and I built such a close rapport with 8/BB that it was difficult any longer to view them as the Devil's disciples. Although wary and suspicious at first, they gradually engaged with the content of their P.S.H.E. lessons, and as we moved away from sex to discuss other important topics, they remained focussed and eager to discuss and learn. It reinforced for me the importance of winning trust by personal hard work and consistency, and by providing for the kids a learning environment where they are respected and valued.

My initial apprehension upon agreeing to teach P.S.H.E. to 'Beelzebub's Babies' had been transformed into an eagerness to continue their education, making our Tuesday afternoon lessons the highlight of the week.

Chapter 14

Work Experience

During my entire time teaching 8/BB, and despite covering some potentially controversial topics, I received very few comments, or complaints, from offended or outraged parents. This may have been because most of the kids were reluctant to discuss matters at home, especially sexual matters, which were often a taboo area in family discussions.

The only real complaint had come from Peter Dibley's mother, who'd had to deal with a major crisis, when Peter had told Doris, his maternal grandmother, during a family dinner party that I'd told him that frequent masturbation did not send you blind, and that the information Doris had imparted to him when she'd caught him wanking last Boxing Day was a load of rubbish.

Considering the highly charged nature of much of the content of 8/BB's lessons, I felt fortunate to have survived without greater parental censure. My teaching colleagues however, were a different matter and responded in a vindictive, but predictable manner.

It became something of a talking point in the staff room, how well 8/BB were responding to their P.S.H.E. lessons, and I became the target of suspicion and malicious gossip for commending their behaviour and effort. Nothing produces resentment among one's colleagues half so quickly as success, especially if that success is in an area where they themselves have failed. The more I expressed approval of 8/BB's achievements, the greater was the staff's denigration of my teaching methods, which most thought at best unorthodox, and at worst dangerously subversive. I enjoyed their disapproval immensely, and fanned the flames of their resentment by praising 8/BB's improved attitude at every opportunity, and by smiling knowingly at their hostility. Nothing increases professional jealousy faster than high achievement, and nothing fuels its growth more effectively than responding to it with wry good humour. To achieve staff room popularity it is very important not to outshine one's colleagues, or attempt to rise above the extremely low expectations and defeated idealism endemic in British education. Teaching remains one of the few occupations where genuine talent is rarely praised, and where the comfort of mediocrity is pursued and valued above the challenges of excellence. It amounts to a national tragedy that we fail to make teaching the natural home for our most skilled and intelligent people, and continue, generation after generation, to entrust the education of the young to those who often lack the skills and courage to work in 'The Real World', where ability is valued, and high achievement is well rewarded.

To give our Year 11 pupils the opportunity to briefly experience this real world of work and to expose them to the demands and obligations of employment outside of school, we send them all, on a two-week work experience placement. This is designed to provide them with a tiny taste of what they will face when they finally leave full time education, to begin the daunting process of trying to build a successful career.

I had always enjoyed the two weeks during which the entire Year 11 were absent from school on their various work placements. Firstly, because it relieved me of my Year 11 teaching commitments, and secondly, because it provided an opportunity to visit selected pupils in their place of work, and so enabled me to leave school for a few hours and to enjoy, however briefly, contact with people working outside the claustrophobic atmosphere of education.

I was especially happy this particular year for, as the Head of Year 11, I was expected to spend most of their two week work experience out of school, visiting them in their many and varied placements. The overall responsibility for these placements had traditionally lain with Sylvia Francis, our popular and perceptive Head of Careers. Unfortunately, she had recently moved to a new position as an adviser on post-sixteen education and training within UNESCO, and was now travelling the world attempting to promote intercontinental educational exchange visits. It was a gravy train of profligate proportion, which provided earnings light years beyond what she had ever achieved as a teacher.

I was delighted by her success, but also disappointed that she had left school just before she would have been responsible for my Year 11's two week work experience. However, my disappointment turned to trepidation and concern when Dr Douglas and his cohort of incompetents appointed Christine Dimchurch as her successor. Christine was a long serving teacher in the Food Technology Department who, ever since her application to become the Head of VI Form had been rejected in favour of Bonnie Butler, had nurtured a profound and dangerous resentment which had, I'm sure, caused Dr Douglas and other members of the S.M.T. many sleepless nights. Her initial response upon learning of her failure had been to run off home in tears. Her next and more worrying actions had consisted of becoming the school's representative for the most militant and troublesome of the teaching unions, and loudly expressing her unstable and threatening Marxist views at every opportunity. She became a persistent and painful thorn in the flesh of all who acknowledged her paranoid grievances, or sympathised with her disappointments. She was an unstable and vindictive failure, who would have been out of her depth in a damp footbath, and who would have been better employed within the fetid darkness of a mushroom farm. Instead, she had been promoted to a position of responsibility for the future careers of many vulnerable and uncertain youngsters. She typified the S.M.T.'s failure to appoint the best and most talented person to the available position and as subsequent events would prove, she became yet another example of their monumental misjudgement.

It was obvious from the outset that, with Christine in charge, Year 11's work experience was likely to be less than successful. The major objective of the whole exercise was to attempt to place each pupil in a working environment which bore some relationship to their interests, skills and ultimate ambitions. It was relatively easy to achieve this for the A* high flyers, who could readily be placed with solicitors, doctors, accountants, etc. The real difficulty was in managing to place the disruptive and unmotivated no-hopers who often came from homes where the very idea of work was an alien concept, and where living on state benefits was the career option of choice.

Over the years Sylvia had built a large and loyal network of local employers willing to cater for this challenging and disaffected group, and her very significant achievements in running the work experience programme could be largely attributed to her success in finding suitable placements for kids whose ultimate career prospects were extremely bleak.

However, it was obvious from the very start that part of Christine's incompetence could be laid at the door of her liberal and totally unrealistic notions of social justice. She was Old Labour by inclination and viewed the advantages bestowed by talent and high intelligence to be socially divisive, and an offence to her notions of equality and social justice. This insane view of the world was compounded by a sentimental attachment to the wellbeing of the thug, criminal, or social dropout. Consequently, she abandoned the long established tradition of trying to fit round pegs in round holes and went for what she considered the egalitarian option, of giving our future university entrants the benefit of experiencing the lowliest and most boring jobs; whilst sending many of those who were as bright as a dying candle, into work situations which required skills far beyond both their abilities and imaginations. Sending kids who view learning as un-cool, and high achievement as an excuse for ridicule into a city centre law practice, where brilliance, dedication, self-belief and ambition are the ultimate values, is not to be recommended; not even as an idealistic experiment in social engineering.

The inadvisability of such a course of action was forcibly brought home to me, when on the first Monday of Year 11's work experience, I received a telephone call at 10.30am from Nigel Winston-Jones, a senior partner in the prestigious law firm of Jessop, Jenkins, Jones and Jones, to regretfully inform me that Tracey-Ann Smith and Nathan Hyde were temporarily locked in their strong-room awaiting the arrival of the police; Tracey-Ann for smoking what was believed to be cannabis in the female staff toilets, and Nathan for damaging their recently installed and massively expensive Xerox Work Centre Pro/90 by attempting to photocopy his erect penis to illustrate the birthday card he'd been making for his girlfriend Stacy.

By the time I had sorted out their little escapade and retrieved them both from police custody, it was early afternoon, and upon my return to school, I was immediately asked to go and collect Crystal Devine from the flagship headquarters of an international bank, where she had called the assistant deputy manager of the foreign securities division a 'fucking perve', and had accused him of looking up her skirt, when she was climbing a step-ladder to file some documents in the bank's archives vault.

When eventually I was ushered into the manager's very impressive office, I was informed that, upon being told that her behaviour was unacceptable and that her work experience placement was at an end, Crystal had called him 'Banker the Wanker', before flouncing out to disappear into the lunch-time throng of busy shoppers. I did my best to apologise on the school's behalf, but was left in no doubt that the bank was, in future, forever closed as a work experience placement for the kids of Gruffudd ap Cynan Comp.

Thinking that things could not get any worse, and worried that Crystal was now on the loose somewhere in a city full of the unsuspecting and innocent public, I set off to try and find her before she was presented with an opportunity to cause some real damage. With many of our girls; had they been alone in this cosmopolitan and potentially dangerous city, I would have been concerned for their safety. However, Crystal's disappearance made me fearful for the welfare of anyone whom she may perceive as a threat. The last thing I wanted was to have to explain to some poor well meaning hospitalised Samaritan that approaching Crystal with good intentions, and anything less lethal than a sub machine gun, had been a monumental error of judgement!

Before my concerns had time to blossom into panic, I received an urgent phone call from school on my mobile, asking if I was any where near St Winifred's Residential Home, and that if so, could I please go and rescue the two paralysed and confused residents who'd been persuaded by Kyle Bowman and Jack Reynolds to stage a downhill wheelchair race from outside the gates of the home to a local off-licence, where the winning invalid had been coerced into purchasing a gallon of strong cider and forty cigarettes, so that they could all celebrate a memorable race. It was only because Jack had dropped his letter of introduction to the home when he and Kyle fled the scene to consume the cider, that the manager of the off-licence knew where to phone to report their actions.

When I finally turned up, the police had returned the two traumatised wheelchair charioteers to St Winifred's and arrested Kyle and Jack, who'd been discovered by the Reverend Morgan-Jenkins, drunk and disorderly in the bottom of a recently dug grave in the churchyard of 'St Vitus' in the Valley', where they had been attempting to locate the final resting place of Kyle's grandfather, Bert.

It was still only 3.00pm on the first Monday of Year 11's work experience, but I was already totally convinced that Christine's experiment in social engineering was a complete and predictable disaster.

The final saga of this first day occurred when Miles Manson, one of our less sensitive art lovers, decided he could improve a complex glass and chrome mobile sculpture, which had been specially commissioned at enormous expense, to hang in the impressive atrium of the newly opened Law Courts, by firing at it with the .2 Webley air pistol, he'd concealed beneath his Tommy Hilfiger hoody that morning prior to leaving home for his work placement as an assistant to the Clerk of the Court. It was to be the only time in his life that his attendance at Court was as anything other than as the prisoner in the dock, and it was the first time in my life that, I'd dreaded the dawn of the second day of Year 11's exposure to the world of work.

Blessedly, the Tuesday was slightly less traumatic, but did result in phone calls from the very dissatisfied parents of Hannah Austin, Mark Vaughan and Sophie Stewart, who complained that their extremely intelligent and highly capable children had been most disappointed with their work experience placement in the local authorities department of Parks, Graveyards and Sanitation; where they had been variously employed in weeding flower beds, removing graffiti from defaced headstones and emptying septic tanks on a remote hippy commune near Abergavenny.

If any proof were ever needed of the inadvisability of attempting to improve social equality by promoting the dim and blighting the aspirations of the bright, then this Year 11 work experience experiment was it!

An occurrence for which I *was* grateful was the sight of Crystal Devine waiting outside my room when I returned to school Tuesday lunchtime, after I'd experienced a stressful morning trying to placate the sales director of the city centre Porsche dealership, who'd only just managed to stop Josh Palmer from taking a brand new black 911 for an unauthorised test drive.

My relief at Crystal's presence was, however, short lived when I discovered that she'd been taken home by the police at 1.00am, after being arrested for threatening to rearrange the features of the unfortunate barman in Pat O'Connor's Irish pub with a broken bottle, when he'd ill-advisedly refused to serve her with a large vodka and coke, because he'd thought her drunk and under age.

As I approached her I knew that she'd sneaked into school across the field, as she wasn't in school uniform, and was I assumed, still wearing her work experience outfit, which was about as inappropriate for the world of international banking as it's possible to imagine. She was wearing a see-through cream silky top over a black bra, and a black skirt so short that it made a pelmet seem concealing. Her legs were encased in sheer black spandex tights and her feet were supported by five-inch platform stilettos, which must have been an extreme rarity outside the porn industry.

Her greeting was, as usual, brief but laconic.

'What's up Sir?' she asked, as I unlocked my door. I motioned her into the room and told her to remain standing, as I feared that any attempt on her part to sit, would have revealed more than I deserved to see!

'What's up Crystal,' I replied, 'is that you have accused a very senior international financier of improper behaviour, called the manager of one of the UK's greatest merchant banks 'a wanker', run off into the city and been arrested for threatening extreme violence to an innocent barman who was only doing his job. In addition, your actions have forever denied future generations of pupils at this school the opportunity to experience the privilege of working in one of our most prestigious financial institutions. This, you have managed to achieve, single-handedly, and in less than twenty-four hours. I think that in the circumstances "What's up Sir?" is a little inadequate, even from you!'

Her response began with the annoying, but predictable 'Yair but', which usually preceded teenage explanations of disapproved of behaviour.

''E was a perve sir, this geezer in the bank, 'e looked up my skirt. 'e was ogling my arse. I could feel 'es eyes all over me!'

'If Crystal,' I observed, 'you were wearing a skirt as short as the one you have on at the moment, then looking up it, as you say, would be impossible, since it is so brief the concept of up is inapplicable, and the distinction between looking at your skirt, or up your skirt, no longer exists. In fact, we are stretching the elasticity of the English language beyond its breaking point, by describing what you are wearing as a skirt at all; since it would probably be more accurate to describe it as a belt, and as such, can hardly be an article of clothing which would give rise to accusations of perverse behaviour, as no-one, to my knowledge, has ever been accused of looking up someone's belt!'

I could tell from her expression that she was about to disagree, and so I quickly continued, 'And if, as the bank manager indicated, you were up a step-ladder in the archive vault at the time of the alleged incident, then looking up your skirt would have been the poor man's only option, and for him to have avoided ogling your arse, as you so delicately put it, he would have required a blindfold! And then, to add insult to injury, you were obscenely offensive to the manager.'

'Yair but, it was a rubbish job anyway and none of me mates was close enough to meet up with at lunchtime and they said I had to work till half-past five so I'd have to catch the ten-past six bus and wouldn't have got home till half-past seven, so I did a runner, coz I didn't want to be there anyway.'

'Crystal,' I said, to prevent her explanation growing longer than her list of misdemeanours, 'as you failed to return home until 1.00am, and then in the company of the police, I cannot see how the hour of your return home was of any concern to you at all!'

'What's going to 'appen now then?' she asked. 'I'm not going back to that stupid bank.'

'Crystal, the only way you'd be allowed back into that stupid bank, would be if you had well over a million pounds to deposit, and even then, you may not gain entry if the manager recognised you. I suggest you go home, and do some work experience helping your unfortunate mother, I'm sure she could find plenty of jobs for you to do around the house.'

She looked at me in amazement, before she asked, 'You mean I can just go home and come back when it's all over?'

'Yes!' I confirmed. 'You can just go home, but I'll be telephoning your mother to ask her to give you lots of horrible jobs to do, and to make sure you do them, and go back over the field. I don't want you walking through the school dressed as the teenage lead in a porn movie!'

'I'm not a slag sir!' she protested, as she gleefully left to serve out the remainder of her work experience doing domestic chores.

It was only minutes after Crystal's departure before I received a phone call from the R.S.P.C.A. Animal Rescue Centre, to inform me that Dixie and Trixie Turner, who'd been unwisely given responsibility for the cattery and dog kennels, had liberated the fifteen cats and eight dogs awaiting sterilisation, transferred six rabbits and five guinea-pigs from their hutches to roam free in the lush grass of the donkey sanctuary, and most seriously of all, had released two rottweilers and a pit-bull terrier from death row, where they had been confined, since a judge had ordered their destruction following their vicious attack upon the court official trying to serve a restraining order upon their irresponsible owner.

What Christine Dimchurch had obviously not cared about, when she made this disastrous placement, was that the Turner twins were the offspring of Zoltan and Melody-Jane Turner, two of the most militant and extreme animal rights activists in the country, who had run foul of the law on numerous occasions for threats of violence against many who worked in areas of medical research involving animal experimentation. If anyone should have been kept well away from distressed and vulnerable animals, it was the Turner twins; whose misplaced sentiments were going to do more harm than good to the creatures of their concern, than a mere loss of liberty; and although their setting free the condemned dogs was motivated by a desire to save their lives, it did nothing for the well being of Barney Budgen, the unfortunate local butcher, who'd been found locked in his own cold store, suffering from advanced hypothermia, when he'd been forced to escape the ferocious attack the dogs had mounted in an attempt to devour the side of beef he'd been carrying at the time.

Dixie and Trixie became the latest kids whose work experience was to be spent at home helping their mother.

By the Wednesday of the first week I'd had fifteen kids sent back to school as totally unsuitable, twelve told not come to work the following day; ten who never bothered to turn up in the first place; eight who'd been collected from their place of work by the police; six who'd absconded; five who'd been dismissed for insolence; four who'd damaged, vandalised, or stolen something; three who'd threatened, or insulted customers; two who'd make improper sexual advances to their work colleagues and one who'd destroyed an egg packing factory by tossing a still lit cigarette into a store room full of egg boxes. Altogether, it was a catalogue of disasters rarely equalled in the entire annuls of work experience failures.

Almost all the problems had sprung from Christine's insane notions of social justice, and were directly attributable to her catastrophic experiment in social engineering. This first year of her stewardship as Head of Careers became known as 'The Great Work Experience Fiasco' and was forever after a beacon illuminating the consequences of promoting tenth rate minds to positions requiring first rate thoughts.

Nothing had made the beacon burn as brightly as the results of sending drug dependent Elvis Evans to work in the pharmacy of Abercwmtwerp General Hospital. Here, he managed to steal sufficient class A drugs to allow him to rise rapidly through the ranks of local druggies from pathetic user to valued supplier; a role which, due to his low intelligence and almost permanently stoned-out state, he was ill-

205

equipped to fulfil, and totally unable to sustain. Consequently, he missed his opportunity to become the local drug supremo, and his very brief career as a valued source of supply was permanently ended when he was arrested for attempting to sell morphine, Viagra and nitrous oxide to the bewildered residents of the Twilight Towers Nursing Home, where his long suffering mother worked as a part-time breakfast cook.

All these very unfortunate incidents occurred in the first week, and by the end of the working day on the Friday, there had been sixty-seven kids sent home to complete their work experience as domestic assistants to their mostly, very reluctant mothers. It had been impossible to find any of them alternative placements, and most of my week had been spent apologising to employers, placating the police and dealing with an increasing number of reporters who wished to further their careers by investigating the value to the community of sending Year 11 pupils on two weeks work experience.

As I arrived at school on the Monday of the second week, I was hopeful that the worst was over, and that I would enjoy a trouble free final few days, visiting successful pupils who were a credit to themselves, the school and, who had proved a valuable asset to their employers. What I did not anticipate was walking into the staff room to be told by Vic Davies that, due to an incident which had occurred very late on Friday, Christine Dimchurch was in hospital, and would be unable to take any further part in the supervision of Year 11's work experience.

Apparently, Christine had kicked Leon Lugardi, the owner of very high class hairdressers, in the bollocks when he had attempted to cauterise her brains by sticking the red hot spike of a Vidal Sassoon curling wand up her left nostril, for sending him the nightmare Leigh-Anne Morrison to learn the basics of hair design. In the ensuing fracas, where they had been locked in combat, Christine had suffered a badly burned cheek and a broken rib and collar bone, and Leon had sustained a serious injury to his scrotum and banged his head on a black mock granite wash basin he'd recently installed to impress his more gullible clients.

Normally, Christine's injuries would not have necessitated an extended stay in hospital, but her encounter with Leon had proved to be too much for her overfull stress bucket, and came at the end of a traumatic week where, like me, she had been castigated and attacked from all sides for her disastrous work experience placements. Consequently, while she was being kept in hospital overnight for observation, she had attempted suicide, by trying to drown herself in the large water storage tank on the hospital roof. Unfortunately, earlier that day the tank had been emptied and steam cleaned, due to a recent outbreak of Legionnaires disease, and instead of experiencing the soft water-borne landing she was expecting, fell fifteen feet to the steel floor, shattering her right ankle and breaking her left tibia. She was however, very fortunate that men arrived early the following morning to refill the tank, as when she fell she had lost consciousness, and it was only the high pressure flood of cold water entering the tank and swirling her about like a piece of flotsam which revived her sufficiently to enable her to scream and cry out; thus alerting the men outside to turn off the tap.

Obviously, it was going to be some considerable time before she would be fit enough to resume her duties, and so I faced the prospect of having to deal with all the future consequences of her misplaced idealism, and having to undertake total supervision of Year 11's final week.

Thankfully, things began to settle down, and on this second Monday, I only had one serious issue to deal with, and that, was unrelated to Christine's social experiment. It involved Maurice Smith and Ian Oakley, two of our dyslexic boys, who'd been unusually well placed on a hill farm helping the shepherd round up a large and well dispersed flock of sheep in preparation for their annual bath in the sheep-dip. Both the boys, despite their illiteracy and learning difficulties, had performed their tasks well, and had been a tremendous help to Mopsy and Megan, the two sheep dogs sent to the far hillsides to bring in the flock. Even the first session of dipping had gone well, with both of them making sure that each animal had been fully submerged before leaving the dipping-pool.

The problem arose when the shepherd supervising this exciting activity was unexpectedly called away, to supervise the unloading of a delivery of animal feed. Apparently, the boys misheard his parting instruction to 'feed the sows' and mistook it for an order 'to dip themselves'; and when he returned, he found them both stripped down to their underpants, and rolling around in the mud and slurry outside the milking shed, in a vain effort to stop the pain and discomfort of their burning skin.

I visited them both later in the hospital, where they had been treated with steroids and bathed in calamine lotion. Thankfully, they both made a full recovery, and joined the ranks of mother's little helpers, who'd already been sent home.

As the second week progressed, there were no further serious issues or complaints, and I began to relax and enjoy my visits to monitor and assess their various work placements. Most employers reported favourably upon each pupil's effort and behaviour, and the only further complaints I received were about lack of punctuality. Despite this improvement however, I was very relieved by the Friday evening, when work experience came to an end, and I looked forward to a restful and trouble free weekend.

At 11.00pm, even before the weekend had properly begun, I was summoned to Abercwmtwerp Police Station, where a distraught Mr and Mrs Roberts were anxiously waiting for news of their daughter Kelly, whom they'd reported missing when she failed to arrive home from her work experience placement, working as a trainee secretary in the portakabin, which acted as the headquarters of 'Honest Eddie's Used Car Emporium'.

Kelly, who had grown into a wilful, and if rumour was to be believed, a promiscuous thrill-seeker with numerous male conquests, had stayed out late on most of her work experience evenings, but when she had failed to turn up at all on this last day, her concerned parents had searched her bedroom for possible clues, and discovered that some of her favourite clothes and her make-up bag were missing. Further police enquiries had also discovered that Johnny 'Badboy' Bonetti, the super-smooth forty-two year old salesman that 'Honest

Eddie' employed to shift the clapped out bangers on his forecourt, had also failed to return home to his wife Maria and their five children.

An APB was swiftly issued, and just after 1.00am, an observant local police patrol in Cleethorpes spotted Johnny's red 1970 Ford Mustang in the car park of 'The Harbour Heights Motel', a seedy run-down, no questions asked establishment, owned by Johnny's second cousin Geraldo.

When, at 2.00am, the police raided chalet 14, they discovered Johnny and Kelly asleep, and locked in a lovers embrace between the faded bri-nylon sheets covering the well used mattress of their queen sized double bed.

Both were taken into custody, and Kelly awaited the arrival of her parents, who immediately took her home. Meanwhile, the police reluctantly released Johnny, as Kelly was just past sixteen and had insisted that she loved him, and that there had been no coercion to get her into bed. The evidence of her willingness was borne out when, four days later, they both fled the country to set up home near Alicante, where Johnny owned a small holiday villa.

Of course, Mr and Mrs Roberts blamed the school for failing to ensure the suitability of Kelly's work placement, and Dr Douglas was questioned by the school governors regarding his appointment of Christine Dimchurch to such a responsible and sensitive position. Despite their concerns however, they lacked the appetite for a vote of no confidence in Douglas's judgement and ability, and so, after brief expressions of regret, things were allowed to drift back into their usual pattern of vacillation and incompetence.

Finally, the Monday arrived, and with it the return to school of all the Year 11 pupils who'd managed to somehow survive their first real experience of the world of work, together with all those who'd been sent home to annoy their parents, or other unfortunate family members. Within a few days, and with the return of their familiar routine, the kids settled back into school-life, and began the last leg of their slog towards the tortuous challenge of their looming G.C.S.E. examinations.

Chapter 15

Special Needs

For many, Year 11 marked the end of their full-time education and signalled their departure from Gruffudd ap Cynan Comp, where their aspirations and future hopes had been dashed upon the triple rocks of an academic curriculum, low teacher expectation and irrelevant examinations. For others, more fortunate in their ability and motivation, it marked the final stage in their transition from callow pupil to successful student. For them all, it was the final year on their journey from child to adult, and was the last year where society would forgive their transgressions, and tolerate their mistakes to quite the same degree.

Toleration, always an important attribute for any teacher, was even more necessary for those dealing regularly with kids deemed to have 'special educational needs'. SEN kids, as they were more frequently labelled, were a varied and diverse group, whose special needs were more specifically identified with a whole plethora of more defining categories. Each of these labelled problems occurred on a continuum of possible further subdivisions of increasing severity. This made the entire field of special needs a jargon filled nightmare, designed to obfuscate the issues, and make it almost impossible for parents and non-teachers to comprehend.

I shall not however, leave my readers in the same state of baffled ignorance and incomprehension, and therefore, I list below a lay-person's translation of some of the more common acronyms used by special needs professionals to confuse and confound the uninitiated.

MLD. (Moderate Learning Difficulties) = Finds many tasks difficult.

SLD. (Severe Learning Difficulties) = Finds all tasks difficult.

SpLD (Specific Learning Difficulties) = Difficulties with reading/spelling/arithmetic

EBD (Emotional and Behavioural Difficulties) = Disruptive

ADHD (Attention Deficit Hyperactivity Disorder) = Medically diagnosed as disruptive, with Ritalin prescribed as the chemical cosh of first choice.

D (Dyslexic) = Difficulties with language, particularly reading and spelling.

DP (Dysphasic) = Problems with written and verbal communication.

DS (Dyspraxic) = Can't tie shoelaces.

DEL (Delicate) = Frequently ill.

AUT (Autistic) = Frequently non-communicative, but often good at drawing.

ASPS (Asperger's Syndrome) = Like autism, but often with the added complication of making inappropriate and weird comments.

In addition to this selection of problems, we must add the more obvious conditions such as: partially-hearing, deaf, profoundly-deaf, partially-sighted, blind, totally-blind, dumb, deaf and dumb, deaf, dumb and blind, plus all the many and varied physical disabilities that the human frame is subject to. In its totality, the term 'special needs' covers such a huge range of syndromes, disorders, disabilities and difficulties that the commonly expressed opinion that around twenty percent of the population has some sort of 'special need', has always struck me as a wildly conservative estimate!

Certainly, we had considerably more than twenty percent at Gruffudd ap Cynan, even discounting the staff. The kids with special needs all had to be classified as SA = School Action, or SA+ = School Action Plus. Kids labelled SA were usually taught in normal classes, but received some additional help from specialist teachers within the school, and those on SA+ were more commonly taught in small discrete groups within the Special Needs Department, often receiving specific help and support from outside agencies, such as specialist teachers employed by the LEA or Health Authority.

Presiding over this empire of chaos, was the menopausal matron of mediocrity, Miss Pamela H Potts, a fifty-two year old former R.E.

teacher, who had lost her faith in God's infallibility at precisely the same moment that she discovered an unshakeable belief in her own! She was as convinced of the superiority of her opinions, as she was dismayed at their lack of acceptance by others. Since losing her religious faith and the affection of the only man who'd ever showed the slightest interest in her, she'd become a male hating harridan, whose only satisfaction remained the residue of power, which she mistakenly believed she exercised over those teachers unfortunate enough to work in her department. These included Lofty Lewis, who despised her and who totally ignored all her instructions and attempted initiatives; Cindy Beaumont, a timid, atrociously attired non-entity, who was her obsequious acolyte and Chris Reed, the teacher in charge of the Pupil Referral Unit, who always undermined her, by refusing to acknowledge her status, or authority. In addition, there were also two part time female teaching assistants called Dolly Oliver and Audrey Barnes, who worked two and a half days each, supporting specific pupils in mainstream classes. This motley collection of failures and misfits made up the Special Educational Needs Team, and due to their daily exposure to the most challenging, disruptive, insolent and unintelligent pupils, had themselves, in their various ways, become infected with the debilitating SEN virus of low expectation, immature attitude, puerile opinions and infantile sense of humour. The only way to protect teachers against the effects of this insidious affliction is to limit their contact with the legions of under-achieving pupils who are its natural carriers. This, however, is extraordinarily difficult to achieve, due partly to the untested opinions of self-styled experts, who argue that the best way to understand and cope with disruption and low intelligence, is to be constantly exposed to it, and the reluctance of most intelligent and competent teachers to take on any difficult and challenging task without massive rewards. These twin forces conspire to ensure that those paid to teach the most difficult and, potentially, the most lethal of our future citizens are frequently the embittered failures, who find refuge in the massive quagmire of underachievement which swamps so many of our schools.

It certainly swamped the self-opinionated Pamela, whose effectiveness as a special needs teacher was seriously undermined by her own very special needs, which in many ways were more varied and profound than any suffered by her unfortunate pupils. These ranged from her desperate, but unacknowledged, need for a loving relationship with a man, to her more obvious requirements for a skilled hairdresser and personal shopper. She had the same mistaken and inflated view of her own sartorial elegance and good taste, as she had of her own opinions. Her only confidante on the entire staff was Cindy Beaumont, who over the years had been cowed and browbeaten into reluctant compliance, and who now accepted Pam's dominance with nauseating subservience.

Everyone else held her in varying degrees of contempt and tried, whenever possible, to ignore her. She always had something to contribute to the twice-weekly staff briefing meetings, usually led by Dr Douglas, but frequently taken over by Pam, as she explained and lectured us all upon some new earth-shattering initiative, which she had introduced to enhance the effectiveness of her department. These initiatives usually led to a marked and rapid decline in the behaviour and attention span of all those special needs pupils for whom she was responsible.

One such memorable initiative was her attempt to improve the behaviour of the most disruptive pupils in Year 7, by bringing in from the LEA a newly appointed behaviour counsellor called Jemma Jewson, who was that all too common phenomenon in LEA staffing, a person appointed to satisfy a politically correct agenda, and who was consequently, totally unsuited and unqualified for the role to which they were assigned.

For the enthusiastic Miss Jewson was a thirty-four year old failed ex-social worker who, a year previously had retrained, and had only recently returned to the job market with her newly acquired diploma in child counselling, and a very idealistic and dewy-eyed view of her mission to improve the behaviour and attitude of some of the most disturbed and disruptive eleven year olds in the country.

It was inevitably to prove a mission impossible! Miss Jewson was assigned a half-hour slot with each of the pupils selected by Pam, as likely to benefit from her dubious intervention. The most marked, and entirely predictable, outcome of these counselling sessions was a very marked deterioration in the behaviour of each pupil who attended. This was hardly surprising, since all reputable research has concluded that giving poorly behaved pupils extra and special attention will simply reinforce the very behaviour one desires to eliminate.

Of course Pam, The Senior Management Team and the LEA were unwilling to admit that the increase in poor behaviour among those attending counselling was in any way attributable to their sessions with Jemma. This was understandable, since such an admission would have exposed the entire initiative and reflected extremely badly upon the intelligence and judgement of those, responsible for its implementation.

It would be interesting to research, how many pupils' lives had been blighted by the reluctance of educators to admit the negative impact of their many, and infinitely varied, crackpot ideas and well-meaning initiatives; almost all of which are introduced without rigorous research, and continued with long after there is massive evidence of their obvious harm. We sacrifice so many of our children on 'the altar of bad ideas', and it is only incompetence and self-serving arrogance which condemns them to suffer long after such ideas are consigned to the dustbin of educational failure.

However, more than in most fields of human endeavour, education is renowned for its ability to recycle failed ideas and discredited theories. Anyone with twenty plus years teaching experience will have seen most theories and initiatives come around several times, often with different titles, fresh funding and new advocates, but with the same depressing failure rates. In the face of such evidence, no teacher of intelligence can avoid cynicism, or escape the conclusion that the education of all future generations is in the hands of enthusiastic educational experimenters, who latch on to ludicrous theories as a means to hoped-for promotion, and who, like all zealots who passionately embrace a new belief, do untold damage to the recipients of their blinkered enthusiasm.

Thus it was, that despite massive evidence to the contrary, the disastrous consequences of the Year 7 counselling intervention was allowed to continue and inflict upon the staff, a disruptive band of privileged and pampered performers, who knew that their insolence, disruption and ill-manners would be rewarded with time-out from lessons to tell their troubles and moan about their perceived victimisation to the silly, but sympathetic Miss Jewson.

This deplorable situation continued, until even those responsible for it began to appreciate its cataclysmic consequences and, searching for a way to end it without loss of face, they decided to stop counselling Year 7 pupils, and to shift the focus to Year 9, where many of the most disturbed and disruptive pupils had already gained a firmer foothold on the hillside to hell, and who were therefore in greater need of help and advice.

The major error of judgement in shifting the targets for counselling from Year 7 to Year 9 was the failure to appreciate that Year 9 contained, and was, the familiar and designated domain of the Empress of Evil herself, the terrifyingly lovely Layla Moon! Placing Layla into counselling with a well meaning innocent like Jemma Jewson was a mistake of monumental proportions, and its consequences would reverberate in the corridors of educational catastrophes for decades to come.

Despite all the evidence that Jemma's counselling sessions led to a significant worsening in pupil behaviour, Pam Potts decided that, because Layla's behaviour was considerably worse than any other pupil in the entire school, she should receive a double session with Jemma. It never occurred to Pam that this was very likely to exacerbate Layla's problems and lead to a predictable disaster. Of course, no-one could have predicted its scale, but all the signs that placing a youngster so disturbed as Layla in counselling with someone so naïvely incompetent as Jemma, would result in a tragedy, were plainly there for all to see.

Layla, who was as uncertain of her own emerging sexuality as she was of the reasons for her aggression, anger and delight in the suffering of others, found Jemma's interest in her motives and behaviour a heady aphrodisiac, and it was not long before she developed a profound fixation and intense crush upon Jemma, who quickly became an object of powerful and dangerous desires.

Most of Layla's psychological problems stemmed from her early abandonment by her parents who, unable to cope with her deviant and controlling behaviour, had given up their attempts to understand her increasingly inexplicable demands and tantrums. In fact, they were relieved when she was finally placed in the care of the local authority. This had occurred when Layla was eleven, and was subsequent to an unspecified incident which had occurred during the school summer holiday, when she had been making a very rare visit to stay with her mother and her stepfather at their country estate in Northumberland. Whatever had occurred had obviously been very serious, because instead of returning to stay with her father, she was taken into youth custody and eventually handed over to local social workers in Abercwmtwerp.

The nature of her offence was sufficiently worrying for Social Services to decide that she could no longer remain at home with her father.

They also very wisely decided that she was not a suitable candidate for fostering. They reached this conclusion after the emergency foster parents, who had been reluctantly persuaded to give her a temporary home, had returned her the very next morning, together with the shoe box containing the stiffened corpses of Brandy and Shandy, their own daughter's pet hamsters, which Layla had dispatched with the business end of her school compass.

Following this incident, Layla was, for a short time, in the hands of psychiatric professionals in the secure ward of St Joseph's Hospital, where new treatments were attempted with increasing desperation, and with diminishing success.

However, inexplicably, the onset of puberty marked a real, if brief, improvement in her behaviour, and by the time she reached twelve, she was considered to have made sufficient improvement to be placed back in local authority care, and they found her a place in 'Prospect House', the only secure childrens' home in the area. Here she seemed to settle in well, and right up until the time she started her counselling sessions with Jemma, her behaviour, although still disruptive and unpredictable, was just about manageable.

Unfortunately, after only a few weeks subjected to the intensity of Jemma's naïve concern, Layla began to re-exhibit some of her less welcome behaviours. In an attempt to gain even more time in

216

counselling and less in the classroom, she became increasingly insolent and unco-operative, frequently disrupting lessons and verbally abusing her teachers and others in her form. She threw a plate of chicken curry at one of the mid-day supervisors in the canteen at lunchtime, and when Miss Monk tried to restrain her she accused her of assault. Predictably, this deterioration in Layla's behaviour had the desired result, for Pam agreed with Jemma that Layla was in need of more counselling and recognised that many of her teachers were close to breaking point and desperately needed a break from her.

Layla, of course, viewed the increase in her contact time with Jemma as a total vindication of her bad behaviour, and saw no reason to improve, especially if this might mean a reduction, or even cessation of her counselling sessions. Finally however, after she trashed an 'A' level art exhibition in the school foyer, stole Frank Baldwin's wallet and car keys, set fire to some paint tins in Angus Paisley's Art Room and called Dr Douglas a 'fucking sad old git!', she was excluded from school for a month. Everyone but the staff in 'Prospect House', breathed an enormous sigh of relief, and were delighted by her absence.

Tragically, in their wisdom, the educational psychologists employed by the local authority, thought it advisable that Layla maintained her links with the school by allowing her to keep her contact with Jemma, and they arranged for Jemma to visit 'Prospect House' each day to continue her counselling.

Jemma, who was by nature a naïve and trusting soul, who believed in the innate goodness of children and the redeeming power of love, and who always tried to see the best in people, was horrified by the conditions in 'Prospect House', and viewed them as a cause, rather than a consequence of Layla's poor behaviour. She was also flattered by Layla's desire to continue in counselling, and totally misread her increasing dependency as a positive sign.

Jemma, who since her acrimonious divorce from Bobby Bucknell, a failed mobile upholstery and carpet cleaner from Pontypridd, had been somewhat lonely, and conscious of her childless status, was herself in need of counselling, and was also desperate for someone to love. This desperation, coupled with an increasing desire for a child, prompted her to offer to act as Layla's foster parent, and to give her a more stable and loving environment, than could possibly be provided by the staff at 'Prospect House'!

Jemma's offer, although unexpected and slightly unorthodox, was just too good to refuse, and was for the staff at 'Prospect House', better than a huge win on the National Lottery. Their desire to be rid of Layla was so acute that most of the usual checks and pre-fostering procedures were dispensed with, and in their eagerness to finally see the back of her, they failed to realise that her intense enthusiasm for the placement with Jemma, was the product of a powerfully developing lesbian desire, and not the needy response of a lonely and unloved child.

This misreading of Layla's real motivation in wishing to be fostered by Jemma, was not simply an unfortunate error of judgement by social workers and the staff at 'Prospect House', it was also a serious failing in their duty of care, not so much to Layla, who already possessed a vast and impressive range of survival skills, but to Jemma and the community at large, who were placed at risk by their desire to be free of Layla's demonic presence.

All the required paperwork for Layla's placement was completed in record time, and her transfer to Jemma's care occurred within a few days of her stated desire to give Layla a new start and a secure and loving home.

When Pam Potts announced in the staff room that Jemma had offered Layla a secure home, I thought that providing a secure home for Layla was a brilliant idea, but I doubted that the required cells, bars, locks, alarms, searchlights, razor-wire and permanent dog patrols within electrified high security fencing, could be easily installed in and around Jemma's two bedroom maisonette on Appletree Drive.

Named for a distant and more rural idyll, Appletree Drive had long since lost the trees which once grew in a small orchard adjacent to the sixties developed block of eight two-bedroom maisonettes, which made up the uninspiring block known as 'Orchard Court'.

Jemma resided at number 6, which occupied the first floor on the left side of the building. Outside was an external concrete staircase, which led to a red paint-chipped door on an enclosed landing, containing Jemma's small potted geranium, which struggled to survive the bleakness of its sad and sunless position.

Since her separation from Bobby Bucknell, Jemma had endeavoured to make a home of 6 Orchard Court, but despite her best efforts, the results were lamentable, since she possessed neither talent, money, or taste. Unfortunately, her idea of contemporary living had been heavily influenced by the design gurus responsible for the Argos catalogue, and Sid Burke, the geriatric and opinionated sales assistant in the home-ware department at her local B&Q. Consequently, the fixtures, fittings and décor of 6 Orchard Court were a perfect example of the 'catalogue catastrophe' school of interior design, and provided a suitably cheap and tasteless setting for the final flowering of Layla's loony lesbian desires.

Much later, Layla was to blame her emerging lesbian tendencies on her early exposure to internet porn-sites, which she was encouraged to view by other kids, whilst she was resident at Prospect House. Whatever the truth of her influences and motivation, the results of her actions became all too painfully obvious. For, only a week after her move from Prospect House to become Jemma's fantasy daughter, she left the warmth and security of her recently purchased IKEA chrome and pine single bed and crossed the small landing at 1.00am in the morning, to acquaint Jemma with the nature and intensity of her own, and as yet unfulfilled, fantasies.

Jemma, who was sound asleep in the queen sized double bed she had bought in an unwarranted moment of optimism, was happily enjoying an erotic dream about Manuel Mendoza, the Spanish waiter with whom she had experienced a torrid, and all too brief an affair, during her recent holiday in Majorca. Such was the power and eroticism of her dream, she remained blissfully unaware that Layla had silently slipped beneath her hypoallergenic duck down duvet and was now lying beside her, and skilfully increasing the reality of her dream, by imitating moves she had learned from a website called lesbianlovlies.com. It was an encounter which may not have ended so tragically and abruptly, if Layla had not misread Jemma's small whimpers of satisfaction as a sign of acceptance, and moved to try another, much more invasive erotic technique she'd once witnessed on a much more extreme site called anal virgins. The results of this miscalculation was Layla's immediate return to Social Services and Jemma's three month incarceration in the secure wing of St Joseph's Psychiatric Hospital, where she struggled to recover from the traumatic consequences of her doomed attempt to provide Layla with a secure and loving home.

Staff at the hospital said later that Jemma's recovery would have been much quicker, had it not been for the additional tragedy of the total destruction of her home, for, a few days after her admittance, Layla escaped from the young offenders unit where she had been temporarily placed, and posted a petrol bomb through the front door of number 6 Orchard Court. The resulting inferno left both Jemma and two other residents homeless, and the burnt out and smoke blackened shell which remained served as a tangible reminder of the sometimes tragic consequences of an unshakeable conviction in the essential innocence of the young.

Layla only felt her revenge complete when the doctors signed her committal papers to St Joseph's, from where she was able to observe through the bars of her first floor padded cell, the forlorn figure of Jemma being impatiently fed baby food in the rose garden beneath, by Myrtle Smith, an obese and brutal ward orderly with bad breath, foul body odour, and an utter contempt for all manifestations of mental illness.

Still, the one positive outcome from this series of very unfortunate events was the final abandonment of all the special needs counselling sessions, and as a consequence, a steady improvement in the behaviour of all those pupils who'd been selected to participate.

Gradually, things within the SEN Department returned to their usual status, of muddled, but largely benign incompetence, although Pam Potts still refused to acknowledge the true reasons for the cessation of the counselling sessions, choosing instead to blame LEA budget cuts as the explanation for their cancellation.

Most teachers were however, very relieved that the sessions had ended, and I was thankful that most crackpot educational experiments, although blessedly non-effective, did not end in such tragedy, as Jemma Jewson's counselling sessions in behaviour improvement!

Chapter 16

The Year 11 Prom

Apart from the production of the Year 11 Year Book, the other mixed-blessing legacy bequeathed to all subsequent Heads of Year by the short, but dynamic reign of Davina-May Dallas, was the Year 11 Prom.

This ubiquitous American import, was now an annual event, and ever since its introduction had proved to be a heady mix of seething anticipation and potential disaster.

The first, but by no means the only difficulty was finding a venue large enough, and where the management were sufficiently naïve and reckless as to allow nearly two-hundred, highly excited and inexperienced sixteen-year-olds to attend a formal dinner and dance in their well cared for and valued premises. Most of the suitable venues locally had already been victims of their own folly in hosting a Year 11 Prom and consequently, had banned all future events from their establishments. The closest and most convenient venue, 'Duke's Court Manor Hotel and County Club' had unfortunately, been off limits to all school events since they'd hosted a prom for a comprehensive school in a neighbouring valley, affectionately known as 'Coalpits Castle,' after its comparison by pupils in the fifties to a certain notorious German POW camp.

Apparently the experience had been so traumatic, and the consequences so horrendous, that the general manager was still in therapy and the young female banqueting manager, who had fled the premises in tears during the food fight in the Marquis Suite, was struggling to come off invalidity benefit and resume what was left of her shattered career. It was common knowledge that a small party of established and valued clients, who'd been enjoying an al-fresco wedding anniversary celebration dinner on the South Terrace, had been forced to swim the eighty metre wide, weed infested ornamental lake, to escape a large crowd of inebriated teenage marauders, who thought it would be fun to help themselves to the Dom Perignon pink champagne, which the party had ordered to toast their host's anniversary. All in all, what with the impromptu striptease by members of the school's rugby team, the vomit filled toilets, the missing valuables from several of the guest bedrooms, the couple caught fornicating in one of the small conference rooms and the dead swan discovered the following morning in the recently refurbished indoor spa, it was little wonder that the venue was forever closed to any future school proms. This was a great pity, since it was one of the very few local establishments which could accommodate the numbers and was isolated enough to ensure that the kids couldn't visit local hostelries to top up on alcohol.

Having promised the kids a prom when they were in Year 7, the one option not available was to abandon the whole enterprise and allow them to simply leave school with no end of Year 11 celebration. The problem was, finding a venue where the management had not yet experienced the pleasures of hosting an event for a very large number of socially incompetent and hormonally rampant sixteen year olds, and so, might just be naïve enough to be persuaded that the event would be both profitable and relatively risk free. As you may imagine, not an easy assignment, especially with the added responsibility of ensuring that the occasion would be a sober affair, with a total absence of alcohol. Attempting to keep British schoolchildren, steeped as they are in a deep rooted culture of drunkenness and binge drinking, away from the temptation of alcohol, was a task on a par with trying to prevent a bunch of Tottenham supporters from verbally abusing the referee when he's just awarded a penalty to Arsenal in the final seconds of extra time in an FA cup final. In fact, as close to impossible, without actually being impossible, as it's possible to get!

Of course, most hoteliers were aware of this, and rightly viewed the combination of teenage revellers and alcohol with understandable alarm. For this reason, all city-centre hotels were out of the question, since they all occupied positions close to numerous pubs, clubs and dangerous drugs. The difficulty of finding a suitable venue was so daunting and time consuming, that quite a few schools of my acquaintance had refused to organise a Year 11 prom. Others, less unsympathetic to the kid's enjoyment, had been forced to hold their prom in their unattractive, inadequate and depressingly familiar school halls. This did have the advantage of severely limiting the number of kids who wished to attend, but it possessed none of the impact and excitement generated by a night out surrounded by the sophistication and mystery of a swish hotel.

If education is about anything, then it ought to be about widening horizons and giving kids exciting and challenging experiences. I'd promised my Year 11 a prom, and the very least I could do was to ensure it was a very memorable event, and not a depressing disaster, held in the appalling environment of the school hall, with its spit stained windows, plastic chairs and tables, harsh lights, inadequate and filthy toilets, crap sound system, unswept and dirty floor, and dinner prepared by the cabbage catastrophe cooks from the school canteen and the soft drinks bar staffed by the well intentioned, but inevitably censorious, ladies of the P.T.A..

Knowing that it was imperative to find an alternative to this nightmare scenario, I began my search early, and started approaching possible venues whilst the kids were still in Year 10. I tried golf clubs, country clubs, tennis clubs, yacht clubs, rowing clubs, rugby clubs, flying clubs, cricket clubs, football clubs, snooker clubs, athletic clubs, Labour clubs, Conservative clubs, Liberal clubs, social clubs, British Legion clubs and strip clubs; large hotels, small hotels, resort hotels, seedy hotels, temperance hotels and motels; town halls, civic halls, village halls, masonic halls, concert halls, church halls, scout halls, music halls, dance halls, assembly halls and drill halls; museums, art galleries, castles, antique centres, leisure centres, shopping centres, garden centres, art centres, holiday camps, army camps, caravan parks, municipal parks, theme parks and science parks. In desperation, I contacted The National Trust, to see if they would provide one of their fine country mansions, but all to no avail. I even investigated the cost of hiring a luxury marquee, but when told that my requirements would cost in excess of £30,000, I resumed my search for a more affordable venue. When, by the start of Year 11, I had still not managed to find anywhere, and just as I was beginning to despair that I would be able to fulfil my Year 7 promise, I had an amazing and totally unexpected piece of good fortune.

An old boyfriend of my eldest daughter Lauren was unexpectedly appointed the manager of a soon to be opened local hotel close to the M4 Motorway to be called 'The Lakeside Palace Resort Hotel'. I realised immediately, that this would provide the perfect opportunity to place the Year 11 Prom in a venue which was new, exciting and which I was certain could be coerced into agreeing to host the event, and do so for a reasonable price; for the manager designate and Lauren's ex-boyfriend was a larger than life professional Irishman called Cormac O'Malley. Cormac was a thirty-five year old, black haired, blue eyed, handsome and admirable rogue, originally from the wilds of County Galway. He was as full of Irish charm as he was of Blarney Stone bullshit. He was a first division drinker, who'd cut his considerable teeth in the catering trade, by first managing, and then owning, several pubs in various counties; always managing to move on and further his career just before the breweries' auditors had an opportunity to thoroughly examine his books. Eventually, he abandoned the role of publican after his insurance company finally paid his huge claim for the total loss by fire of The Stag and Stoat, a grade two listed, thatched county pub in the picturesque English village of Woolbury-under-Wenge; where he'd angered the county set by banning the local hunt from crossing a paddock which he owned at the rear of the pub's car park and refusing to allow them to gather outside the pub for their traditional Boxing Day stirrup-cup. He also managed to alienate most of the local residents by holding regular Irish theme nights, where Guinness and Jameson's Whiskey was half price and numerous itinerant Irish musicians of his acquaintance would turn up and play accordions, fiddles, guitars, banjos, bodhrans, flutes, whistles and the Uilleann pipes long into the night. These regular jamborees attracted into the village numerous ex-pat Irish vagrants, who set up a kind of New Age Celtic village in his paddock, complete with caravans, tepees and benders, where the revelry and music would often continue until dawn. Needless to say, his tenure as

224

the owner and landlord of their ancient inn was most unwelcome among nearby residents and his departure would have been universally applauded, had it not been occasioned by the total destruction of their beloved local.

His next venture was as banqueting manager for a large newly opened hotel on the outskirts of Bristol. From here, with its many opportunities for wheeling and dealing, he gradually earned a reputation for filling all the hotel conference and banqueting facilities for every available slot. In less than eighteen months he was promoted to assistant manager and at the commencement of his second year he was made general manager. He swiftly became the most successful manager in the group and when the group's directors were faced with selecting someone to manage The Lakeside Palace, their new resort hotel and the group's flagship establishment, Cormac was their unopposed choice.

I learned all this during my first visit to see him in his swish new Scandinavian style office to persuade him to host our Year 11 Prom. It was a request he could hardly refuse, since his lovely wife, Siobhan, was blissfully unaware that his brief spell as my daughter's boyfriend had begun less than a year after their marriage, and had continued for some four months, until Lauren learned the truth regarding his marital status. At the time I was mindful not to destroy his family by telling Siobhan of his infidelity and I was now very grateful that at the time I'd also persuaded Lauren to remain silent.

After we'd exchanged the usual pleasantries I enquired about Siobhan and was informed that they now had three children and were happy and very much in love. I expressed my congratulations and said that I sincerely hoped that nothing would occur in the future to disrupt their happiness. I then outlined the immense difficulties I was having in finding a suitable venue for my Year 11 Prom and, that I would be extremely grateful for anything he could do to help. I drove away an hour later with the assurance that, not only would the hotel be delighted to host the prom, but that we could have the entire Hawaiian Suite, their finest banqueting room, free of charge, that the selected menu would be subject to a 50% discount and the hotel would also happily provide a disco, photographer, cartoon artist, professional video of the event and a complimentary non-alcoholic drinks reception without additional charge. It was an offer far beyond my most hopeful expectations and was a powerful reminder that our infidelities are seldom without cost.

Back at school there was a palpable ripple of excitement and anticipation when, at the next year assembly I informed the kids that, not only would they be having their prom, but that it would be held in the luxurious and highly exclusive surroundings of the Hawaiian Suite at the Lakeside Palace Resort Hotel. It was undoubtedly an achievement of heroic proportions, and my announcement sent many staff into a paroxysm of resentment and envy. It was a triumph equal to the dreams of a conquering Caesar, and elevated my reputation among the kids to a status not enjoyed since the insane emperor Caligula elevated his horse 'Incitatus' to the rank of Consul of Rome.

However, before the kids could enjoy the fleeting euphoria of their forthcoming prom, they first had to endure the far larger and less pleasant experience of their G.C.S.E. examinations. These narrow and uninformative markers of supposed academic excellence were valued by the S.M.T. and the government as indicators of the school's achievements. The bench mark of this success was the much vaunted five 'A' to 'C' grades. Any pupils who failed to achieve this very well publicised standard was branded as unsuitable for the more rigorous demands of 'A' levels, which were also very poor indicators of talent or potential. In fact, extremely high academic results were rarely a reliable guide to earnings, fulfilment, social acceptance, achievement, or happiness and contentment. Considering that they indicated so very little, it was always a mystery to me that they were valued so highly. It was, however, indicative of the immense failure of imagination, which prevented so many professional educators from appreciating those immeasurable qualities and gifts, which are the true markings of human value, and the genuine signs of individual worth.

I remember very clearly, being extremely depressed when invigilating a G.C.S.E. examination, as I witnessed the intense concentration of so many earnest and furiously scribbling students, who'd been suckered into believing that, this was there one and best opportunity to demonstrate to the world, their parents, their teachers and potential future employers, their knowledge and achievements. Of course, after so many years of relentless indoctrination, most of my kids were also seduced by the G.C.S.E. propaganda machine, and so, inevitably joined the ranks of those striving to succeed. I knew that, for every eventually supposed triumph, there would be future failures and for each imagined failure, there would be future success. Certainly life's a bitch, but thankfully it's a bitch which cares not a jot for exam results!

Eventually, the long and largely meaningless ordeal of their G.C.S.E examinations was over and the evening of The Prom became like a beacon of fun and sanity in a world of disappointment and dross. There were just over one hundred and sixty pupils attending The Prom. Months previously I'd barred those most likely to cause a major problem, even so, it was a risky business to take such a large number of highly excitable sixteen-year-olds into sophisticated and expensive surroundings, where they would be expected to display new and unfamiliar social skills.

My main concern was the easy availability of alcohol and the need to keep it, and the kids, well apart. The obvious sources of supply were the stretched limousines which the kids had hired to transport them from their homes to The Lakeside Palace Resort Hotel. It was customary for the companies operating these tacky American imports to offer package deals, where their over-excited passengers were plied with cheap champagne to enhance the experience of being wafted to their chosen destination in the plush bowels of these mobile tart's boudoirs, where, in addition to the heady mix of alcohol and sexual tension, was added the extra stimulation of flashing lights, throbbing music and seductive perfume. It was a deadly combination, designed to heighten anticipation and lower inhibitions. I'd long since arranged that no alcohol would be available within the Hawaiian Suite of the hotel, but short of searching every pupil upon arrival, it was impossible to ensure that no-one had smuggled in a secret supply.

When at last the long awaited evening finally arrived, my wife and I ensured that we were at the venue early, to check all the arrangements and to be there to greet the kids as they arrived in their stretch limousines beneath the Grand Portico. This impressive entrance to the Lakeside Palace was decorated in mock Grecian splendour and provided the perfect setting for the arrival of our guests. At the hotel's expense I'd arranged for a professional photographer to record the evening and also hired a company to film the event for posterity and the kid's absent parents. With the photographer stationed on one side of the pillared entrance and the film crew on the other, the scene resembled a set for a Hollywood film premiere.

Fortunately, it was a glorious evening, bathed in the revealing light of mid-summer. The grounds of the hotel were a stunning mixture of immaculately manicured lawns, distant woods with glimpses of marble temples bathed in the sun's amber light, and closer to, an enormous ornamental lake, with islands, waterfalls, weeping willows and twelve specially imported black swans, which glided serenely past, silhouetted against the silver surface of the gently rippling water. A wide gravelled drive snaked its way through this idyllic landscape from the unseen lodge which stood nearly a mile distant, by the huge wrought-iron gates which marked the entrance to this mock earthly paradise. The road crossed a beautiful white stone, twelve-arch bridge, which spanned the lake before dividing around a large, pristine circular lawn, in the centre of which was a fountain, where countless plumes of water rose and fell in perfect synchronisation with the sound of Vivaldi's Four Seasons. Completing the scene, four magnificent peacocks displayed their shimmering iridescent tails to a disinterested and dowdy peahen, which seemed totally unimpressed by their macho posturing.

It was into this breathtaking setting that, a few moments later, the leading car in a long procession of gleaming limousines delivered the first contingent of over one hundred and sixty over excited Year 11's to the very imposing entrance to the Lakeside Palace. They spilled out onto the gleaming white Italian marble reception area. The boys, stiff and uncertain in their first ever dinner suits and the girls, outshining even the brilliance of the peacocks in their stunningly coloured evening dresses and ball-gowns. Many of the girls wore tiaras, and, as is the current fashion, also sported a corsage of flowers at their wrists. It was amazing to see how fabulous they all looked. The transformation from the depressing and sexless anonymity afforded by their school uniforms into infinitely desirable young men and women was almost complete. All that stood between them and genuine sophistication and elegance was youth and inexperience. However, this lack of mature self-awareness only added to the intensity of their emotions and the absolute charm of their naïvety.

As they spilled out from their limousines, they were all excited and voluble, greeting their friends and commenting enthusiastically on each others suits and dresses. Two memorable outfits were Ben Jacobs, who wore a white suit with a shot-silk black waistcoat decorated with white sequins, which he wore over a black shirt and white bow tie, and Hannah Austin, who'd developed into the prettiest girl in the school, and who was attired in a simple black backless sheath dress, with a black multi-stringed jet necklace and matching tiara set in her long blond hair. They both proved the exception to the truth of the saying 'youth is wasted on the young'.

Once all were assembled, they were ushered through the stunning foyer with its mock Greek statues, brilliantly lit marble fountains and verdant palm trees into the reception and bar area of the Hawaiian Suite, which had been designed to replicate a South Sea island paradise. It was as far removed from their normal experience as it was possible to get. Unfortunately, they were all far too excited and inexperienced to fully appreciate the splendour of their surroundings. They were all given a glass of non-alcoholic sparking white wine, to which I'm sure, many added large measures from the miniature vodka bottles they had secreted in a pocket, evening bag, or other more intimate hiding place.

The photographer and film crew had now moved inside, and were busy photographing and filming groups and individuals. The kids looked the equal of any gathering of Hollywood A list celebrities and easily outshone most of the teachers, who had obviously just dusted off their tired and out-dated dinner suits and unflattering dresses, bought when most were a size 12 and now struggling to contain the results of years of over-indulgence and failed diets.

Angus Paisley had even turned up in a charcoal-grey lounge suit, which had what appeared to be dried egg on the lapel and looked as though it had come from the bargain rail of an Oxfam shop. I felt very tempted to ask him to leave! The one very noticeable exception to this motley collection of fashion catastrophes was the silk burgundy Grecian style dress worn by Concepta O'Conner, who looked ravishingly gorgeous, and who had been every male member of staff's fantasy since her memorable erotic nun act in the recent talent show.

Whilst everyone was busy drinking and socialising I took the opportunity to check the final preparations for dinner in the Hawaiian Suite. I was pleased to see that all was ready. The twenty circular tables were all draped with pristine white linen table-cloths with silver and lilac balloons floating above central table decorations of sumptuous baskets of tropical fruit. Soft music was being piped through the PA system and the maître d' and his team of immaculately dressed staff were all ready to serve the first course. The stage was set, ready for the later appearance of the eight piece rock and blues band, and off to one side the DJ was making final adjustments to his very impressive rig. All that could be done to ensure that this was a successful and memorable evening was now finally in place, and so I asked the maître d' to announce that dinner was served.

Everyone had already consulted the large table plan in the reception area, and so, knew their table number and where it was located. Their admittance into the splendour of the Hawaiian Suite was a joy to behold. Young and inexperienced as they were, they were obviously impressed by the sight which greeted their entrance. It was immensely gratifying to realise that all the months of planning and hard work were now finally appreciated.

During the meal, which was, due to Cormac O'Malley's fear of my possible revelations to his unsuspecting wife, surprisingly good, the film crew and photographer constantly circulated, recording every small event for the future viewing pleasure of the kids' absent, but extremely interested parents.

The room was buzzing with excited conversations, somewhat too loud atmospheric background music and the steadily increasing inebriation of one hundred and sixty alcohol intolerant teenagers, many of whom had been surreptitiously adding the contents of their concealed vodka miniatures to the sparkling grape juice, which I'd persuaded Cormac to supply free of charge.

By the time the meal had ended and the speeches had begun, most of the kids were at that heady stage between sobriety and sickness, where the intensity of the moment obliterates reason and fails to recognise false emotion. They were at that alcohol-fuelled time of fantasy and excitement; just beyond the reach of responsibility and not yet cognisant of consequences. They were experiencing that very small window of illusory promise, which intensifies the present, dims the past, and blanks the future. The seduction of such moments is so great, that despite the awful experience of intense hangovers, many are persuaded to pursue such brief moments of delusional immortality time after time, after time. It is the desire for such fleeting intoxication which makes the vintners rich and their victims grateful. There are in life, very few experiences which confound life's disappointments quite as effectively as the power of alcoholic euphoria, which fills the space between responsibility and regret with a brief, yet deluded vision of what, at their very best, human beings might just be capable of.

It was extremely unlikely however, that any of the increasingly inebriated kids would have had the faintest perception of such philosophical musings. Most were only just capable of describing the state of alcoholic ecstasy as 'getting bladdered', or 'rat arsed'; revealing the ineffectiveness of their English lessons to raise their linguistic ability to a higher level.

By the time the few mandatory speeches were over, most of the kids were anxious for the commencement of the music and dancing. I signalled the music to begin and within moments the atmosphere in the Hawaiian Suite changed from an elegant dining room to a pulsating night club. It was not long before the room was littered with discarded bow ties, abandoned stilettos and cast aside sequined evening bags, as one hundred and sixty variously intoxicated teens took to the dance floor.

It was time for the staff to move to the bar in the Hawaiian Suite's reception area to enjoy a well deserved alcoholic drink and escape the tuneless insanity of 'Dynamite Dan's Dynamic Disco'. Dan, whose idea of volume, rhythm and melody had been heavily influenced by his day job as a pneumatic drill operator in a motorway road gang,

231

was in his element, as he spun a selection of contemporary sounds, which bore as much relationship to music, as did the kid's insane gyrations, to any sort of recognisable dance. As all of us 'responsible adults' left the Hawaiian Suite for the relative calm of the bar, the scene behind us rapidly descended into a pulsating, gyrating, heavily perspiring riot of colour, noise and flashing lights, as the flamboyantly dressed and intoxicated kids careered and stomped around the dance floor in a display of youthful exuberance and energy which made a Sioux war dance seem sedate by comparison. It was an exhilarating scene, which lived on in my memory long after the even greater chaos which was to follow.

For, as I enjoyed my first and only drink of the evening, perched on a mock leopard skin bar stool and struggling to show an interest in Angus Paisley's plans to create 'living art' by persuading his VI Form students to allow themselves to be utilised as living canvases, upon which his most talented Year 7s could express themselves with fluorescent body paint; Nathan Hyde, who'd been excluded from the Prom on the grounds that he was a dysfunctional and unpredictable maniac, was breaking into the Hawaiian Suite's male toilet through an open Velux roof window and was busy selling cocaine, ecstasy and cannabis-resin, to all the dinner suited drunks who strayed into his well prepared drug dispensing cubicle. What Nathan was totally unaware of, as he casually tossed what he falsely imagined was a spent match into the waste bin for the soft cotton hand towels, was the very sensitive and inappropriate setting assigned to the hotel's smoke detection system by Melvin Flood, the incompetent fire prevention engineer, who'd been responsible for the installation of the Lakeside Palace's fire protection system. Unfortunately for us all attending this most marvellous evening, Melvin had set all the smoke detectors at their lowest possible setting and they were so sensitive that they would have responded to the smoke residue of an extinguished candle. Faced, as they now were, by the intense smoke and fumes from a flaming bin, they went into full operational mode and in addition to emitting an ear piercing alarm, activated the new and highly efficient sprinklers installed throughout the hotel.

This event sadly coincided with the police raid organised by Chief Inspector Bradley and his team of twenty officers and five dog handlers from the drugs squad, who'd been waiting months for the opportunity to apprehend Nathan in the act of supply and his clandestine visit to the Prom, had finally provided them with their chance.

At precisely the moment they burst into the frenetic and pulsating chaos of the Hawaiian Suite, where at least one hundred and forty teenagers were leaping and whirling to the manic and unearthly noise of Dynamite Dan's Dynamic Disco, the huge array of overhead sprinklers proved the manufacturers claims regarding their awesome power and effectiveness. For, had there actually been a fire in the Hawaiian Suite, it would have been extinguished in seconds. As it was, the immediate effect of this gigantic power shower, was to rapidly cleanse the sweat and quell the ardour of the stunned, screaming and increasingly panicked dancers, who found themselves plunged into semi-darkness as the main lights went out and the emergency low level escape lighting took its place.

Equally nonplussed, and arrested in their purpose, was Chief Inspector Bradley and his drenched drug squad team of over enthusiastic officers; but by far the worst affected by the madness and mayhem were the five fearsome police dogs, who in the confusion, noise, deluge and the explosions now issuing from Dynamite Dan's Drowning Disco, had broken free from their handlers and contributed a new and unwelcome element to the scene, by enthusiastically joining the mess of bodies ineffectively struggling to remain upright on the inches deep water slick, which had transformed the highly polished dance floor, into a surface as slippery as a police skid pan. As girls collapsed in clouds of wet taffeta and boys slid and slipped in a vain effort to save them, the dogs barked, snarled salivated and tore into everything which moved. Fortunately, this was mostly the hems of brightly coloured ball gowns, which fluttered and flapped before them like distress flags in a high wind.

Myself, and all the staff, who'd been enjoying our drinks at the bar in the Hawaiian Suite's reception area, fared slightly better, for thankfully, the torrent of water which flooded from the numerous sprinklers was rapidly absorbed by the luxurious deep piled wine red carpet, and all the dogs were fully occupied on the dance floor, but we still all received a thorough soaking, before most managed to escape via the large double door fire exit adjacent to the bar.

Aware of my responsibilities as the organiser of this rapidly deteriorating event, I headed back into the hell of the Hawaiian Suite to save as many as possible from the deluge, the demented dogs and the dangers of Dynamite Dan's Disco, which was now crackling, spitting and exploding like renegade jumping jacks at a firework display. The dogs were barking and snarling in a most terrifying manner. The police, some of whom were now collapsed on the floor, struggled to remain upright, as they shone their torches into the melee in an attempt to illuminate the utter chaos which was now the Year 11 Prom! They were desperately trying to call off the dogs and calm the panicking kids. Girls were screaming, boys were shouting, dogs were howling and yelping as police riot batons descended on their skulls in a vain attempt to persuade them to release their grip upon some unfortunate teen in imminent danger of being torn to pieces.

As I stood in the doorway, surveying this scene and considering what action I could possibly take to alleviate its worst effects, the alarm unexpectedly ceased, the sprinklers stopped and the main lights came back on, to reveal the true scale of the devastation.

It was a scene which was to live a very long time in my memory and haunt my sleepless nights into my well deserved retirement. Kids were weeping and wailing. Once stunningly beautiful dresses were tattered and torn. Discarded shoes and sequined handbags floated by on a slick of fast receding water. Lurex tights were ripped and spotted with blood and canine saliva. Dynamite Dan was sobbing uncontrollably, as his £5,000 disco deck and light show spluttered their final sounds, and then died! Chief Inspector Bradley uttered an unrepeatable expletive, as the last and largest of the still uncaptured police dogs sunk its well cared for canines into the soft flesh of his inner left thigh, as he desperately tried to rise and re-establish some semblance of order. It was a vision of hell, which would have made a suitable subject for the terrifying imagination of Hieronymus Bosch.

The only sight which provided any relief from the general despair and mayhem was Concepta O'Conner, whose skin tight burgundy dress was now so wet that it was almost transparent, and revealed quite clearly the fact that she had dispensed with both bra and knickers, in her desire not to spoil the smooth outline of her very expensive and wonderfully revealing gown. She was a vision of such divine loveliness that, for years afterwards, I was able to summon the memory as a counterpoint to the nightmare end to my Year 11's final event, and my very last, and in many ways most successful, attempt to ensure that they all had a memorable send off!

Chapter 17

Goodbye to all that!

Following the end of the Year 11 Prom and the kid's departure, some to hospital, others to the comfort of their chaotic and untidy bedrooms and a very few to the holding cells of Abercwmtwerp Police Station, there was, unfortunately for me, still four weeks to endure before the end of term and the arrival of the day when I could commence my new and eagerly anticipated status as a retired teacher, with no further responsibilities for the education of the young.

As Head of Year 11, and with Year 11 no longer in attendance, I was suddenly free of all my pastoral responsibilities and with retirement attractively looming like the last and longest holiday of my entire life, I determined to relax and enjoy my final few weeks in the confusion, chaos and endemic incompetence that is British education!

If my attitude and demeanour was previously considered as maverick, obstructionist and unhelpful, I now added to my already renowned and well deserved unpopularity, a demob happy attitude of monumental unconcern, indifference and cynicism, which only those who are fireproofed by circumstance can afford to exhibit.

Determined to enjoy my final month and convinced that a little subversion is always good for the health of any organisation, particularly schools, I made a public display of incinerating all documents I possessed relating to the National Curriculum, all circulars offering unhelpful guidance from the DfES, all the unread handouts foisted on me during many wasted days attending ineffectual and irrelevant in-service training courses, and sweetest of all, Dr Douglas's tedious and uninspiring School Development Plan.

During the remainder of my English lessons, the kids were treated to many new and unfamiliar topics, as I totally abandoned the straight

236

jacket of the National Curriculum, and strived to make my last weeks the most sustained and intense retirement party in the annuls of British educational history. I encouraged all my classes to express their appreciation of my teaching career with cards, gifts and tearful goodbyes. The most expensive and appreciated presents I deliberately displayed on a long side table, suitably and prominently labelled with the name of the giver, accompanied by a sentimental personal thank you card from me, extolling the generosity and worth of the pupil responsible. I actively manipulated this orgy of present giving by focusing on its competitive element, awarding the most generous pupils with house points, gold stars and free time.

As the gifts, cards and good wishes grew, so too did my determination not to tolerate any behaviour likely to sour my long goodbye. Consequently, when Giovanni Demarco and Onslow Jones disrupted a class discussion of Shakespeare's sonnet number 18 by comparing Aimie-Lee Harris to a fucking slag whose tits were more tempting than the darling buds of May, I asked them to leave the room, and when they refused I physically removed them, with the rest of the class whooping and shouting their approval and encouragement. By the time I'd man-handled them both into the corridor, they were completely nonplussed and uncomprehending of what was occurring. Used as they were, to no challenge or consequences ever being offered in response to their obscene and loutish behaviour, they were at a loss as to how to proceed.

Finally, Onslow mumbled 'You can't touch me', to which, I responded; 'pardon?' The irony was totally wasted on him, for he replied,

'I'm going to get my mum on to you.'

'Your mum,' I bellowed. You'd better get your father, your useless brother, your dreadful sisters, your uncles, aunts, cousins, neighbours and your friends, if you have any, because, you spotty faced, obnoxious little oik, your mother'll be no match for me!'

Before either of them recovered sufficiently to reply, I informed them they were no longer welcome in my class and that if they dared to appear for their next lesson I would eject them with sufficient speed and violence to make their eyeballs bleed, and with that I returned to my class and the roars of unanimous approval of the other kids, who were as fed up with Demarco and Jones as were the rest of the staff.

My anticipated summons to Douglas's office came just before lunch, and I arrived promptly, passing the subdued figures of Demarco and Jones, who were sat on a couple of chairs just outside the door. As I knocked I glared at them both and said how much I was going to enjoy the final three weeks free of their revolting presence.

When I entered, I was delighted to see that Douglas had invited Bert Bowen and Vic Davies to provide him with support.

'Good afternoon gentlemen,' I smiled, sensing their nervousness and discomfort, as I took the proffered seat and awaited their condemnation.

It was Bert who opened the proceedings, by asking if I'd physically thrown Giovanni Demarco and Onslow Jones out of my English lesson.

'Yes,' I said, 'their behaviour was insulting and unacceptable and when I told them to leave the room they refused, saying that I couldn't make them. So I decided to disabuse them of the notion that they were untouchable.'

'But you can't just throw them out of your lesson,' Bert protested.

'Pardon?' I replied, for the second time that day and with a similar lack of appreciation of my irony.

'They have a right to be educated,' Bert said, obviously influenced by some crackpot clause in 'The Children Act' or some lunatic provision in European human rights legislation.

'Yes,' I agreed, 'they do have a right to be educated, but I have a right not to be abused and insulted in my place of work, by a couple of moronic low-lives, whose educational aspirations rise no higher than their testicles, which unfortunately, seems to be the location for what laughingly passes for their brains. It's simply a question of whose rights take priority here. Is it their right to be educated, or my right not to suffer abuse and insult?'

'That's all very well,' Douglas chirped up, 'but they said you kicked them out for the rest of the term and that they couldn't come back into your lesson.'

'Correct!' I agreed, 'In case you hadn't noticed, the rest of the term consists of three weeks, during which, they would attend twelve more lessons, it's simply that, during those three weeks Demarco and Jones are not going to be taught by me.'

'But you can't do that.' Douglas responded, now obviously beginning to be annoyed by my attitude.

'Look gentlemen,' I said, 'I appreciate your dilemma, but it is *your* dilemma, so let me help you resolve it. You have, as my employers, a legal duty of care for my health and safety at work. A duty of care, which, for the past several years, you have singularly failed to fulfil; in view of this, I have reluctantly been forced to take the steps necessary to protect my well-being and mental health. I thought this action preferable to contacting my union, my doctor, my MP and the local and national media, to highlight your collective and persistent failure to protect myself and other members of staff from continual disruption, insolence and stress, but of course, if you insist upon Demarco and Jones's rights to an education over and above my rights to work in a safe and secure environment, then I shall be forced to reconsider my decision to provide you with this opportunity to exercise your responsibilities.'

As the implication of my remarks sank in I told them that my resolve not to teach Demarco and Jones for the remainder of the term was no idle threat, and that if they appeared for their next scheduled lesson I would refuse to admit them.

Douglas spluttered, but was clearly now almost incapable of rational discourse. Bert's mouth was opening and closing like a fish out of water, and Vic Davies had long since lost interest in pursuing a confrontation they were not going to win.

Before they'd sufficiently recovered their composure to continue their defence of pupil rights, I said that if there was nothing further I had a lesson to prepare, and left them to deliberate their future actions.

It was with a satisfied sense of victory that I taught 10/BB their final twelve lessons without Demarco or Jones making an appearance.

Finally, the last day of term arrived, and with it my final day. There was a long standing tradition at the end of the summer term that the kids finished school at mid-day, so the staff could have a buffet lunch in the main hall, where Douglas would say an official 'goodbye' and an insincere 'thank you' to all those staff who were leaving to take up new posts, or who were, like me, fortunate enough to be heading into the child and responsibility free realm of retirement. Undoubtedly, the retirees were the most envied of those who'd not be returning, since the others would mostly be swapping one dirty uncared for and stressful environment for another, and one set of scruffy, unimaginative and depressed colleagues, for yet another bunch of incompetent senior managers and defeated and deflated staff, who disliked children and who had long since abandoned any idealistic notion they may have once nurtured about becoming an effective and respected teacher.

It was an occasion which I had reluctantly attended many times, listening to interminable, tedious and witless speeches, while impatiently watching the clock to determine the earliest moment I could leave without causing too much offence. Today however, I'd be forced to stay, at least until I'd been called to the front to receive whatever tacky and unwanted retirement gift had been purchased with the money reluctantly contributed by my resentful colleagues. This would be their last opportunity to demonstrate their meanness and insensitivity, by presenting me with the most unwelcome and irrelevant present their limited imaginations could devise.

Finally, after numerous lengthy and mind numbingly anodyne speeches of thanks and departure, Douglas made a few insincere remarks about how sad he was to be losing an effective and valued colleague and how the school was losing a popular and dynamic Head of Year, before he called me to the front of the hall to receive my retirement gift. I deliberately placed the gift unopened on the stage and waited until the last sound of the desultory and half-hearted applause had faded before I spoke.

'I have,' I said 'always admired brevity, (long pause) in others.'

There were the expected groans as they anticipated a lengthy and uncomplimentary goodbye.

'So,' I continued, 'in my only attempt to be admirable, I thank those who contributed to my gift and bid goodbye and good luck to you all!' And with that, I judged it time to make my exit.

I retrieved my gift from the stage and before anyone had the opportunity to say any personal goodbyes, I left the hall and headed rapidly to my car, which that morning I'd parked two streets away to avoid the inevitable pupil vandalism which occurs on the last day of term.

I drove out of Abercwmtwerp for the very last time at 3.23 pm on Friday 26th July, never to return, and at least twenty minutes before any other member of staff had managed to summon their vehicle rescue service to fix their graffiti covered, vandalised and disabled cars, which stood silent and immobile in the school car park, as a final testament to the thoughtful attitude and well mannered behaviour of British youth.

Afterword

My leaving gift, which I finally opened just before the Christmas following my retirement, as I desperately needed the wrapping paper, turned out to be a large and lavish coffee table book entitled 'Sailing in the South China Seas'. Like many such volumes designed for the 'what the hell can we buy so and so market', it contained minimal text accompanied by the kind of chocolate box idyllic photographs usually found as the subject for large jigsaw puzzles. Obviously purchased at a knock down price from a remainder bookshop, it was almost, but not quite, the most undesired and irrelevant present I'd ever received. That distinction was unfortunately still held by the chrome-plated tea-caddy spoon with a compass in the handle and crowned with the Hastings coat of arms in cheap enamel, which my mother had given me in 1974 as a memento of her SAGA seaside touring holiday to the sunshine resorts of the south coast; where she and my luckless father were transported in a coach full of whining geriatrics from one tired and tawdry hotel to another, all the way from Ramsgate to Torquay. As my father said later, it was a tour designed to make death appear as an attractive and desirable alternative, and the transition from holiday to hellfire seem like a welcome change.

For me, the transition from work to retirement had moved in the opposite direction and I reflected on the joy of a holiday free of kids, as for the first time in many years I was able to go away during term time. The satisfaction I felt as I stood on the aft deck of Cunard's flag ship liner the Queen Mary 2 watching the sparkling wake created by her four huge propellers, as she sailed through the azure blue of the South Pacific, was made infinitely more intense by the knowledge that back home thousands upon thousands of teachers were trapped in the miserable mediocrity of mainstream education and were struggling to survive the triple forces of uninspired and unsupportive management, incompetent politicians and disinterested and disruptive pupils. Life is all contrasts and profound personal satisfaction is often more easily attained when contemplating the misery of others. Success without failure is, after all, a meaningless and unachievable concept.

Standing as I now was, in the warmth of a perfect evening, lit by the dying rays of a Pacific sunset, on the deck of probably the finest and most luxurious ocean liner ever built, anticipating a superb dinner in the splendour of the Queen's Grill and contemplating late night cocktails in the plush interior of the Commodore Club on deck 11, it was difficult to imagine that my satisfaction index could possibly rise any higher. Yet, only a few short weeks later, when I was back home watching the early morning news on breakfast television, an event was reported, which raised my level of satisfaction to a state beyond rapture and brought my contentment with the world to its highest point since June 1958, when Edna Paget had treated me to my first blow-job on the back seat of the coach returning us all from a school trip to Colchester Zoo, and although the current news did not result in the ecstasy of a messy orgasm, it nevertheless gave me that wonderful feeling of comfort, which comes when events reward one's unspoken desires.

The report, which held me transfixed by its awful beauty, was the news that, during the small hours of the morning, a huge fire had engulfed the comprehensive school at Abercwmtwerp, and due to cutbacks in fire cover for the Welsh valleys, there was absolutely nothing left to salvage. Blessedly, due to the very late hour at which the fire had been started, the police and the fire brigade were confident that no one had been injured or killed. This naturally pleased me immensely, since I did not wish my satisfaction at the total destruction of the most filthy and uncared for school in Britain to be diminished by the knowledge that someone had been hurt or badly burned.

The police stated that they strongly suspected arson as the most probable cause and were investigating the possibility of a link between the fire and the recent release from the secure ward of St Joseph's Psychiatric Hospital of an ex-pupil of the school, suspected of holding a grudge, and who, from their known history, was certainly capable of starting the fire.

They had no need to name the suspect, for I knew, with absolute certainty that the culprit was none other than Layla Moon, and I was also certain that the world had not heard the last of this particular Devil's disciple; but that, as they say, is another story!

Coming Next

If you have enjoyed this book then look out for the next hilarious novel from the pen of James Rainsford. Entitled, 'The Incredible Layla Moon,' it is a black comedy telling the life story of Layla, a highly intelligent, manipulative and charismatic child whom you've already briefly met. It relates her fascinating story from conception to adulthood and details her early life before her short, but eventful time at Gruffud ap Cynan Comprehensive School; continuing through her teenage years, until as an adult she finally achieves her full and awesome potential. Unimaginably evil and suspected of possessing demonic powers, Layla in turn, astounds, impresses and affects all who meet her. She is quite simply 'Incredible!'

The beginning of her story is printed here for your amusement and delight. Enjoy!

The Incredible Layla Moon

Chapter 1

Beginnings

Layla Lucrezia Moon entered the World at precisely 6.00pm on June 6th 1986. Years later, many would assert that the time and date of her birth was highly significant, as it occurred at six-o-clock on the sixth day of the sixth month. This fact alone was sufficient to convince the gullible that she was marked for a life of evil from the moment of her birth. They undoubtedly, would have been even more certain of her demonic origin, had they also known that she had been conceived at exactly 6.00pm in room 666 on the sixth floor of the Hexagon Heights Hotel on Kailua Bay Hawaii, where Joseph and Mary Moon, her ecstatic parents, had spent their idyllic six week honeymoon. Others, less easily influenced by the mystical nonsense in the Book of Revelation of St John the Divine, became reluctantly persuaded of her satanic powers by her subsequent deeds.

However, at the very beginning there was nothing to indicate the scale and nature of the events, which later, were to make her so notorious and universally feared. Her very first appearance in the small, yet fabulously well equipped delivery room of the maternity suite of St Vagina's private birthing clinic, was a joyous occasion, filled with optimism, hope, gratitude and the relief which usually accompanies a successful and trouble free birth. Even Ramona De'ath, the senior midwife and Damian Brimstone the consultant gynaecologist on duty that evening, agreed that they'd rarely witnessed such a swift and trouble-free delivery.

Mary and Joseph Moon, Layla's luckless parents, were excited and delighted at the arrival of their first, and as subsequent events determined, their only child. They were even more pleased by the easy birth and the unbelievable beauty of their daughter. For without doubt, Layla was the most perfect baby ever delivered in St Vagina's state-of-the-art maternity suite. Everyone who saw her in these early days remarked upon her perfection. She never cried and appeared to smile months before medical textbooks said this was possible. The entire clinic's staff was amazed at Layla's progress and Mary and Joseph were allowed to take her home the evening of the day following her birth.

Home was a newly constructed modern eight-bedroomed detached house in an exclusive development of six individually designed dwellings on a wooded hillside above the deprived South Wales valley-town of Abercwmtwerp. The Moons had purchased their impressive house on this new and prestigious development, just three months before their wedding and had moved in immediately after their return from honeymoon. Their house, now complete and filled with expensive Scandinavian designer furniture and fittings, stood in four acres of wooded gardens at the head of a beautifully landscaped cul-de-sac called 'Paradise Pastures.' It was in this luxurious and pampered child-centered environment that Layla passed the early years of her very eventful life.

To keep her amused and stimulated there were attractive mobiles above her Dreamland Brazilian mahogany cot. Her bedroom was full of the most expensive soft toys and colourful visual experiences to help develop her perception and imagination. There were mirrors, concealed lighting and subdued music to stimulate or calm her changing moods and her every need was catered for by her doting mother and by Ingrid Johannson, the attractive, blond eighteen year old Swedish au-pair and English-language student, who'd been interviewed and appointed by Joseph to assist Mary in her domestic duties and to act as a live-in babysitter to Layla, so he and Mary could continue to enjoy their busy and familiar social life.

This life, which prior to Layla's arrival had consisted of parties, meals in expensive restaurants, visits to casinos, exclusive nightclubs and foreign holidays in secluded and exotic resorts, was funded by Joseph's extensive business interests in the timber and joinery trade. Due to the tragic early death of his father Maurice, when he was unfortunately decapitated by a rogue bandsaw in one of his own timber yards, Joseph had, at the tender age of eighteen, inherited a very large fortune and total ownership and control of his father's considerable business empire. This consisted of a timber importing company, four sawmills in Wales, two in England and Scotland, one in Ireland, a chain of twenty joinery companies throughout the UK, which, in honour of his birth eighteen years previously, his proud father had renamed 'Joseph's Joinery', and most profitable of all, ownership of thousands upon thousands of acres of prime forest in India, Brazil, Norway and Finland.

By the time he first saw Mary at the poolside of the Pagoda Palace Resort Hotel while holidaying in the Seychelles he was a single, handsome twenty-six year old playboy with a large penis, extensive fortune and expanding business empire. Mary, who'd been forced to accompany her wealthy Texan parents on their vacation to this Chinese owned exclusive beachfront hotel, was by contrast, just sixteen and bored to distraction by their turgid company. She was instantly smitten by Joseph's charm and conspicuous wealth. Until her meeting with Joseph she had lived what her parents had falsely imagined was a sheltered and protected existence as a pupil at St Theresa's private Roman Catholic girls' boarding school, in the secure and monitored grounds of the Convent of Our Lady of the Passion, located within a walled enclosure in an exclusive Dallas suburb. Far from protecting her innocence however, St Teresa's was a cauldron of repressed and frustrated sexuality, which found unfortunate expression by actively encouraging the formation of intense lesbian liaisons between pupils and pupils, pupils and staff, and even worse, by turning a blind eye to the many girls regularly and systematically abused by Father Brendan Murphy-O'Malley S.J., the fat, balding, myopic, middle-aged Jesuit Priest who served as spiritual mentor, to both the nuns of the convent and the girls of St Teresa's School. For Brendan, his pastoral role within the convent and the school was the perfect appointment, as it allowed him to indulge his sexual predilection for uniforms, schoolgirls and religious symbols – a powerful trio of stimulants which provided him with so many opportunities to sin that he spent a large part of each weekend in self mortification and unanswered prayer.

It was in this environment of seething and rampant sexuality that Mary was, at the tender age of fourteen, first introduced to the intimate delights of lesbianism by Isobella-Consuela Diaz, a stunning black haired half-blood Spanish senior prefect and Sister Maria Magdalene a young red headed and stunningly beautiful Carmelite novice on a years teaching exchange from the Covent of the Sacred Heart in the depths of County Galway. For Mary, this early initiation into the many and various methods of lesbian gratification ignited an intense sexual fire, which manifested itself in a powerful sexual curiosity and a heightened awareness of her own attractiveness and desirability. This early and obvious flowering of her sexual interests quickly made her a very desirable target for the attention of Father Brendan, who, after using his accustomed ploy of blackmail by threatening to expose her lesbian liaisons to her parents, introduced her to his extensive and vast repertoire of fantasies and perversions. Therefore, by the time that she was sixteen and on holiday with her unsuspecting parents, she was already an accomplished and knowledgeable sexual predator of considerable skill and experience. This, together with her stunning good looks, toned and youthful body and panther like grace, made her totally irresistible to Joseph Moon when he first saw her by the heart shaped pool which graced the fabulous tropical gardens of the Pagoda Palace Resort Hotel.

When he first noticed her, she was lying on a lemon sun-lounger, wearing a tiny black satin bikini. His eyes were immediately drawn to the small embroidered golden crucifix, which was stretched to an erection inducing tightness across her prominent mount of Venus. Her bronzed, lightly oiled skin shimmered with sensuality in the sunshine of this perfect day and with her long natural blond hair, intense blue eyes, inviting and seductive smile, she was a vision of such rare desirability, Joseph knew instantly that if he could not marry her, he would forever remain single.

Her parents, Chuck and Charlene Sherman, were at first very concerned at the obvious interest which Joseph showed in Mary, as they considered him far too old and experienced to be a suitable boyfriend for her, as they mistakenly believed her to be their innocent and uncorrupted baby. However, their initial anxiety quickly evaporated, once they had made urgent enquiries concerning Joseph and had been reliably informed by Walt Maverick the discredited ex-Texas-Ranger now running the Maverick Private Dick Detective Agency, a Dallas investigators, part-owned by a recently imprisoned tele-evangelist friend of theirs known as 'Salvation Sid, the kid with the ear of God'. The only ear now listening to Sid belonged to Boss Man Benson, the brutal anti religious head-warden in charge of D Block in Cottontail County Penitentiary, where Sid was serving a five year stretch for defrauding the devastated members of his T.V. congregation of some ten million dollars, donated in the vain hope that the power and efficacy of his prayers would ensure their salvation.

It had been Sid's dollars however, which had enabled Walt to set up his detective agency following his dismissal from the prestigious ranks of the Texas Rangers, for assisting Sid to shred documents relating to his improper use of the charitable donations made to his T.V. church. Despite this, Walt was a very reliable P.I. and when he phoned the Shermans in their luxury penthouse suite in the Pagoda Palace with his detailed report on Joseph Moon, they were delighted to learn that his assets and personal wealth exceeded their own by a considerable margin. Their view of him as a potential suitor changed instantly from one of horror, to active approval and encouragement. In fact, within twenty minutes of receiving Walt's call they had approached Joseph, who was in his usual position at the pool bar, from where he had a perfect view of their divine daughter, as she made every effort to stimulate his obvious interest by deliberately adopting the most

251

tantalising and provocative positions whilst she oiled her sleek body with expensive sun lotion.

Joseph, who'd spent the two nights since he first saw Mary by the pool, in such a state of sexual arousal that he'd been unable to sleep, was now so hooked by his desire for this teen-temptress, he'd decided that no matter what the consequences, he just had to have her! Imagine, therefore, his delight, when just as he was formulating a plan to transform his fantasy into reality, an unexpected opportunity was offered by Chuck and Charlene when they invited him to join them, and Mary, for dinner that evening in the internationally renowned Pagoda Palace prestigious restaurant called 'The Terrific Pacific Prawn' This was run by Marcel-Pierre Poulet, a three Michelin starred chef from Scunthorpe, who'd adopted his current nom-de-plume after he'd unexpectedly won a T.V. cooking competition to prepare the main course at a Gatcombe Park garden party hosted by The Princess Royal in honour of Mojobo Hippolado the President of Western Zargoninia, and attended by her mother, The Queen. He'd felt that his real name of Charlie Chicken lacked the gravitas demanded by such a royal occasion. His ex wife Beryl, forever after maintained that his subsequent rise to fame owed more to his poncey new name than to his dubious cooking skills. She was cruelly dismissive of his talent and referred to his two great signature dishes of foie-gras with pear and walnut jus on a bed of crushed caramelised swede and Crown of Welsh mountain lamb in apple and cherry butter, with smoked Greek olives and black truffles, as 'Pretentious Pâté' and 'Rip-off Ribs'. Fortunately, her contemptuous dismissal of his skills did nothing to depress his confidence or affect his culinary arrogance, an arrogance which had served to raise the reputation of many mediocre chefs to the status of celebrity prima donnas. As his fame increased, so too did his prices and popularity and he consoled himself with the knowledge that, his ex-wife's food preferences and opinions had been nurtured and developed in her father 'Percy's Pie and Chip Shop' where her taste buds had been destroyed by years of stale steak pies and curried chips.

None of this secret history impacted in the least upon Joseph's heightened anticipation as he contemplated dining with Chuck, Charlene and their ravishingly desirable daughter. In fact, any sensual dining pleasure Joseph may have experienced in the slightly kitsch atmosphere of 'The Terrific Pacific Prawn' was totally overwhelmed by the almost unbearable proximity of Mary Sherman, who'd arrived with her parents, dressed in an iridescent cream silk backless top, black pleated mini-skirt, sheer black silk tights and strapless five inch stilettos decorated with jewel encrusted butterflies. Her long blond hair cascaded across her flawless shoulders and flowed down her naked back like a water-fall of golden rain and her delicate finger nails were adorned with tiny diamonds and crimson polish. She was a vision of such heart stopping sexuality that Joseph was finding it difficult to breath. She was possessed of completely unblemished skin, intense azure blue eyes, dazzlingly white – perfectly even – teeth, and exuded female sexual pheromones of such power that Joseph was grateful his obvious and rampant erection was hidden beneath the generous overhang of The Terrific Pacific Prawn's pristine white linen tablecloth.

Subsequent to their discovery of Joseph's considerable wealth, Chuck and Charlene Sherman were very keen to encourage his interest in their youngest and most treasured child. Slight initial concern regarding what they innocently imagined would be the early loss of her virginity, was outweighed by the prospect of welcoming Joseph's riches into their under developed Texan oil business. Consequently, they made no objection when he asked their permission to take Mary on an island hopping trip the following day in his recently acquired Riva speedboat, which was conveniently moored in the resort's exclusive marina.

That night, Joseph lay awake, not remembering anything of Marcel-Pierre Poulet's expensive cuisine, but in feverish anticipation of the day he was about to spend in the company of the most beautiful and desirable creature he'd ever seen. Mary too, was restless and relaxed herself with a particularly effective masturbation routine, only recently learned from Sister Maria

Magdalene beneath the rough horsehair blanket in her somewhat Spartan cell. She quickly achieved a shattering climax imagining how Joseph would enjoy her fellatio technique, which she'd practised and honed to perfection on the pathetic penis of Father Brendan in the dank and curtained privacy of the convent's confessional, and not employed, since she'd deep throated Miguel Ramiro Mendoza, her parent's part-time Mexican gardener and pool attendant on the morning prior to her departure for the Seychelles. Miguel, who was a forty-five year old illegal immigrant with a wife and six children to support, worked for subsistence wages and was terrified that unless he complied with all of Mary's sexual demands, she would carry out her threat and reveal his illegal status to the immigration department. Her blowjob had, for him, been a rare treat, since she usually forced him to gratify her desires in ways which allowed him no opportunity to relieve his own desperate and intense sexual frustration.

Mary, who saw Miguel as no more than a convenient and easily manipulated sex object, was infinitely more interested in the prospect of sex with Joseph, whom she found much more appealing and attractive. He became even more desirable the following morning when he introduced her to 'The Spirit of Ecstasy' his new forty-four foot, twin 800 hp Rivarama speedboat. Mary's obviously pleasurable reaction to the sight of this sleek and stunningly beautiful craft was matched by Joseph's enthusiasm for her own fabulous appearance. When she'd arrived, he'd been sitting on a low bollard, trying to appear casually nonchalant as he studied her approach down the long run of the marina's floating pontoon. She was wearing a white lawn shirt tied high on her right side, a short white and lemon pleated Dior tennis skirt, a pair of lemon coloured calfskin Prada mules and an Armani white and silver scarf draped across her tanned shoulders. As she came closer, Joseph was aware that he'd never seen such a lithe and graceful girl. Her long legs were tanned and lightly muscled, as she moved towards him with all the grace and poise of a thoroughbred mare being taken to stud. She possessed a confidence in her own sexuality which, despite her tender years, was buttressed by her extensive experience and made irresistible by the deadly combination of her apparent innocence twinned with her obvious awareness of the effect she had upon every heterosexual male between puberty and death.

By the time she finally stood before him, Joseph was so excited by the prospect of being alone with her for the entire day he was momentarily struck dumb and missed his cue when she greeted him in her slow and slightly husky Texan drawl.

'Hi, Joseph!' She smiled. 'Is *this* your boat? My, my, it is a big one, isn't it? I just love big ones,' she continued, as she licked her lips and focused her full attention upon the obvious bulge in the front of his navy-blue Henri Lloyd yachting shorts. Joseph licked his own lips, but it was an ineffective gesture, as his tongue was as dry as a sheet of sandpaper in a microwave. Before he'd even had time to swallow, Mary had planted her long tanned legs on either side of his right thigh and deliberately lowered herself, until he experienced the almost unbearable sensation of her silk panties against his warm skin. She perceptively applied pressure, by gripping his leg between the oiled smoothness of her upper thighs and leaned forward so he could smell the sweetness of her breath and feel her obviously naked breasts beneath the thin material of her shirt. She lowered her beautiful mouth to his right ear and whispered suggestively 'Are you going to take me for an exciting ride, Joseph?' Just before he was able to ensnare her in his arms, she swiftly stood and took a couple of steps back, so she could assess the effect of her unexpected embrace. She was delighted to see that Joseph was so shaken by her move he was panting like an aroused dog in a hot desert and struggling to regain his poise and composure. Mary was completely aware of the turmoil she'd caused and was in total control of her seductive powers. She looked forward intensely to the pleasure she would derive from making Joseph a willing and docile slave to her sexual favours.

By the time he'd recovered sufficiently to properly introduce her to the stunning delights of 'The Spirit of Ecstasy' she had readopted the irresistible persona of an innocent and naïve convent schoolgirl and she flattered him with her comments and expressions of approval as he pointed out all his boat's very expensive fixtures and fittings. Mary was the perfect audience for his display of the Riva's impressive features and as they left the entrance of the small marina, he opened up the throttles to demonstrate the awesome power of the craft's twin 800hp engines and glanced back, to where she'd spread herself across the curved cream hide luxury of the aft seat. With her long blond hair streaming behind her and her even longer legs parted just enough for him to have an entrancing view of her white panties, he felt more fortunate than a tom-cat in a creamery.

They were headed for the nearby island of 'Sainte Anne', an unspoiled tropical paradise, with palm-fringed pristine white sandy beaches, kissed by the gently lapping waves of an azure blue sea. Earlier that morning, Joseph had arranged for a sumptuous picnic to be brought aboard and his large galley fridge now bulged with Marcel Pierre Poulet's finest selection of al-fresco fancies, including, Pacific oysters, beluga caviar and Dom Pérignon vintage champagne. He was determined Mary should be as impressed by his good taste and refinement as she was by his conspicuous wealth.

With the Riva's enormous power and impressive top speed, the trip seemed to take no time and Joseph was soon dropping anchor in the calm of a secluded and deserted bay, where the water was so transparent the sandy bottom was clearly visible some five metres below. Once the boat was securely anchored and Joseph had silenced her huge engines they both changed for a swim before they ate. Being a gentleman Joseph showed Mary into the fabulous forward cabin so she could change in private. She was pleased at this, as she did not wish him to experience the pleasure of watching her undress until the moment of her choosing. When she emerged, Joseph was thrilled to see that she was wearing the black satin bikini with the golden crucifix adorned pants which had so intrigued and excited him when he'd first seen her by the pool.

'What's the significance of the cross?' he asked as his eyes were irresistibly drawn to where it decorated the gentle swell of her perfect pudendum.

'Oh that!' she responded, as she glanced down to acknowledge the object of his gaze. 'That was embroidered for me by one of my friends at school.' The friend, had in fact been Sister Maria Magdalene, her Irish divinity teacher, who'd given her the bikini as an Easter present to celebrate Christ's crucifixion and to mark their first mutual masturbation session using the large cream alter candles, which Maria had managed to steal from the locked candle cupboard of the convent's Chapel of the Holy Virgin. However, before Joseph could pursue the matter further, Mary descended the short ladder to the aft swimming platform and executed a perfect dive, to enter the inviting water with scarcely a splash.

It was much later that afternoon when, following a refreshing swim and the pleasure of a fabulous lunch with champagne that Joseph finally had Mary lying next to him on the satin ivory sheets on the queen-size double bed in the Riva's luxurious forward cabin that he discovered it was not only her bikini pants which were enhanced with religious symbolism. For, to mark Christ's resurrection she'd allowed Sister Maria to dye her pubic hair red and to cut and shave it into a scarlet cross, which matched in shape and position the one embroidered on her pants. Joseph, who possessed no knowledge of the dark and potential sexual power of the passion of our Lord, was easily persuaded to accept Mary's account that her pubic art was simply the result of naïve convent schoolgirl enthusiasm. Still, he did find the cross slightly disconcerting and it strangely heightened the intensity of his desire to imagine beautiful schoolgirls fashioning each other's pubic hair into symbols of religious faith. He may have been seriously disturbed however, had he known that the real architect of this example of blasphemous art was Father Brendan Murphy O'Malley, who'd ordered Sister Maria Magdalene to cut and die the pubic hair of all the girls who acted as his sexual acolytes and who'd been initiated by him into the darkness of his profane perversions. Certainly, Joseph was the fortunate recipient of all the erotic skills and tricks which Mary had acquired as Father Brendan's favourite pupil and by the time she finally left his bed, he was, sexually at least, a much weaker, much wiser and much happier man.

Within six months of this first sexual encounter Mary had left school, Joseph had invested more than sufficient cash into Chuck and Charlene's oil business to ensure its future success and he'd been fast tracked to salvation by his swift conversion to Roman Catholicism. In less than a year, they'd enjoyed the most wonderful wedding on the vast sunlit lawn of Chuck and Charlene's new mansion on the outskirts of Fort Worth and departed with great hopes for their future, to the bridal suite of the Hexagon Heights Hotel, where the sperm and egg – which was to become Layla Lucrezia Moon – met and began the process, which later, was to have such unexpected and catastrophic consequences.

To be continued...